BY R. F. DELDERFIELD

R. F. DELDERFIELD

All
Over
the
Town

SIMON AND SCHUSTER · NEW YORK

For *ROBERT* and *JULIET*
who enjoyed the hors d'œuvre
and demanded the full dish

Published by Simon and Schuster
A Division of Gulf & Western Corporation
Simon & Schuster Building
Rockefeller Center
1230 Avenue of the Americas
New York, New York 10020

Manufactured in the United States of America

1   2   3   4   5   6   7   8   9   10

Library of Congress Cataloging in Publication Data

Delderfield, Ronald Frederick, 1912–1972.
  All over the town.

  I. Title.
PZ3.D37618Al   1977   [PR6007.E36]   823'.9'12   77-24561
ISBN 0-671-22920-6

ONE

Some people are born with the faculty of reasoned, consecutive thought—that is, thought bidden to commence at a certain point and to travel along certain lines. Others, under the stress of business requirements, develop the faculty and use it when occasion demands. Nathaniel Hearn was born without this faculty, and at the age of thirty-three had long since abandoned any hope of acquiring it. His was the type of brain that ranged, that projected lines of thought without conscious beginning and without effectual end, that meandered here and there along the avenues of his imagination like an untidy brook reaching not the sea, nor even a broader stream, but losing itself more often than not in a water meadow, where it spent itself to no apparent purpose.

Perhaps this failing, if failing it was—for it gave him a local reputation for excessive amiability—was responsible for his returning to Sandcombe at all. He had received Samuel's letter weeks ago, asking him point-blank: did he or did he not wish to return to his prewar post as assistant editor to the *Sandcombe and District Clarion?* If so, would he reply immediately, as the post, while reserved for him, could not be held open indefinitely.

Nat had considered this letter. At any rate, he had begun to consider it, but he got no farther than the word "assistant," which made him indulge in one of those slow, rueful grins for which he was already famous in Sandcombe, the grin that made local councillors, stationmasters, club secretaries and rectors say, "Hearn? That reporting chap? He's all right—do anything for you if you tackle him the right way. What sort of stuff does he write? Mostly what Old Sam Vane lets him, but he cooks it up brightly enough. He won't ride a hobbyhorse, if that's what you're after—been there too long—always gives you both sides of the question. Can't afford to do otherwise."

On the whole, this was a fair estimate of Nat and of his paper, the *Clarion*. With a four thousand circulation, a general stationer's shop and a busy little printing works behind, the Clarion Press (the word "Press" embodied the lot, even to the sidelines, such as sale of toilet rolls to the urban council) was not in a position to take sides. Ever since its foundation, the week General Gordon was cut up in the Sudan, the *Clarion* had pursued such a middle course that it seemed to be no course at all.

Sam Vane was a realist. His bread was spread with printer's ink, and the sources of that ink were confined by the SUDC boundaries. The strain of maintaining this course throughout the greater part of his life was not as great as one might imagine. Within a year of settling down in the converted livery stables off St. Luke's Road, Sam Vane had realized that the one obstacle in the way of making a steady living in Sandcombe was to hold an opinion. With every Friday—the day the *Clarion* was published —the balancing trick became easier. At sixty-six he was incapable, not only of saying anything in his editorials, but of imagining, for one instant, that he had not said a great deal.

Sam had told himself for so long that his regular clients were right, his possible clients might be right and outsiders (who took printing orders elsewhere) were wrong, that he never hesitated a second in writing as much in his "Round About Town" column, which served as his editorial. And he wrote, if necessary, in direct contradiction to fact. Facts never bothered him. Facts could not be taken to the bank every Saturday in a little gladstone bag. Nobody questioned facts in a comment column, and in the hard news—accidents and the like—both Sam and Nat had been liberal with "alleged." There was no need to worry unduly while that word was still in the *Oxford Dictionary,* and if it didn't quite fit there was always "we learn on good authority." (Nat had never known what authority, and none of the readers ever asked.)

Nat's habit of ragged thought had driven him, on this first morning of demobilization leave, to make a wide detour on his way to the office. Leaving his bed-sitting room near the promenade, he could have cut straight into the town at the junction of High Street and Pilot Street, pursuing his way up the former thoroughfare to St. Luke's Road, where the Clarion Press sprawled away in a range of uneven slate roofs to the edge of the Beck, which ran behind the premises.

The realization, however, that within a matter of minutes he would be making a decision that would shape the remainder of his life, forced him to walk quickly past the head of High Street and along the seafront, where the seasonal orchestra—an octet of women in Russian tunics, "Sonia and Her Rhythmettes"—were playing excerpts from *The Gondoliers.*

It says little for Nat's powers of concentration that the sight and sound of the octet, penned like circus apes in the cast-iron cage of the bandstand, reminded him of his first evening at Sandcombe, in June 1928, when another band had been playing "Carolina Moon" to a half-empty enclosure and a dozen youths who used the gravel path round the stand as a mating corridor and sniggered greetings to the same girls a dozen times the same evening. The girls walked round in the opposite direction, and thus both groups avoided the chair-money collector.

How long ago was that? Nearly eighteen years, and it seemed like eighty, although it struck him as curious how many tiny, inconsequential events he could recall of those intervening years. The indomitable little Bostock woman taking five prizes with five children at every autumnal baby show. The tubercular laborer at Fanshawe's farm, who lived dismally enough but died originally, having ended his life by hanging himself with a lavatory chain. The fuss Mrs. Betterby-Stuart had made when her name had been omitted from the list of helpers at the St. Luke's League of Action sale of work. The occasion he had slipped up on a date and published a wedding, using all the customary adjectives—"pretty," "dainty," even "smart"—before the wedding actually took place. The marathon debate in the council over the projected removal of the Crimean cannon from the Headland View battery. The cannon had since gone for salvage, but in those days, when railings were railings, and not potential munitions, Councillor Grimstone-Beech, a veteran of the Dargai campaign, had saved the motion to sell the cannon by declaiming that such an act constituted a direct insult to the heroes who wintered before Sebastopol.

Ah, ancient history. People would laugh at it now, no doubt, but in those days it had been the topic of the week, and he had written two columns on the debate for the *Clarion*'s inside news-pages.

Nat wondered if Sam had kept advertisements on the front page during the paper shortage. He must have been forced to replan the wasteful layout somehow. Had he cut out the front-page block of "Sandcombe, from Galleon Hill," a blurred seascape displayed under the words "Established 1884" and showing pedestrians promenading in crinolines that had been laid aside years before the first issue of the paper?

These were the currents and eddies of Nat's thoughts, as he sauntered on beyond the lifeboat station and on to the Flats—that section of the Sandcombe foreshore which was always due for development, but remained for each succeeding generation a triangular wilderness of wiry grass.

He had reached the concrete blockhouse, where a batch of German prisoners were clearing tank traps built to hinder their advance inland six years before, when he made a final effort to marshal his thoughts, to force his mind to accept the fact that here, for him, was the true finish of the war. Was he to accept, passively, this return to normal, to Sam's grating fussiness, to gathering of names at the lych-gate of St. Martin's Church during funerals, to jotting down the details of the team race at the local swimming galas, to compiling pages of notes on the date, place, time and circumstances of minor road offenses?

He didn't know, couldn't tell. It depended. But on what? He didn't even know that. Perhaps Sam had changed, perhaps he was tired and didn't argue so much when presented with obvious facts; perhaps Gerald, Sam's forty-year-old son, had lost the irritating habit of polishing finger and thumb on the lapel of his black "business" jacket; perhaps Skinner, the gnomish little foreman printer downstairs, had taken to washing himself once in a while; perhaps *Clarion* readers had allowed themselves to be swallowed up in the wider issues, plugged on the front pages of the dailies and over the air, bulletin by bulletin, since that overcast Friday morning in 1939 when Bumble, the mop-headed office-boy apprentice, had rushed into the editorial office over the shop and screamed, "Nat, Nat, 'e's gorn for 'em!" and Nat had sat back and said, in common with so many other men in their late twenties, "This is it!"

Of course, it hadn't been. For six months little or nothing had changed. Sandcombe saw snow for the first time in two decades. Evacuees came and went. Nat had tracked down and interviewed two or three local seamen who had helped to sink the *Graf Spee*. An elderly reservist, who had been a market gardener out in the Leas, had gone down with the *Royal Oak* at Scapa, leaving a mountainous wife and five indifferent children in Lower Beck Street. The pictures of these men appeared in the *Clarion,* and Nat wrote potted biographies, heading the Scapa story "Sandcombe's First Sacrifice."

Spring had arrived, very much as usual, with high tides cascading over the Promenade and damage to a council snack bar under the cliff. Then came the German advance into the Low Countries and the nagging match with Sam over joining the RAF, with Sam gradually giving way, after one or two of his prominent customers, with sons already in uniform, had dropped hints about Nat's age. Sam seemed to derive a new impetus from the vague tide of satisfaction that stole over all elderly men during these months—the feeling of being wanted in business once more, the quiet satisfaction of a come back, a rolling up of sleeves, a getting back into comfortable harness, with national shortages in all consumer goods to excuse a little stiffness and disinclination to work too hard.

A week later and Nat was one of millions, with the same story, down to the last detail. Bell tents at the reception center, stale jokes at the recruit center, North-Country billets, a clerk's desk in an empty hotel, carpetless stairs thudding all day with the impact of recruits' shiny boots. Airfields in the Midlands, the drone of aircraft all night, rain pattering on the tin roof of the Nissen, queues for meals, endless shuffling along the concrete avenues of hutted camps. Gas drill, sorting the In and the Out tray in a steaming respirator, lighthearted and obscene slogans on latrine walls—*We Bull while Russia bleeds* and *Joe for King, Betty Grable for Queen!*

Years of it. Waiting at the top of hills for a hitch into the town, a visit to the cinema and a cheap meal at the canteen. (Sam, who had ultimately smiled on enlistment, had said nothing about balance of civilian pay.) Camp Shows and Welfare officers with ginger mustaches tapping his shoulder, "Jolly good show, old boy," and returning to their mess armchairs and whisky at reduced rates. A feeling of detached bitterness by the late summer of 1943. A slackening of interest in the news and cynical appreciation of Jane's strip in the *Mirror*.

Postings without purpose, to camps often hard put to find him a job. Envelope addressing in accounts sections. Pep talks by officers for whom he worked out servant allowances. Fits, starts and stops like ceremonial drill. Morale drives that petered out in forty-eight hours. Long railway journeys up and down the country. Leave with nowhere to go but hostels. Abstract discussions in the hut, lighted by the glow of cigarettes. Bickerings over precedence in NAAFI queues. A gradual descent to primitive standards of life—food three times a day, a bed not too near the radio, which moaned and chattered from 6 A.M. until midnight. Dirty nails and unutterable boredom.

Autumn 1943. The long-delayed commission, hidden three years in an AM pigeonhole. The OCTU and a nervous attempt to display table manners, long since forgotten. The agony of squad-drill direction. Ultimate posting as an assistant adjutant and the smug letter from Sam, "... glad to hear you are at last an officer ..." The transfer to a photographic unit. D Day and the real war. Pitiful towns in Normandy, crushed, reeking, hopeless. Journeys through a land that had once been civilized where now nothing worked, not even locks and taps or washbasin stoppers. Penetration, as CO of a small unit, to the land beyond the Loire for bomb assessment. Freezing French hotels and *lodgements militaires.* Provincial mayors offering pitiful civic welcomes, no food, no petrol, no warmth —nothing but smiles and cognac and embarrassed requests for soap. A land where, it seemed to Nat, the ordinary people had gone beyond hate and patriotism and self-pity, and dismissed both past and future with a characteristic shrug, the music-hall shrug of the Latin, a shrug that said, "Mend the bridge? But why, monsieur? We have a raft made of two old barges and some planks. It serves. Besides, we have no girders, no tools—nothing. And the men are prisoners or playing soldiers in the hills."

May 8th and forty-eight-hour pass in London. A sense of high expectancy which turned, as the evening wore on, to a blind pity, not far from contempt, for the solid phalanxes of sheeplike people who stood about waiting for stragglers to climb a lamp standard or throw a cracker at a shuttered window. An awful anticlimax, shared with millions of people who had forgotten how to enjoy themselves when the cinema box offices were shut.

The long waiting weeks in the camp, pretending to work. The only real thrill of the whole business, the thrill of hearing his number called at the demob center. Sam's letter read and reread. And now this, full circle.

Nat scratched his nose and turned back from the Flats. How old? Nearing thirty-four. Halfway to the biblical span, although that meant nothing in Sandcombe, where the Medical Officer of Health was always quoting the average age of mortality as being seventy-six (excluding one year olds)—a shade higher than that of Cragport, a few miles along the coast. But if not the *Clarion,* what? Some other paper? Some other trade? Put in his name at the resettlement center. Go abroad, oil, publishing, civil service?

Suddenly Nat realized that he was happy to be back. The air smelled good. People had grinned and waved to him all along the prom. There was a good deal to be said for Sandcombe. Its very smallness (nine thousand in 1931) meant good-fellowship—important to a man without a family background. He had got his old digs back for the asking. The bed-sitting room, stacked with his favorite books, had a good smell. Mrs. Bannister, his landlady, liked him. He was an all-the-year-rounder and a "good-class" lodger—much better than letting the room over and over again to casuals you couldn't trust. She did her best to mother him, and Nat was a man who liked to be mothered.

Sam hadn't said anything about money. He never did until he was forced. It had always appeared to Nat that he was hoping against hope that someone, some day, would serve on the staff for nothing, or pay a small premium to learn the trade. But Nat's money—four pounds ten before he enlisted—was enough. In Sandcombe there were few opportunities to spend and, anyway, he seldom had time enough to buy inessentials. Perhaps the Old Man would add another pound. He would ask him, just for the fun of seeing the hunted look that always came into Sam's face when anyone mentioned money.

Nat turned into High Street and made his way through a string of nodding acquaintances to the Clarion Press offices. After all, perhaps Sandcombe had changed, perhaps Sam's streak of snobbery would induce him to choose his words now that he was dealing with an ex-officer. Nat thought it unlikely, but the possibility aroused his curiosity, and he passed in through the plate-glass door and nodded at a strange shop assistant, in the act of telling an elderly customer that her employers refused to stock rude picture postcards.

TWO

The Clarion Press was organized in three interlocking departments. There was the shop, on the corner of High Street and St. Luke's Road, the printing works, occupying the converted stables and loft, with a covered yard and a ramp sloping down to the stream, and there were combined offices on the first floor. The larger office, immediately over the shop, was marked "Editorial," the smaller, across a landing stacked with stationery, was marked "Printing Enquiries—Mr. Gerald Vane."

The shop was a modern affair, with two mahogany counters and innumerable racks, displaying a good class of stationery, office knickknacks, local publications, maps and a limited number of school textbooks—a new line introduced by Gerald.

The printing works was by no means modern, and Gerald sensed, accurately enough, that it gave customers an impression of slackness and inefficiency. It was badly lighted, and the machines, with the single exception of a secondhand automatic Heidelberg press, were sadly outmoded. One or two, notably the flatbed, invariably referred to as the "Big Machine," had been giving trouble for years, and Skinner, the foreman, was always prophesying that it would "never lars the run"—that is, it would never survive the final rush of the week, when the two inside pages of the *Clarion* were printed between 6 and 9 P.M. on Thursday night.

About half the work done in the works was connected, in one way or another, with the newspaper. The rest was jobbing—an assortment of programs, double-demy posters, small magazines, such as the parish affair, *St. Luke's and St. Martin's Messenger*, overprinted stationery, visiting cards, draw tickets, menus and timetables. The craftsmanship was good, notwithstanding the age of the machines, for the habit of working solely for money had not yet reached Sandcombe. Most of the men took a certain amount of pride in their work, and two of them, Skinner and the keyboard operator, Burton, were unusually conscientious employees. The trouble lay with the juniors, who would never stay long, moving out and seeking jobs where they were not expected to work overtime three nights a week—a preference on their part which gave Sam an opportunity to write one or two slashing leaders on the "Something-for-Nothing-Cult of Modern Youth." Modern Youth was unimpressed. It was still represented, at the Clarion Press, by Bumble, an untidy combination of apprentice and office boy, and Marlene, a pert seventeen year old, serving in the shop.

Bumble hung on because, deep down, he was fascinated by newspapers, which for him were linked, however remotely, to sleek young men in devil-may-care hats, who sat on the tables of district attorneys in gangster films and always came back to the office with a headline and riddled remains of a big shot. His longing to join this swashbuckling brotherhood was like the yearning of other boys for the circus ring or the footplate of an express. He felt that if he stayed on long enough Sam would die and the new editor would send him out to describe bodies washed up on the beach, or into blazing hotels to gather details of how the local brigade, now, alas, a mere unit of the NFS, "saved the staircase in the nick of time."

In readiness for this call he had even attended night classes at the Sandcombe Institute, and tried to learn shorthand. He had always liked Nat, not because he considered the latter his ideal of a newshawk according to Sam Goldwyn, but because Nat was the only person in the firm who treated him as an equal. Since Nat had gone overseas with the air force his liking had developed into mild admiration. If Nat had been accepted for aircrew it would have been adoration, for Bumble was one of the keenest "types" in the Sandcombe ATC.

Next to Nat, of whom he had seen little enough these five years, Bumble admired Marlene, who seemed to him to have the makings of a "smashing Judy." (Bumble preferred to talk in 1940 RAF slang.) Marlene, however, had other ideas. She had worked a year in Sandcombe's most up-to-date hairdressing salon, Pompadour. She was an observant girl, and Pompadour had given her a surface polish, lost upon her family, which inhabited a cottage down by the docks, but good enough to pass muster with Bumble, who thought it gave her "class." It was a pity Bumble did not "work clean." In a black coat he might have stood a chance. As it was, he was kept hovering behind two or three of the sixth form grammar school boys, who were earmarked for banks.

The whole of the firm's printing output, including the *Clarion,* was carefully supervised by Gerald, Sam's only son. It was unfortunate for Gerald that he had just missed the last call-up. A year in the services, or even in an armament factory, might have prevented him from becoming a prig. Nat was always prepared to admit that Gerald had many good points. He was a hypocrite, but a conscious one. Unlike Sam, he could relax when the customer was downstairs. He was ambitious and extremely hardworking. He was genuinely interested in the art of commercial printing, and always tried to ensure that a job was as good as he could make it with old and unreliable tools.

Gerald had never married. His desire to impress always made him awkward with women, and his slavish devotion to the business left him little or no time for outside interests. He read a good deal, mostly adventure novels and travel. Never having left Sandcombe for more than a week at a time, he found pleasure in penetrating, by proxy, the upper reaches of the Amazon or trekking across the plateaus of Tibet, always remembering, when he laid down the book and removed his gold-rimmed glasses, that explorers who actually made these journeys didn't have an exacting business to run or a certain position to maintain. Gerald's "position" in Sandcombe was not as important as he would have wished, but it was improving year by year. People from the Ridge were beginning to nod to him as he walked down from his home, in Cliff Terrace, to the office. The Clerk of the Council, Mr. Angel, often asked his advice in publicity matters. He was only forty, and if he looked after himself he had thirty years of active life ahead of him. He might even get on the council or become a justice of the peace. Thinking of these things, he was always careful to crease his pin-striped trousers under the mattress before he retired, and he was never seen without a gleaming white collar and a black tie. He looked after his fingernails—quite an effort when one worked in a printing office all day, but easier now that he seldom touched type, busying himself instead with costing and the daily maintenance of output and stock charts, a dozen of which were pinned to his office walls. He was delighted to explain these charts and graphs to patient customers. "This little red feller," he would say, tracing a galloping curve with his ebony ruler, "this is a price guide —just to make sure I don't overcharge, you know. That gradient there, for instance, it constitutes the fourteen percent rise in the cost of paper, but you'll notice it's a gradual rise. We share the increase, get me? Seven percent you, seven percent me. . . ." And so on. All Gerald's graphs had one thing in common. Each showed a tendency to climb off the page, but whether this was optimism on Gerald's part or an indication of continually increasing turnover on the part of the Clarion Press was something no one except Sam could say, and he never looked at them. Sam seemed to get along very well without charts, but constantly glanced at his passbook.

It was Gerald who found Mollie Thorpe, the girl who had partially filled Nat's post during the war. Although he would never have admitted it, even to himself, Gerald rather admired her smile and the quick way she had of looking at him when he came into the office and said, "Ah, Miss Thorpe . . . and how much are we giving the Buller case?"

Mollie Thorpe was not really a journalist. When war broke out she had almost persuaded her father, the local Midland Bank manager, to send her to Paris for a course in commercial art. She had a good eye for line and color, and had made a certain amount of pin money before the paper shortage killed her small connection.

She had never lived much in Sandcombe, having been away at school until 1937. On leaving school she joined the local dramatic society, and came into local prominence as a juvenile lead.

It was while Mollie Thorpe was acting as prompt mistress for one of the thespians' shows early in the war that Gerald, knowing that the doctor had forbidden his father to go out after nightfall, contracted the society and asked if a member would write the notice. Mollie complied, submitting a neatly typed column, which Gerald read and approved for that week's *Clarion*. Mollie, who understood the theater and, what was more important, was not insensible to temperament among local thespians, had sent in a good, straightforward commentary. Gerald, who could not write himself but felt he had sound judgment in these matters, was impressed. The girl had used phrases which he did not fully comprehend and which, therefore, appealed to his snobbery.

He wrote to her, asking if she would be interested in the post of assistant editor during Nat's absence on service. She came in the next day and inquired about the wage. He offered her two pounds ten, but she stuck out for three pounds. Gerald paid her the extra ten shillings, momentarily thrown off his guard by one of her quick, easy smiles, and despite Sam's grumblings the girl had been worth it, and more. All the same, Gerald heard of Nat's impending return with faint relief. He had made one or two guarded attempts to break down the strictly business relationship between Mollie and himself, but, although the girl had always remained civil, she had a smiling reserve that amounted almost to insolence. There was something about the way she looked at him—an unblinking, even patient glance—that made him feel slightly uncomfortable. It was as though she was saying to herself, "Have your say, little man. Then I'll do it my way."

Mercifully she was not concerned with important issues on the paper. His father still handled the council meetings, big social gatherings and indictable court cases, Mollie covering only the brief reports—anything from a funeral par to a half-column inquest or a Girl Guide rally. She wrote them up well enough, quickly and clearly, without any evidence of the journalese to which *Clarion* readers had become accustomed; but if they noticed a change in style they still bought papers, and Mollie stayed on, working in Nat's chair near the window.

The day Sam had informed him of Nat's impending return Gerald had spoken to Mollie.

"Ah, Miss Thorpe . . ." She looked up from her typewriter, and he crossed to the bow window to avoid her calm stare. "We've heard from your predecessor, Flying Officer Hearn. He's coming back."

"Yes?"

Damn the woman! Why didn't she help a little? He was trying to tell her that she would be getting her notice. There was no point in keeping the two of them on. Even if paper rationing was annulled, that would be quite impossible.

He added, "We're keeping his job open, of course—have to, it's law, I understand."

She had said, "That's all right, Mr. Gerald. I was always aware of that."

He relaxed a little, his forefinger and thumb beginning to move slowly up and down his lapel.

"There's no need for you to leave us altogether."

Why had he said that? When he came into the room he had no intention of re-engaging her. She continued to keep her brown eyes on him—eyes that looked soft enough, but were as he was aware, far from indicating the helplessness he liked to find in young women. That quality always made him feel more of the big, generous, helpful employer.

"There'll be no room on the paper, I'm afraid. . . . I thought perhaps my office. . . . I need a . . . secretary rather badly. We've been so busy."

He had been going to say "shorthand-typist," but checked himself. She did not look like a shorthand-typist. Secretary was so much more impressive for both of them.

As she made no immediate reply he went on, "You haven't taken another job yet?"

"No."

There she was again. No help whatever.

"Well, perhaps you'll think it over. . . . We—Mr. Samuel and I—we've been very satisfied during all this time."

"Thank you."

He turned and went out quickly, his finger and thumb gathering speed.

Mollie grinned into a bundle of uncorrrected proofs. One of the few things that gave her pleasure at the office was baiting Gerald. Unkind perhaps? But the fellow was so comically transparent and pitiful. He simply stood there and asked to be embarrassed.

And now what? The Paris course? Hopeless, with clothes rationing still in force. London? An office job? They were paying good money in town for shorthand-typists. Not enough personal freedom—not so much as at this place. Provincial journalism, something bigger; in a city, perhaps? That might do, and then it might not. It would be good to leave Sandcombe for somewhere less cramped and parochial, but good lodgings were at a premium, even when they could be found. Mollie had a comfortable home, a detached villa on the Paxtonbury Road, with a striking view of the Channel and an acre of wild country garden. After all, one did not spend all one's time at work. City lodgings in the Midlands or North could be desperately dreary. Here one had few friends, but there was always the sea and the moors behind and the maze of rides leading through the pinewoods as far as Paxtonbury, the nearest county town.

She turned back to her typewriter and squeezed Lady Malden-Payne's bazaar opening into eight lines, using the piece about the decapitated Chinese missionaries as a lead-in. Hang on here a while, but not as Gerald's secretary—not for double the money. When this Hearn fellow came back she might have a holiday and arrive at a decision sunbathing in Spaniard's Cove. In the season she did most of her thinking down there, while she was tanning herself an attractive golden brown.

THREE

During the morning that Nat spent wandering along the Flats, making up his mind to present himself at the office, and completing the last half inch of the circle begun in the early summer of 1940, Gerald Vane had two visitors. They arrived at his office within a few moments of one another.

This was somewhat irritating, as the second to arrive was Baines, a local councillor, and proprietor of Sandcombe's local bus and charabanc routes. He was Gerald's most important customer. Gerald was then engaged with Frost, the milkman—a customer of sorts, but one whose errand did not appear to have much to do with the printing of billheads.

Frost, a tall, stooping man, with unpleasantly small eyes, was depressed. He had come straight from the petty sessions at Sandcombe Police Court, where he had been fined two pounds for working a horse with open sores. The case had been brought by the RSPCA, and the Chairman of the Magistrates' Bench, Major Fenwick, had been somewhat outspoken, for he was an outdoor man, reputed to love horses, and he knew Frost of old, having endeavored without success, to get an extra pint of milk out of him during a period of acute local shortage a few months before. He told Frost he "had the makings of a vicious brute," and expressed a wistful longing to have "had it in his power to send him to prison."

Frost did what any intelligent Sandcombian would have done in the circumstances. He went straight to the *Clarion* office and asked Gerald to "play it down, old man." He knew the case would have to be reported, but he was not a regular reader for nothing. There were toe-lines and headlines.

Gerald, having asked Baines to discuss his new time-table layout with Skinner, assured Frost (who paid last quarter's printing bill) that he would speak to Sam about the case, and hurried into the editorial before Baines returned upstairs.

He found Mollie at work in the bay window, hacking out a half column on the Silverstone inquest. His father was bent over the heavy mahogany desk, scribbling away at his "Round About Town" notes, and getting a good deal of satisfaction out of the job, to judge by the firm, unbroken set of his clean-shaven lip, and the way he punctuated each full stop with an "Ahhh!" or "There!" as though he was beating a carpet.

Gerald coughed. He had to get Mollie out of the way.

"The surveyor's in the shop, Miss Thorpe. Would you mind getting Monday's golf scores out of him? He asked me to take them, but I'm rather busy."

Mollie got up and went out, under no illusions as to why Gerald had suddenly recalled the golf scores. Sam, who was used to this sort of thing, went on scribbling, but he said, "Well, what is it? I'm as busy as you are, Gerald!"

"I've got to have a word with you—it's about Frost the milkman."

Samuel let fall his pencil and looked up, severely enough.

"Don't talk to me about that scoundrel," he rasped out. "I'm giving him what for in the editorial this week. Not a word to say for himself. Working a horse with . . ."

Gerald cut in. At times like these he was not afraid of his father. They were realists, both of them, but Sam's memory was beginning to fail. He seldom looked at the ledgers, relying more and more upon Gerald's twelve-hour day.

"He's a customer," said Gerald.

"Wasn't aware of it," mumbled Sam, the slightest bit ashamed of himself for forgetting.

"He's not all that good," went on Gerald, more sure of his ground, "but there's no sense in rubbing it in. If we can do something to make him grateful . . ."

Sam knew his son was right. Secretly he was rather proud of him. It flashed through the older man's mind that, even as Gerald was reining him in at the moment, so might he, as a young man, have cautioned his own father if the latter had been anything but a shiftless, indigent fellow, who had continually borrowed from him until Sam's mother had died and Sam had fended him off and struck out for himself. Gerald was right, of course, but it went against Sam's principles to surrender without protest.

"It's a bad thing, Gerald, letting the printing influence our policy. This fellow's got himself to blame . . . bad supervision at the stables . . . he ought to have a lesson of some sort, you know."

Gerald allowed himself a swift, sidelong grin. Really the Old Man was quite incredible sometimes. But he played up to it, for Sam had no secrets from Gerald, though he considered he had many.

"He's had his lesson," he said. "Chairman of the bench made him smart. Besides, he's got his costs and the fine to pay."

Sam picked up the sheet he had been covering. It began, "Seldom in the history of local jurisdiction has a local tradesman been found guilty of a more callous offense toward a four-footed helpmate. . . ." Pity. It struck a sound note. The vicar might have preached a sermon on it, as he had preached one on the leader Sam had written about two-piece bathing costumes last summer. He crumpled the sheet and tossed it into an over-full wastepaper basket.

"We don't want to be unduly hard on the man," he said.

Having won a minor victory—if the bringing of his father into line with the firm's financial interests could be called a victory—Gerald expanded a little.

"About Hearn," he began.

"Well?" grunted Sam, disinclined to open a subject which might occasion a second climb-down.

"He's home," said Gerald, and waited.

Sam had expected this. Something about wages now, unless he was much mistaken. Gerald had always been inclined to side with Nat in the countless little controversies that had been played out in this office during the last fifteen years. It was not that Sam disliked Nat—he found him pliant and efficient—but he resented what he termed being "got at" by a Gerald-Nat alliance. He knew that, behind his back, Gerald had gone to Nat for sympathy when his father had contemptuously turned down one of Gerald's new ideas ("wheezes" Gerald called them) for modernizing the plant or increasing turnover. He knew that Gerald, outwardly a respectful son for these disrespectful days, considered him old-fashioned. Old-fashioned he was content to be, if it was old-fashioned to protest against the dribbling away of hard-earned profits on silly little pieces of chromium-plated rubbish for desks, and complicated systems of costing that filled fat notebooks (notebooks out of stock, mark you) with a maze of meaningless figures.

But Gerald was not to be caught. He merely waited for his father to lower his guard.

"I suppose he'll want more money," said Sam at last.

Gerald said he supposed he would.

Sam burst out, "These ex-servicemen; they're coming back asking the earth. Whippersnapper from Coates, the ironmongers', had the impudence to ask seven-ten. He was getting three-fifteen before he went away. What's to become of us all, if we carry on like this?"

Gerald, who was neutral, not having served in the forces (a circumstance which afforded him mild regret now that it was all over), made a little sound which might have been sympathetic, but was, in fact, an expression of boredom. He was getting very tired of discussions with the Old Man. It would be good to begin again discussing him instead with Nat.

Chipping away at a hard piece of skin at the base of his thumbnail, he said, "He's got to have his job back. It's law."

Sam suddenly tired of the subject. Offer him six," he grunted, "not a penny more. I have to see the vicar about his Church Services adverts; they're too cheap."

He went downstairs, passing Mollie Thorpe on the way up.

Gerald drifted into his own office and closed the door. He wanted to work out his paper reserve. Mollie went back to her desk to find Bumble, frowning down on a blurred pull of Nat Hearn, in a flight-sergeant's uniform.

"What they want to use that old block for?" He pointed to the three chevrons and crown. "He had his thick ring a long time ago."

Mollie yielded to a desire to know more about this man Hearn, the man whose ghost she had encountered so often in the town bazaars and in the parlors of little terrace houses where she called for funerals, weddings and the careers of local servicemen. They all knew Nat. They never pretended to regard her as anything more than a wartime substitute for Nat. They fumbled among handbags and bureau drawers for creased newspaper cuttings from bygone *Clarions* and told her, "Nat wrote that when my husband died" or "This is Nat's account of Letty's wedding. Quite a nice little bit, we thought." Mollie felt he must have understood these people very well, but wondered whether this would make him any more human than Sam or less fidgety than Gerald? For a long time now she had been curious about the fellow.

"You were here with Nat Hearn?" she asked Bumble. "What was he like—I don't mean to look at—what was he like to work with? Fussy?"

Bumble looked slightly pained. "Gosh, no! 'Course 'e wasn't. Nat? 'E was wizard; always the same. It was better here then. Got on with everyone, 'e did. Bit absentminded. Often used to 'ave to speak to 'im twice 'fore he'd look up."

"He's coming home," said Mollie.

Bumble grinned. "You're up to date, aren't yer? I 'eard that Monday night. Are *you* stayin' on?"

"I don't know. Haven't made up my mind."

"Oh? Well, there's the last pull of the inquest. What a screwy thing to do at 'er age—drown herself in a bath!"

"It won't ever happen to you," said Mollie; but Bumble had already drifted down the works stairs, and her voice was lost in the clatter of the platen, piling up mountains of pink programs for Tuesday's Fruit, Flower and Vegetable Show.

Mollie was still at the desk, when the landing door opened and softly closed again. She looked up, and saw a square young man, wearing new flannels already baggy and

24

spotted. It took her a full half minute to realize that this was Hearn. He looked older than she had imagined from his RAF picture, and somehow much more friendly. His mouth was curving upward a little, as though he had enjoyed creeping in on her and putting her at a slight disadvantage. She liked his eyes—gray and restless, as though permanently looking round for odd details he had overlooked in write-ups. He was slightly sunburned, but that would wear off, as she knew he was only recently back from Italy. He had nice hands and fingernails. He looked a good deal taller than he was, for he seemed to her altogether too thin, only broadening out at the shoulders.

"Hullo?" she said, and smiled, not wanting to give him the impression that she realized her career as subeditor-cum-reporter to the *Clarion* was over, cut short by his silent entry into the office.

He moved across the room, lounging rather than walking, and sat on the edge of the table. His restless glance took in what she was doing. She felt he knew, down to the last colon, the stuff she was writing on the sheet of foolscap that hung from the platen of his rackety old typewriter.

His glance left the table and traveled round the untidy room, moving from the open 1936 *Clarion* file, spread on the floor, to the calendar a month out of date and the curling three-color poster advertising *Outward Bound* which Gerald, proud of his first three-color job, had pinned up as an exhibit years ago. Mollie watched, interest taking the place of initial embarrassment.

Nat took a long, nostalgic sniff. He looked at the bow window. It was shut.

"Old Man still as frightened of fresh air?" he asked her.

"Hates it. That top bit's been screwed up!"

Nat nodded. "I'm not all that keen myself," he admitted, "but he's the outside limit. Loves a fug. You should see the amount of underclothes he wears!"

Mollie smothered a little giggle, but Nat went on, with mock seriousness.

"Thick pants," he said, "right down to his boots. And vests, with sleeves, all the year round. Wonder he didn't melt in here sometimes."

He got up and added, more to himself than to her, "Funny chap Sam. Bit pathetic, I suppose. Never seems to have got much fun out of the job."

"Did you?"

He looked hard at her, as though trying to make up his mind whether she was really interested or merely trying to make polite conversation. He decided she was interested, and sat down in Sam's chair, shooting his long legs under the desk and thrusting his hands deep in his pockets. She could see why his clothes lost their shape so quickly.

"Dunno. I've been out along the Flats trying to figure that out."

"Well," she said, "you ought to know. You were here long enough. I've been following you round. You're a sort of legend."

"Am I?" She saw, instantly, that he was pleased. "They remember me?"

"All the little ones do."

"I'm glad." He smiled across at her, and she thought how much younger he was when he smiled. He seemed quite a different person. "I think I'll let that decide me."

"Decide you?"

"To come back. I wasn't sure, you know, right up to now. I hate making decisions of any sort. It's difficult to make decisions when you haven't any convictions. I had a lot of convictions when I came here. I was a socialist—the booky sort—and I thought the police were incorruptible. I even thought innocent people sometimes went to jail."

"Don't they?"

"Never. But guilty ones sometimes get away with it. But you ought to know, you must have attended a good many sessions."

She looked across at him, and it struck her again how different he was from the man she had imagined. He was bitter, but his bitterness was softened by humor—a bitterness against causes, not against people. She felt he liked people and was always faintly exasperated with them for not being more successful as a race. She felt justified in risking a direct question. Bumble and others had been right. He was an approachable person.

"Were you happy here?"

He grinned, withdrew his long legs and, standing, walked over to the window, where he could look down on the High Street.

"Are you?"

She looked at his back and knew he was still grinning.

"I asked first."

"Yes, you did. All right." He turned and sat down on the littered window recess, piled with proofs, old *Clarion*s, two empty glue bottles and all the rubbish that had overflowed from her "Deal-with-Sometime" tray.

"I suppose I was," he admitted, "at any rate, after the first year or two."

"Did it take so long for your hide to thicken?"

"No; but it's no use judging the place from your standards. You see, Sandcombe isn't a bad place for a man with no background."

"Weren't you born here?"

"No. I'm not sure where I was born. I only know my mother wasn't smart enough to collect father's address!"

So that was it. Illegitimate. Why hadn't someone told her? Or did anybody know? Surely he wouldn't blurt out a thing like that.

He answered her question for her.

"Sam doesn't know that. Nobody here knows it."

"Why should you tell me?"

"God knows. Perhaps its just because you've been *me* for so long."

Somehow the answer seemed adequate. Looking at him, sitting there among the litter, she was conscious of a growing liking for this lean, gauche, gentle man. She knew, without his explaining further, why he had come back to Sandcombe. All those people in the terrace houses and all the shop assistants and artisans who came into the shop with little pieces of paper, containing whist scores, In Memoriam notices, the results of swimming races, they were the people he regarded as his family—a family she had nursed through the war years and was about to hand back to him. Small wonder he didn't sneer.

"Gerald wants me to stay on as his . . . secretary."

"Going to?"

"What do you think?"

"Gerald's all right when you get used to him. I never quarreled with Gerald. But you wouldn't last in his office. You'd crown him with a ledger inside a fortnight. Why don't you stay on with me?"

"Neither Gerald nor Sam would wear that."

"You leave it to me. I'm rusty. I can't even remember the vicar's initials. You'll have to hang on for a bit. If I can fix it, will you stay?"

Why not? she thought. There was no pressing alternative, and working here, with this odd man, promised fun. She felt intensely curious to see how he went about his professional job.

"I'll try it for a month."

"Good." He got up, still restless, and lounged over to Sam's desk, picking up the blotting pad and holding it to the light. "I used to be able to see what he had in mind for an editorial from this," he told her. "Here we are. See these jottings? 'Vicious beast,' 'un-English,' 'nudity.' . . . He's having a go at someone. I never knew anybody who could say nothing so emphatically. There's a streak of genius somewhere in Sam."

His mind went off at a tangent again. "Tell me," he said, with another of his slow grins, "does that little Mrs. Bostock still exhibit in five of the ten classes in the baby show?"

"In all ten now," she told him. "Her husband wasn't called up."

He laughed out loud, and was still laughing when the works door opened and Gerald came in, followed by Baines, the garage proprietor. Gerald stopped short on seeing Nat, and, before he could recover himself, Baines pushed forward, extending a huge red hand—a hand that Nat had always thought should belong to a sadistic pork butcher rather than to an organizer of half-day trips to the Druid's Cave at Cragmouth.

Baines greeted him enthusiastically. He had been on good terms with Nat before the war. In those days Baines had not owned the garage in High Street—it had been run by Vetch, Baines' senior partner, a man as small and insignificant as Baines was large and aggressive. Vetch had had the money, and was known to be close with it; Baines was always saying old Vetch would have it buried with him, till and all; but apparently Vetch had thought better of it in his codicil, and died leaving Baines plenty of capital and a free hand. Notwithstanding petrol shortage and restricted car deliveries, Baines had made the most of his chances, and today he looked as prosperous as he would have Sandcombe believe he was.

He had been co-opted onto the council during the wartime truce, and was making rapid headway, commercially and socially. A beefy, quick-tempered man, he had a huge round head, small eyes and a loud mouth, draped with a straggling mustache dyed ginger by heavy smoking. Nat recalled that Baines believed in Sandcombe's future. He was always at war with the retired class on the Ridge, holding that they alone prevented the town from fulfilling its natural destiny and becoming a West-Country Blackpool. Nat had read some of his speeches in the *Clarions* Gerald had posted to him abroad. He remembered Baines' slogan—"Progress with Taste!" Baines did not look very much like an exponent of taste. He wore a check suit of heavy brown tweed, a blue-and-white shirt and a spotted bow tie. He always kept his bowler hat wedged firmly on the back of his bald head, where it looked rather like a black blockhouse crowning a smooth, pink rock.

"Glad ya back, Nat ol' man," said Baines, and sounded as if he meant it. "We can do wi' some young blood to chivy up some o' them jokers at cahnsel. Dead most of 'em. Died in the 'ungry forties! You get busy on the ol' typewriter, son. I'm with yer, 'ook, line an' depth charge!"

Nat felt this was a promising beginning, and Gerald, who would have curled a lip at this sort of talk from anyone but a first-class customer, nodded enthusiastic agreement.

"Mr. Baines is doing some energetic crusading on the council, Nat. He's aiming at a hundred houses."

Gerald, who clutched a buff order form for ten thousand timetables which Baines had just dropped on his desk, made it sound as though only now and again in the course of the centuries that had elapsed since cave-dwelling communities had as many as one hundred dwellings been seen together in a single area. Nat, who was aware of Sandcombe's housing problem, even before the postwar shortage, which was on everybody's lips, was not unimpressed, for he thought he saw in Baines a man who would do the town some good in spite of himself. He was the sort of councillor who made rash promises immediately before the March elections, and then felt obliged to carry them out because his customers and his electors were the same people—people, moreover, who had ready access to a man with a business in the center of High Street. This could not be said of most of Sandcombe's councillors, who could promise anything before they faced the poll, and then execute a strategic withdrawal behind the creeper-covered walls of their detached houses on the Ridge. Over Baines' broad shoulders Nat thought he detected a swift wink on the part of Mollie, ostensibly proofreading in her alcove, but he ignored this and said, "I was glad they co-opted you, Mr. Baines. And if you're out for a housing scheme, Gerald and I are with you, all the way."

"One hundred percent," endorsed Gerald, already beginning to feel that here was an ally upon whom he could rely implicitly if it came to further wrangles with Sam. He made a mental note to acquaint Nat at the first opportunity with Sam's increased tendency to dictate policy.

Baines reflected a moment before turning back to Gerald.

"Them timetables . . ." he began.

"Yes, Mr. Baines?"

"Better make it fifteen thousan'. Cheaper if the type's set, isn't it?"

"Every time," said Gerald, flourishing a stub of pencil above the order form.

"Now there's something you c'n do for me," added Baines, with a blatancy that Nat found amusing, but almost indecent. "Who writes the "Round Abaht Town" column?"

"I expect Nat will from now on," said Gerald.

"Stress the 'ouses," said Baines. "It'll be comin' up at

the next monthly meeting. I think I've got most of 'em lined up, but you never can tell."

Again Nat caught Mollie's eye over the garage proprietor's shoulder. It disconcerted him a little, for it seemed to say, "Nice going! Amazing how quickly you pick it up again, isn't it?"

He followed Gerald and Baines to the door and, because he felt she was still looking at him, passed down into the works, drifting from machine to machine, until Gerald bustled back and took him by the arm. He was excessively cordial.

"Keep that up with Baines, old man; he's dynamite. Worth at least two hundred and fifty pounds a year to us. Not only that, though I agree with the fellow. Not out of the top drawer perhaps, but go-ahead."

He dropped into the habit of guide, almost forgetting it was not Nat's first visit. He was, however, far more truthful about the machines than he would have been in conversation with a customer.

"Look at that flatbed. It labors like a cart horse. Caster's always breaking down, so's the keyboard. I've been trying to persuade the Old Man to replace them. It would more or less clean us out, I know, but how can I be expected to turn out good work on this rubbish? Sam won't part up with a penny. D'you think he'd listen to you?"

Nat reflected. This was a new approach. Gerald must be getting desperate.

"I never had much pull with him. You know that, Gerald."

"But it's different now . . . since you were made an officer, I mean."

Nat grinned. Different? Because he had changed his serge for gaberdine and a cap that fell off for one that stayed on? It had been different with a good many people— railway porters, hotel and cinema commissionaires, prostitutes. Was it the money or just honest, downright snobbery? Probably a little of both. An idea occurred to him.

"I'll try it on, Gerald; but could you do something for me as well?"

"I've already done it," said Gerald, with a certain smugness. "I forced your salary up to three hundred a year this morning. It was like drawing teeth!"

Nat was neither elated nor disappointed. If he had thought about it at all, he would have been rather surprised by a thirty-shilling rise, but money did not seem so important in Sandcombe. It never had.

"Thanks, Gerald, but it wasn't that. . . . It was the girl . . . the one upstairs."

"Miss Thorpe?" Nat thought he detected a little stiffening in Gerald's tone.

"Thorpe, is it? How'd she make out?"

"Oh, well enough. I asked her to stay on—in my department, of course, but she doesn't seem keen. Good family and all that, but upstage, old man, definitely upstage for us. She can't take a dressing down."

Nat tried to picture Gerald administering a "dressing down" to the alert, rather arresting young woman upstairs, but the tableau refused to come to life. Gerald might handle the shop girls satisfactorily, or even Miss Morgan, the militant evangelist in the stitching room, but Mollie Thorpe would have probably cut the interview short by telling him not to be such a silly little man. Something told Nat quite emphatically that Gerald was afraid of his wartime subeditor. It made his request easier.

"I've told her," he said, "I shall be rusty. I haven't touched shorthand for over five years. You'd better keep her on in my office a while."

Gerald grimaced.

"If you think it's necessary. . . . I was going to give her the choice of coming in with me or finding another place. Are you sure she'll stop?"

"I think I can promise she will," said Nat, and turned quickly away, for he thought he detected faint pathos in Gerald's expression. "How's Burton?" he asked, to change the subject.

Burton was a dour journeyman who had sat at the keyboard for years, exchanging hardly a dozen words a day with anyone. He lived by himself in a small cottage up on the Paxtonbury Road, pedaling an ancient bicycle to and fro morning and evening, and eating a packed lunch in the boiler house during the dinner break. He was a good printer, punctual and accurate. His work seldom had to be read for literals, but his silent habits made him unpopular with the rest of the staff, who were fond of a gossip over the galleys and typecases. His single extravagance in life was homing pigeons, which inhabited lofts in the outbuildings behind his cottage. He wrote "Homing Notes" for the *Clarion* every week, and was proud of the fact that some of his birds had been used by the military during the war.

"He's about the same," Gerald admitted, "but I've heard he's been thick with Carstairs lately. Carstairs is one of the cranks in his club, but he also happens to be the union representative at Paxtonbury. I daresay he's been giving Burton ideas. The Governor's still dead against union men. Can't say as I blame him when you think of the way the country's going."

"You'll have to come to terms with unions sooner or later," said Nat, and suddenly he felt tired of Gerald's company. "I'll go up and see what's cooking," he told him. "I'll start in this afternoon."

Gerald brightened. Thursday was payday, and so it meant a full week's work out of Nat. There was a good deal of Sam in Gerald.

"Grand," he said, and only just prevented himself from rubbing his hands.

Nat had mounted the first stair when Bumble came out of a stockroom. Seeing Nat, he dropped the paper he was carrying and almost ran across the landing.

"*Nat! Whizzo!*"

Nat regarded the boy with mock gravity. "My, my," he said, "how the children do spring up!" But he wrung Bumble's hand with warmth, for he liked the youngster's sincerity and enthusiasm. It was rare enough among the present crop of adolescents.

Bumble wasted no time. "I'm a sergeant in the ATC, Nat. Can I tell 'em you'll come along to HQ an' give us a talk next Tuesday?"

"What about? The uses of bullshine in the RAF?"

"Give us the gen on Lancs, Hallys—anything you like?"

"I don't know a Lancaster from a Handley-Page," said Nat—a statement almost literally true. Nat hated engines, particularly aircraft. They didn't seem to be able to go near anything without grinding it to a pulp.

Gerald cut in. "Run along, Bumble; Mr. Nat's got other things to think of now he's back with us."

Laying a hand on Nat's arm as he turned to return to the office, he added, "I shouldn't let 'em get too familiar with you, old man. After all, you're more or less one of us. I've had the devil's own job trying to run this place on business lines."

He didn't add that Bumble's father had been sergeant-major in the Home Guard, and had taken a particular pleasure in comparing Gerald's ceremonial march to the waddle of a pregnant duck. That, together with Bumble, senior's, comment, "You fix bayonets like you were givin' birth to a sack o' nails!" took a good deal of living down in a town like Sandcombe. Gerald had hated the Home Guard with a vehemence that his instructors would have had him reserve for the *Wehrmacht*. But Gerald had found it difficult to hate the Germans. They were such an orderly people.

Nat grinned and shambled on upstairs. He had not yet got his second wind in the Clarion Press, and something told him that the getting of it might take some considerable time. He had found some of his Admin. & Special Duties adjutants a trifle parochial, but they were Regency rakes alongside Gerald.

FOUR

Mollie had gone out when he returned to the office. Disappointed, and anxious to miss Sam's greetings, Nat went out into the High Street, and, to avoid a series of aimless conversations, slipped into the Galleon, at once Sandcombe's oldest and most up-to-date public house.

Mrs. Gage, the licensee, was a good business woman, and on taking over the Old Tudor inn many years ago had lost no time in assessing its possibilities. She had attended a number of local auction sales and crammed the three bars with as many antiques and pseudo-antiques as the low-ceilinged rooms could hold.

The bars now looked like little museums. Welsh dressers, warming pans and horse brasses abounded. Sabers, pistols and blunderbusses clung to the distempered walls, crowding out a mass of yellowing prints depicting hunting scenes and steeplechases that featured horses as lean as greyhounds. In the huge fireplace of the saloon bar red electric light bulbs were cunningly ambushed in a pyramid of half-burned logs, which, besides giving the chimneypiece a Pickwickian air, had the advantage of saving fuel.

Outside a monstrous signboard, flaunting a golden galleon that Drake could never have boarded without a crew of steeplejacks equipped with New York fire escapes, swung from a wrought-iron fixture, occasioning thereby a considerable correspondence between Mr. Frobisher, the draper who resided opposite, and the urban district council. For Mr. Frobisher, in addition to being a teetotaler, was a light sleeper, and the rhythmic creaking of the signboard each night that the wind blew in from the sea had led, indirectly, to the composition of many an impassioned sermon preached on the Methodist circuit, the sermons having been hammered out white-hot between the anvil of Mr. Frobisher's bedside table and the hammer of his speechless indignation.

Mrs. Gage greeted Nat as she might have greeted the return of an old customer who had recently renounced the Pledge. He was one of her old-time steadies—none of your periodical bursts, ending in a chorus of ditties and a summary ejection into High Street at closing time, but a regular night-by-night customer, who brought in a good class of trade and reported her darts matches in the *Clarion*.

She was a full-bosomed, florid woman, whose French style of dress, a generation behind the times, might have served as a model for Renoir. She was not a Sandcombian, but hailed from Lancashire, and was aggressively proud of the fact.

"Eeee, tha's back, Mr. 'Earn. This'n on me, laad. Now we'll 'ave somethin' worth reading in t' *Clarion*. We've 'ad nowt but church notes 'n burials since tha' joined t' air force!"

Nat, feeling slightly cheered, sat down in his familiar corner and sipped his beer. He asked after several old friends, some of them still in the forces, others gone away to find work.

"There's nowt here," Mrs. Gage told him. "T' council does nowt to encourage visitors. Trying to keep plaaace select, so they tell me. Blooody nonsense! There's nowt select here, not even enough houses to go rahnd. Ah said to that feller Baines—'e's on'y one with a bit o' go in 'im —ah said—'Wot do you reckon you're goin' t' do nine months from now?' An' he says, 'Nine months? Why nine months?' And I says, 'Eeee, Mr. Baines, it's long time since tha' were young, I c'n see. Tha' wouldn't have asked why, if tha'd been away in t' army five years an' had come 'ome wi' tongue 'angin' out!' "

With this, Mrs. Gage, who was famous for her broad humor, stabbed her customer a trifle painfully with a blunt forefinger and went off into peals of laughter before waddling away to attend to the Jug and Bottle, where she passed on the joke to Mrs. Scratton, Sandcombe's promenade donkey-driver.

Mr. Sleek, Sandcombe's most popular undertaker, now sidled in and, seeing Nat, brought his beer across to the settle. Sleek was an old friend of Nat's, who held for him the strain of affection reserved for some of the more extravagant characters in Dickens.

He was an extraordinary man, who could never be mistaken for anything other than what he was—a jobbing carpenter who had long since abandoned cabinetmaking in favor of coffin-making, an altogether more lucrative profession, and one that, as he was always ready to admit, could never be affected by booms or slumps, confining its mild fluctuations to the vagaries of the damp local climate.

Like most undertakers, Sleek was a naturally jovial man, but he never gave this away, sensing that it was bad for business. His pale face, crowned by a stovepipe hat, had always the expression of the professional mourner—sad, but not overwhelmed by the inevitability of human decay. He told amusing stories, all of them linked in some way or other to graves, trestles, coffins, brass plates, wreaths, sextons and exhumations, without permitting himself to be amused, but leaving it to his audience to decide whether to smile or to shake a doleful head, as they preferred. Most of them, however, smiled or laughed outright, for Sleek was an accomplished raconteur with the drollest way of expressing himself. Now he took a slow, satisfying draft of beer, neatly divided the swallow tails of his shiny frock coat, and sat down, without removing his hat.

It occurred to Nat that he had never seen Sleek without that hat, and he wondered, in his absent way, if countless excursions to Gatton churchyard, where the undertaker would be obliged to stand, in all weathers, bareheaded to the seawinds, had left him any hair. Nat never followed a cortège to the graveside. He collected all his data at the house, or, in the case of popular funerals, at the lych-gate. He now made a mental note to sneak up behind Sleek the next time that gentleman headed the mournful crocodile from the chapel after the service. He would then be able to satisfy himself as to whether Sleek was bald.

"Working, Mr. Hearn?" asked Sleek, greeting the journalist with grave dignity.

"More or less," Nat told him; "I only got back last night."

"Delighted to see you," said Sleek, and meant it, for

somehow he had never felt that it was really in keeping for a woman to accost "others present" as they passed through the lych-gate to attend a ceremony. His own wife had never attended a funeral, but she was an expert stitcher of shrouds, an occupation that kept her at the sewing machine for as many as eight hours a day in wet Januaries and Februaries.

Sleek felt in his pocket and, drawing out a fat notebook, thumbed through pages covered with angular, copper-plate handwriting.

"I've a duty here . . ." he began, and Nat recalled that Sleek always referred to his customers, dead or alive, as "duties," as though he was responsible to the government for making certain of the fact that no dead people were left lying about inside the area of the Sandcombe Urban District, ". . . I've a duty here by the name of Jigger. You'll recollect her—a skimpy bit of a woman; looked like a drink o' water dressed up, my Ellen always said."

"Dead?" queried Nat, who was quite certain of the fact, but derived mild enjoyment from hearing Sleek get into his old, familiar stride once again.

"I'm afraid so," went on Sleek, as though Miss Jigger's death involved him in monetary loss rather than gain. "Went off sudden. Them thin ones don't as a rule. Fat ones do, especially them with short necks." He looked hard and rather ruefully at Nat's collar. "I'm glad to see you've got a long neck, Mr. Hearn. I won't have the pleasure of seeing you comfortable for a long time to come."

"I hope not," replied Nat, very civilly. "Give me the gen on Miss Jigger. I've almost forgotten the routine."

"I put her away yesterday," continued Sleek. "You can get the names from the house. I believe her sister's up there. You might remember her. She used to work at Britton's the baker's, in Conduit Street. She left when she had to get married."

Nat said he recalled the lady very well. She had impressed herself on his memory by calling and dictating a birth announcement, insisting on the use of the words "premature birth." Nat remembered thinking that this was carrying gentility a bit too far, and had gone to Sam about it. Sam agreed to insert it, however, as the additional words were worth two-pence each to the *Clarion*.

Prompted by Nat (who was surprised to find how many of the professional questions he remembered, and how easily they slipped into the correct order after all this time), Sleek went on to give a sketch of the late Miss Jigger's career. "Dressmaker at Paxtonbury, second daughter of old Josiah Jigger, one-time tobacconist in the Market Place, an enthusiastic League of Nations Union member, worked in the canteen during the war," and so on, down to several dark and mysterious hints that Nat did not include in the report. Sleek summed up in the closing comment, "Queer family, but good payers, mind you. Oak coffin—best I could do; no stinting there, like some of 'em, Mr. Hearn. Sure to have the flowers in the paper if you call, sister's preparing a list for you—aye, *and* the inscriptions, not just the names. You'll put me on the bottom, of course?"

Nat, as ever, promised he would, for Sleek paid one-and-ninepence for the insertion of his name at the foot of each obituary he brought in. The undertaker finished his beer, and rose to his feet.

"I daresay I shall have another little job for you next week," he prophesied. "Old Jim Ditton, the pilot, is sinking. He's turned eighty-three, you know." Then, by way of epilogue, Sleek returned to the late Miss Jigger. "You'd 've never a 'thought," he concluded, "that a party of her build would 've weighed so much. *Bones,* that's what it is, Mr. Hearn, *bones!*"

When Sleek had gone Nat experienced a curious wave of depression. People like Sleek and Mrs. Gage and Gerald—indeed, the whole lot of them—had seemed faintly comic, and homely from a distance; but here, in their midst, Nat found them rather pitiful, even boring. Where was that woman? He felt he could do with her to put him on the defensive again, to make him dig down for good reasons for his return to the *Clarion*.

As he was about to get up, the swinging door opened again, admitting a tall, stooping man, with high cheekbones and soft brown eyes. Nat recognized him as Otto de

Vere, one of Sandcombe's proudest possessions, for he earned what was considered to be a fabulous income by writing thrillers, and lived in sin with a somewhat raddled blonde in a big house on the edge of the cliff.

Otto was on intimate terms with Nat. Before the war the journalist had often spent an evening with him at his home. Otto might have been of any age between thirty and fifty. He had one of those narrow, black-browed, Mephistophelian faces that do not register age. His hair was thick, gray-brown and usually rumpled. He ought to have worn spectacles but neglected to do so, having acquired the habit of squinting through half-closed eyes. His clothes were always well made, but somewhat showy for Sandcombe. He drank a good deal of spirits, and was popular in a bar on account of his prodigality and contempt for the money he earned.

Nat liked him. Lazy cynicism made Otto good company. He was known as a wide reader and a man who, while professing to despise world affairs in general and politics in particular, seemed to miss nothing in the newspapers and stored a vast assembly of facts in his capacious memory. He also held his work in genuine contempt, and his comments, on being told by a Sandcombian that the latter had just finished his latest book, were always greeted with a shout of laughter. "You mean you read it to the *end?*" he would drawl, and then, "You poor devil! Have a drink."

There was some sort of scandal attached to the man, quite apart from the presence on the cliff of the ex-musical comedy soubrette with whom he maintained a humdrum but otherwise satisfactory partnership. Sandcombe accepted this state of affairs, partly because Otto was a writer, and writers were expected to live in this manner, and also because Otto was rich beyond the dreams of Sandcombians, even those of Marty Shiner, the local bookmaker.

Nat knew a good deal about Otto. He knew that he had once been a history master at a public school, but had been fired after some trouble involving women. He knew why he continued to keep the blonde. "As far as bed is concerned, she's interesting and interested," Otto had once told him. He knew also that at one time, long, long ago

Otto had dreamed of writing a sensational work on Tudor England, a period in which he had specialized at Oxford. His long string of thrillers, however—*The Case of the Severed Thumb, The Greenhouse Murder,* etc.—had played such havoc with his style (or so Otto, an inherently lazy man, declared) that, although he still read history, he wrote none. Nat had not seen Otto for several years, and greeted him with considerable pleasure. Otto ordered shorts. Mrs. Gage always had something put by for him.

"Never thought you'd come back," admitted Otto. "What's the idea?"

Nat went straight to the point. "You've been here all the time, Otto. They told me your lung had kept you out of it. I had a feeling the town would have changed. Everywhere else has. What is it that keeps this place the same?"

Otto regarded the bottom of his glass. He seemed to hesitate a moment. Then he said, "What makes you think it is the same?"

"I've been back twenty-four hours. That isn't long, I know, but it's long enough. I dropped in at the works. Gerald's still binding about the machinery, Burton still flies pigeons, and the Old Man still runs the paper to suit his printing customers. Then I came in here—that old harridan over there still makes phony Rabelaisian jokes. Sleek, the undertaker, was in here a minute since. He still thinks it's funny to gag about funerals with mock seriousness. The whole setup's the same."

"Oh, *that* hasn't changed," said Otto; "all the poor devils round here have kept their pet idiosyncrasies. Why the hell shouldn't they? It's all they've got. But the town, *as* a town, that's a different cup of tea, young feller-me-lad."

"Why?" pursued Nat. "These people make up the town."

"I'm surprised to hear you say that," said Otto, with one of those smiles that always made Nat conscious of his mental inferiority when he discussed abstract matters with him. "You've been in Bomber Command. Doubtless you met some good types there. Did they have anything to do with Bomber Command's policy? Did what they thought and felt affect Bomber Harris's plastering of Germany?"

"They had to do what they were told. Anyway, I don't see where this is getting us."

"I'll tell you," said Otto, leaning forward on one elbow and speaking more seriously than Nat had ever heard him speak in the past. "This place is like everything else. Finished, washed up, on the way out."

"As a seaside resort?" queried Nat, beginning to enjoy a discussion lazily begun.

Otto made a gesture of impatience.

"As a community, you idiot. Why? There isn't any community spirit left. How could there be? It's been torn out of the people by restrictions, by the fight for rations, by the petty tyrannies of blackout wardens, by fear, frustration and years and years of nagging irritations intensified since the peace. Big places lost their community spirit years ago. London first, about the time of the big expansion five generations ago, then the northern cities during the slumps; but places like this, Paxtonbury up the river, Cragmouth along the coast, they hung on because they were small and interdependent. They had limited populations who took in one another's washing. They were more or less cut off, in spite of the wireless and cinemas and penny dreadfuls from Fleet Street. That was all right until the test came. When it did, they broke up, as you'd expect them to. Everybody struck out for himself. He had to or go under in one way or another. What have you got left? Is there any teamwork? Is there hell! Just nine thousand little egos ferreting round for bits of hake and sausages, snarling at one another in the bread queue, swapping a petrol coupon for a dozen eggs, and then going home and saying, 'I wonder where the hell he gets 'em?' That's Sandcombe, that's anywhere. It's curtains old boy, curtains."

Nat reflected for a moment. Then he said, "All the societies we used to have, all the clubs and organizations I wrote about week by week, they function, don't they?"

"In a way, yes," Otto told him, "but they're not the same. They've all become centralized. Most of the young blood went off. All the old codgers stepped in and hung onto committee places. D'you think they'll give them up?"

"Why not? They'll get old and tired."

"My dear old chap, when is a man old or tired enough to give up something that feeds his vanity? These old people love it; it's the indefinite postponement of the red light. They've got a sort of freemasonry organized. Politics, trade, food, entertainment, it's all intermingled. They'll never give it up. That woman Gelding, at the operatic society, will play leads now until they carry her, shrieking a flat aria, to the churchyard. Baines and the new council setup, they're all in with one another. 'Vote my way and I'll turn my back on the petrol pumps.' It's all too set; you younger fry have had it. You might as well realize that."

"There are plenty of youngsters coming back," said Nat, without much conviction, for Otto's pronouncements seemed to match his mood.

Otto finished his whisky and nodded for a refill.

"I thought you were coming to that, old boy. Well, there are plenty coming back. But, for a start, how long will they stay? There are no houses and few jobs with enough of the ready to keep pace with the rocketing cost of living. They'll soon go off to the cities and get swallowed up. Even if they don't, ask yourself, honestly, how much they care. *You* care; you're professionally interested. It's a hack writer's job to care about trends and all that sort of ballyhoo. But you're in a minority of one. The others haven't the brains or the guts to care. They're not interested in community life, not while Hollywood offers them two and a half hours of paradise for one and ninepence three times a week. Not while morons like me give them a fifth-rate puzzle to solve for a shilling, plus a bare buttock or two on the cover. Stop kidding yourself, son. Get a job in South Africa or New Zealand. They've got longer to go than we have. They might even stagger through another war or two."

Nat stood up. He was grinning, in spite of himself. "Still living with Pam?" he asked.

Otto nodded.

"Naturally. I always told you physical sensations are the only things that matter."

"You're phonier than you ever were," said Nat, and went out into the High Street.

FIVE

Although the full impact of Otto's remarks was not felt by Nat for several weeks (that is, until he had had time to go his rounds and judge for himself if things were as bad in Sandcombe as Otto declared them to be), it is doubtful whether he would have remained there more than two months had it not been for the stimulating presence of Mollie. She stayed on in the editorial office, dividing her time between proofreading, the compilation of news shorts and Gerald's correspondence—an arrangement which seemed to work satisfactorily, largely owing to her own unfailing tact.

Nat found the gathering of news pleasant enough. He liked renewing old acquaintanceships and catching up with the family history of Sandcombians scattered by the war. It took him less than a week to pick up his old threads and to fill a notebook with jottings. The actual committing to copy of the material he gathered proved irksome, however, and he was glad enough to lean back in Sam's leather chair, shoot his long legs under the desk and drop into an easy conversation with the girl in the window alcove.

More often than not they had the office to themselves. Since the war Sam rarely spent more than an hour a day in the building, and was more silent than Nat remembered him, pottering through the stockrooms and grunting over his correspondence, then hastening off to pursue one or other of his outside interests, notably chapel missionary work at North Road Methodist Church, or to visit the clubroom of the Sandcombe Philatelic Society, of which he was chairman.

Gerald looked in now and again to discuss items of business, and Bumble wasted as much time as he was able in the editorial room, popping up from the works with proofs and other excuses. Apart from such routine interruptions, Nat and Mollie sat at their respective desks and sandwiched long discussions on town affairs, the atom bomb, the future of Europe, plays, books, furniture, old china, religion and sex, between the writing up of a church bazaar and the Conservative and Unionist Women's rally in the grounds of Highcliff Lodge (lent by Mrs. Betterby-Stuart).

Nat found her mind quick, receptive and above all utterly logical. Time and again she accused him of inclining to one point of view on the grounds of sentiment. He liked her directness, her quiet refusal to be sidetracked, her deftness in sidetracking him when she was losing ground, but, beyond all, he warmed to her sense of humor, which matched his own. This was lively enough at all times, but hitherto had been damped down by the disadvantage of always having worked alone, for even in the forces he had been engaged upon work of a more or less specialist nature, and had seldom operated with a team.

Theirs was a friendship not entirely intellectual. For his part, he found her attractive, having the sort of attraction that grew on a man. There were moments, when they were not talking and he was quietly regarding her over the platen of his typewriter, in which he felt he would have liked to get up, cross the room, run his fingers through her dark hair and tilt up her face for a kiss, perhaps many kisses.

Nat had not had a great deal of experience with women. In the old days, in Sandcombe, he had never seemed to find time, and in the forces his casual associations with WAAFs, all vaguely unsatisfying, had been played out with the sort of girl who met him more than halfway. Mollie was not that type. She stayed in her alcove and, as far as Nat could divine, would stay there indefinitely.

It had been comforting to reflect, in the first days of their friendship, that there was no hurry about it all; but as the weeks went by and summer gave place to autumn Nat was conscious of a growing brother-sister complex, which seemed to remove her still further physically, while bringing her closer than ever into his mental orbit. He felt that he had started on the wrong foot, and could not help wondering, a little irritably, how he was ever going to get into step with the woman.

He had also an uncomfortable feeling that she was aware of, and perhaps not a little amused by, his dilemma, which warned him that his first attempt to improve their relationship would be so final, one way or the other, that he felt less and less inclined to take the risk. A polite but firm rebuff, he argued, would only result in her leaving the place, whereas if she welcomed the decisive step, Heaven knew what might be expected of him. Marriage, even.

Silly business this sex. Why couldn't things continue as they were, without the slanting sunlight catching the tip of her nose, as she bent over the first pulls of the *St. Luke's Parish Magazine?* She talked about everything but herself. He couldn't even be certain she had ever kissed a man, much less slept with one. He made discreet inquiries in the town, but they only led into cul-de-sacs. If only she had served in the forces he could have asked her outright. The WAAFs had not been so reticent in these matters.

Such, then, was the relationship between the two when they covered the convention together—a big Free Church assembly held in the flat meadow behind Christow's farm on the Paxtonbury Road. Nat always attributed to this expedition the first link in the chain of disguised routine events that led up to the crisis, and all that subsequently transpired at the Clarion Press.

The convention had been a hardy annual in the prewar days. It was organized by a representative committee of the Free Churches in the district, and was a warning undertone to obdurate sinners, a hint that failure to heed the message could only lead to descent into the pit.

Having been deprived of one another's spiritual support for more than seven years, the conveners planned a monster rally on this particular occasion. Chief organizer was Mr. Twigger, secretary of the local Free Church Union and a celebrated dispenser of religious tracts, printed in letters of fire, which he left in unoccupied cars and pasted up in telephone booths. Seen while engaged in this pursuit he looked rather like a neatly dressed Nihilist planting bombs along the route of the Tsar. It was amazing, in these days of acute paper shortage, where he obtained his vast stocks of literature. Some of his leaflets, telling the story of a Liverpool docker's spiritual awakening, or a drunken Glasgow glassworker's acceptance of everlasting life, ran to eight and even ten pages. He was, however, an excellent organizer, and brought the convention's summons into the Clarion works in good time for printing and distribution. Bumble was given the job of setting it, and was intrigued by the buildup Twigger had given the principal speaker, the Reverend Ezra D. Owen-Thomas, of Salem Chapel, who was billed as "The Man with a Flame in His Mouth!"

"Strewth," muttered Bumble to Bennett, across a typecase, "they've even roped the ruddy circus in this year!"

But he knew the convention would be covered by the *Clarion,* and put one of the first proofs on Nat's desk.

After a glance through the program, Nat told Mollie, "You'd better help me out with this. I usually lose grip after the third sermon. Let's tackle 'em together, and then go in to the tea and sale. The tea's usually good, or was. These people are always better trenchermen than the Anglicans."

They found the marquee crammed. The front rows were pressing down on the tiny roped-in enclosure reserved for the press, which was hard by the exit, to the right of the platform. The trestle platform creaked under the weight of speakers and committeemen, the latter displaying huge rosettes and buttonholes, looking, as Mollie irreverently remarked, rather like election agents taking time off for a wedding.

A harmonium (why was it always a harmonium?) had been manhandled up from one of the Sunday schoolrooms in the town, and wedged under the platform. Two neatly dressed Sunday school scholars, a boy and a girl, sat one on each side of the choirleader, clutching huge bouquets which were to find their way onto the platform at a given signal. The signal would originate from Sam, who was already helping himself to water from the carafe, although he had yet to speak.

"Who is the dowager?" hissed Nat, indicating the vast woman in the flowered frock who was occupying Sam's attention at the moment.

"Lady Colham-Porter," she told him, and added, "*Beans!*"

"What happened to Lady Watchley—*stout?*"

"Went to the States in 1940—*cute!*"

Nat relaxed and she gave him an answering grin. A job like this became something of an entertainment when shared with a fellow cynic.

Now Sam was on his feet, announcing the opening hymn. He read the first verse, and the harmonium gave two preliminary chords. Nat noticed that one of the bouquet holders, the boy, was beginning to look pained, and as the hymn advanced his sullen expression hardened into ferocity. He held the carnations and maidenhair fern as though it was mere camouflage for a bomb, the ticking of which he was striving to muffle. A lean woman, doubtless his parent, reached over the front row of seats and whispered something in his ear. The boy's expression did not change, but he surrendered the bouquet without protest.

The first chorus roared across the tent. These people could sing, and few had need of the hymnbooks. They knew their Moody and Sankey by heart, and sang:

> Courage, brother, do not stumble,
> 'Though the path be dark as night!

as if they meant it. The harmonium, grappling with four or five different keys, stumbled now and again, but Miss Thatcher, at the keyboard, had coped with this sort of thing for years, and was in no way put out. She laid on the instrument like a veteran coach driver urging his team up a steep gradient, flogging the pedals and tugging the stops in such a masterly manner that the approving eye of Lady Colham-Porter was caught and held to the last flourish of the last line. The audience sat down, breathing heavily. They had not sung like that since the autumn of '38. Profound satisfaction shone in every face.

Sam did not sit down. He bent over the table thumbing through his notes—notes that Nat knew he would not use, for he had often borrowed them from Sam in years gone by, only to discover that they bore no relation whatever to the speech Sam had made.

The brief silence after the singing seemed unearthly. Then Sam smiled—a wide, genial smile, that revealed one or two gold fillings. It was the general signal to relax.

"Well, friends. Here we are again!"

A polite murmur of assent, assuring the chairman that this was the case. He went on, "It does me good, it does us *all* good, to meet here after a suspension of what is it— five, six, seven years? I said to myself when I heard that the National Emergency had canceled our plans for the 1939 Autumnal Convention, I said to myself . . ." At this point Sam turned abruptly to the Hon. Secretary, sitting on his immediate right. "What *did* I say to myself, Mr. Twigger?"

Mr. Twigger, who hadn't the slightest idea, looked confused, and the audience giggled a little at his obvious discomfiture, as Sam had intended. A little humor, he felt, always started these gatherings on the correct note—a note of cordial evangelicalism. But he soon took his eye off the blushing Mr. Twigger and went on to answer his own question. "I said to myself, '*Now* we've got something to fight for. *Now* we can get busy and vanquish one Fiend before we go on to trounce his Employer.'"

There was a burst of applause mixed with polite laughter. Nat, catching Mollie's eye, bent over his book and began to scribble furiously. He was too near Sam to take any chances. Against "Chairman's remarks" in his notebook he scribbled "Hitler-Satan partnership." It would serve as an adequate reminder.

Having got into his stride, Sam quickly ran through the evangelist's arsenal. Every time he made a point—and he made quite a number, particularly in the field of postwar morals, a topic that had an evergreen appeal for him now that two major wars had been fought in two generations— a tall, white-haired Baptist in the seat immediately behind Nat signified agreement with a thunderous "Hallelujah!" occasionally varied by "Amen, amen!" Sam must have liked these interruptions, for every time one of them punctuated his speech he turned and beamed at the Baptist, and the pair thus encouraged one another throughout the oration.

Nat, whose collar was a matter of inches from the enthusiastic Baptist's beard, also welcomed them, for when he was shouting at the platform the Baptist was unable to breathe down Nat's neck.

One way and another, things were not too comfortable in the press box. Mollie, facing Nat, had her back to the exit, and the gusty wind had torn loose the tent flap, which threatened to envelop her in wet folds. Her efforts to catch the trailing guy rope had already deflected the attention of a large section of the audience, not excluding the boy in the front row. This young gentleman, bereft of his bouquet, was regarding her discomfort with undisguised glee. Only his uncertainty as to what would ultimately take place prevented him from succumbing to the temptation to employ the trailing guy rope as an excuse to get out of the tent.

Nat took careful note of Sam's remarks, not because they carried news value, but because he was well aware that Sam would peruse the report very carefully when the first and second proofs were pulled. The opener, Lady Colham-Porter, was of less account, for no journalist, however ingenious, could have forged a readable paragraph from her brief speech. It began "Well now . . ." and it ended ". . . there now." In between these noncommittal phrases came a jumble of half-completed remarks about good works, Gospel messages, kind invitations, flattering tributes, Godspeeds and warm woollies, the latter, of course, being the exhibits on the Ladies' Working Party stall, which Lady Colham-Porter was confidently expected to purchase outright.

Having allowed a decent interval to elapse between the final "there now" and the reseating of Her Ladyship, in order that she could be quite certain that the opener had finished, the harmonium player prodded the little girl, who skipped up with a neat curtsey and the bouquet. The audience breathed "Ahhhhh!" with fond unanimity. The little boy, his bouquet now being returned to him, also sprang to his feet, but was dragged down again just as Lady Colham-Porter reached out for a second armful. She could not know that this bouquet was intended for the wife of the Man with the Flame in His Mouth, situated eighteen inches to the rear of her husband.

The audience sniggered, Mollie laughed outright, and Nat was observed by Sam to wag a finger in her direction. All through the main address Sam pondered this finger-wagging episode, unable to make up his mind whether it signified a professional reproach on the part of his chief subeditor or an indication that Nat had found grace on the battlefields of Europe.

The second hymn, "Fight the Good Fight," was a wise choice on the part of the Hon. Secretary, Mr. Twigger, for most of the audience knew it by heart, and there was a scarcity of hymnbooks. Nat shared one with Mollie, and was not the first man to be glad of this particular excuse for touching his lady's hand in public. The convention sang the hymn with enormous gusto.

It was during the early stages of the Rev. Ezra D. Owen-Thomas' message that the tent flap behind the press table became unmanageable. A series of loud reports prefaced his text, and the preacher turned a steely eye on the journalists, almost as though Mollie was herself engineering this novel form of salute.

The secretary slipped from the platform and disappeared, returning, a moment later, with a self-satisfied nod which informed the audience that a guy rope had been readjusted by an expert.

Hardly had he sat down, however, when the flapping exit bellied like a galleon mainsail into Mollie's back and catapulted her halfway across the flimsy table. Recovering hurriedly, she edged round beside Nat, and the latter, who found the necessary pressure of her knee mildly exciting, was duly grateful to the tent flap.

The Rev. Ezra took as his flint, steel and tinder a verse from the third chapter of Isaiah:

And it shall come to pass, that instead of sweet smell there shall be stink; and instead of a girdle a rent; and instead of well set hair baldness; and instead of a stomacher a girding of sackcloth; and burning instead of beauty.

51

Halfway through the text Nat had to lean forward and screen Mollie from the platform, for he sensed she was about to be overcome by an uncontrollable fit of the giggles. At the word "stink" he saw, out of the corner of his eye, that she had bitten her lower lip, a lip left unlipsticked on his advice before they set out.

The Rev. Ezra more than justified his buildup. The flame in his mouth was an understatement on Mr. Twigger's part. That gentleman had never had the pleasure of hearing him, or he might have billed the visitor more adequately. From somewhere between the Rev. Ezra's larynx and his widely spaced teeth there issued something far more devastating than a flame—rather a scorching oxyacetylene jet searing and withering everything that it touched. It warmed up on BBC comedians, engulfed Sunday cinemas, licked over charred embers of promiscuity and roared up the walls of the whole social edifice. Peace conferences, the divorce courts, jitterbugging, cinema posters—all were consumed in the fire. Nat began to feel that Sodom and Gomorrah were indeed the Islands of the Blest alongside the Britain of today. The Rev. Ezra drew a lurid but convincing picture of an imaginary returned service girl, staggering home from the pubs on the arm of her paramour, and reeling into the kitchen to find her father and brothers too intent upon dog-racing form to notice her condition. He quoted figures. According to his sources of information the birthrate of natural children was soaring high above that of children born in wedlock. Nat sat there scribbling, dazed by the statistics of sin.

What was the cause of this tumultuous descent to the pit? War? Pah! A cheap payoff (the Rev. Ezra did not scruple to use modern colloquialisms if he found them effective), an easy prescription that drugged the conscience (where conscience still lived) while doing nothing to heal the disease. Ah no, ah no, no, no! The war itself was but a *symptom* of the cataclysm—here Nat pondered on the grace of the shorthand symbol for "cataclysm"—evil thinking and spiritual sluggishness had produced the war, produced Hitler, produced and deified Mussolini, stimulated and organized blood lust that now found illegal outlet in the series of shocking crimes served up in their revolting detail every Sunday morning.... Sunday, when families, unkempt and in dressing gowns, were scavenging through the papers instead of preparing for worship.

Worship! Ah, there was a sign of the times! Did they know how many people attended a place of worship on Sundays? Did they know that petrol consumption on Sunday afternoon exceeded the petrol consumption, including commercial consumption, of the remaining six days of the week? No? Then he did—he'd read it in the papers, he'd read that ...

"When the blazes does this bloke find time to read the Bible?" muttered Nat, and turned sideways to discover that he was addressing an empty seat. Mollie had slipped through the flapping exit long since.

Nat glanced at Sam, whose gold-rimmed glasses were gleaming up at Ezra. Then, acting on impulse, not unmixed with relief, he squeezed round the press table and emerged onto the lawn. Almost immediately he saw Mollie, leaning against an elm near the abandoned produce stall.

"You'll get me shot," he told her.

She was still somewhat incoherent. "I'm sorry ... I had to come out ... it doesn't seem as funny out here as it does inside, but ... oh, Nat, was it *always* like that?"

"Of course. I told you, didn't I? You didn't see half of it during the war. They hadn't the time; besides, they got split up, and they're never so bad on their own. Come on, we'd better go back."

"Must we?"

"Sam'll demand a verbatim report."

"Oh, let him. He's the most pompous old fool I've ever heard."

Nat pondered. Inside the marquee Ezra's muffled voice was now declaiming against sunbathing and cosmetics.

"There's the tea, the other speeches and all the stall-holders' names to get," he said.

Mollie looked at him, and saw that the habit of years was still exerting a strong pull. She had always known he was a little afraid of Sam, but the knowledge excited sympathy, not contempt. She remembered his years here before the war and his comment the first day they met. "Sandcombe's not a bad place if you haven't a background."

She said, "You'd better say I was taken ill and you had to take me home."

He looked relieved. "That's pretty good. Come on, then, let's go through the wood to the cliffs. I'd like to show you something."

The wind had dropped when they went through the fieldpaths and into the pinewoods that straggled up the long ascent toward the cliff edge.

It was early October, and the way looked inviting. The open patches of the wood were splashed with yellow gorse and purple heather. Ragwort still sprouted among blackberries, long past their best or plucked clean by the townspeople, for this was a favorite spot for pickers. The bracken was turning to bronze and burgundy, and a thick, crisp overlay of dead beech leaves and pine needles rustled underfoot. The wind, blowing in from the sea, was still strong enough to bend the tapering points of the pines and stir the stronger branches of the beeches into low song. But inside the wood it was very still, and neither of them spoke until they had struggled to the verge and stood on the cliff edge, looking down into the wide, white-flecked bay.

"I remember coming up here one day after my first row with Sam," he said. "I'd made up my mind to pack it in. Can you see now why I didn't?"

It was a view worth the climb.

The whole sweep of the coast lay beneath, as gloriously detailed in the sharp October sunshine as anything he had seen over the Continent, flying at less than five hundred feet in a clear sky. The light blue water was enclosed by a curving buttress of red cliffs, gashed here and there by a blaze of yellow gorse where a landslip had occurred and sprouted thick undergrowth within the year. Away out to sea were the sandbanks, exposed by low tide, gleaming like a miser's hoard on a ruffled blue-and-white tablecloth.

There was nothing else—not a single fishing boat—to break the limitless expanse of water until it merged with the low banks of cloud, tinged above and on both sides with the gray threat of rain, twenty miles out to sea.

Away on the right, where the woods began to thin, ran the familiar red cleft, which looked as though a fairy-tale giant, seeking escape into the earth, had split the cliff in two and thus made room for Sandcombe. It held a serried huddle of red, white and gray buildings, staggered along the ledges, dense in the center, thin and uneven on the outer tiers.

From this height they could see the untidy ribbon of High Street, following the course of the Beck into the woods that screened the main Paxtonbury Road.

Peering down on the town like this, Nat felt that it did not look the sort of place to breed and house Sams and Geralds and Baineses and Sleeks. The latter's principal depository could just be seen through the clump of yews that grew in the parish churchyard. It looked green and solemn and comfortable.

He threw down his RAF raincoat on the roots of the tallest beech and they sat, by common consent, Mollie curling her legs beneath her and thrusting forward her tilted nose to sniff the air. The breeze had loosened her hair, and its dark tendrils streamed dangerously close to Nat's cheek.

She was talking about the people they had left. By this time they would be singing "Just As I Am Without One Plea" in the big tent.

"Why don't they come up here in ones and twos?" she asked. "It might help to blow the fug away."

He said nothing for a moment, and then, chancing to look upward, saw a triangle of blue between the straining branches. He said, quietly:

> I never saw a prisoner look
>   With such a wistful eye,
> Upon the little tent of blue
>   We prisoners call the sky?

"Yes?"

> Or on the something clouds that sailed
>   With sails of silver by.

"You don't have to be a prisoner," she told him, and for once he thought he detected a strain of irritation in her voice; "I shall never stop wondering why you don't cut and run."

"I suppose it's because I know, instinctively, that cutting and running isn't the answer."

"Then what is?" She turned and looked directly at him.

"Leadership, Mollie. Those people down there"—he jerked his head toward the cleft—"they're all right, fundamentally. What's more, they've got damned good stuff in them somewhere."

"You'd want a dissecting knife to find it."

"Not necessarily. I'm not pretending I know the answers yet. Otto was like you. He'd given up hope; but, unlike you, he knew he'd never find the answer outside the town, in bigger places like London."

"So you think we're both wrong?"

"Yes. I think the answer's down there somewhere. You see, those people are the same people as the men and women I lived with in the camps. And I happen to *know* that they were OK. We all knew that."

"Don't you see how different it was then? You were all uncomfortable at the same time. You were all united against authority or, in the field, against the Germans and the Japs. You had common interests and common troubles —bad billets, bad food, bullies, even bullets. You were bound to rely on each other and to like one another. If you hadn't you'd have given it up after a week or so, and Jerry would have walked in."

He considered this for a long time. It was the sort of reply Otto might have made.

"Peace isn't much different," he said at last. "There are still dozens of snags, corresponding to the snags we had out there—boredom, complacency, laziness. But most of the people don't know what to do or where to go. They rely on those with the money and the pull—people like Sam, who blows the local trumpet, and people like that Bible puncher down there, who preaches through it and depends on preaching for a living. If someone had a plan— nothing grand or expensive, but just a plan, clear and simple and worked out with common sense—you could still make that town a fine place to live in for the nine thousand within it; then, if everyone concentrated on his own locality, the whole country would crawl back to some standard of dignity and culture and comfort, even kindness maybe. I don't know, I daresay it's pretty hopeless, but that's how it strikes me."

He looked up from the little pile of pine needles he was stirring, and caught her looking at him more intently and more gently than ever before.

"Dear Nat . . . you're going to get terribly hurt before you toughen up."

He gave her no answering smile. "I'll never toughen any more than I have. I just believe in people. You either do or you don't. It just seems a pity to me that you don't, Mollie."

She looked away quickly, surprised to discover that his estimate of her hurt a little. Wasn't he just a little too naïve? Did he really know her? Did he know, for instance, that she had stayed on at the *Clarion* all these weeks solely because he had an attraction for her out of all proportion to his ambitions, his rather gaunt Cassius looks, his almost unbearable meekness when dealing with Sam and Gerald? It seemed not. He talked almost as though he lumped her in with the rest of the town—hard, selfish, greedy, flabby, tired, bored, artificially cynical.

She got up, suddenly.

"Let's go."

He looked so pained and surprised that she laughed. He struggled to his feet, and brushed the dead leaves from his baggy flannels.

"What's the matter?"

"Nothing"; but she still smiled.

"What's amusing you? Is it still me?"

"A bit. You don't belong here really, Nat—no, I don't mean just to the place; you don't belong to the *age*."

"To what age do I belong? Calvin's or Knox's? Preaching a ham social gospel with Tom Paine or tagging into exile with the Tolpuddle Martyrs?"

"Long before that, dear—riding a white horse in plate

armor, perhaps, looking for holy grails and chained-up damsels!" She leaned back against the thick trunk, and her eyes were laughing.

He half turned from her and looked out to sea.

"You find that too much out of date, don't you?"

He seemed to shrink a little as he said this, and it appeared to her that she saw him, suddenly, for the first time, lonely and tragic as an adolescent, but somehow utterly lovable. She moved forward; placing both arms round his neck, she pressed her mouth to his—pressed it so fiercely that for a few seconds he was too moved and surprised to respond. Then joy surged through him—a man's joy at the straining of a woman's body to his, and a little boy's joy in the knowledge that he was wanted. He held her as close as she seemed to demand. The first spatter of rain fell on the yellowing foliage of the beech tree, but it could not penetrate the arbor made by the sagging branches.

She was generous—more generous than she had been with any man, but even at the time she could not make up her mind whether this was because she enjoyed his ardor as much as he seemed to enjoy hers, or whether it was merely a case of soothing a puzzled child. But he never appeared so young again to her as on that pleasantly muddled windy afternoon under the beeches.

SIX

The long interval spent under the shelter of the beech tree that showery afternoon was undoubtedly a big contributory factor to what Nat always described, in later years, as "Sam's Swan Song." Nat's attitude to Sandcombe changed from that moment—changed, curiously enough, in a way that Mollie had never intended, and would never have desired, if she could have prevented it.

It was some time before she discovered this or, indeed, that her attitude toward him immediately before she kissed him had fired smoldering trains of thought gathering in Nat's mind since his first day home—the sudden wave of boredom that engulfed him when talking with Gerald at the foot of the works steps, the faint disgust engendered by the conversations with Mrs. Gage at the Galleon, and with Sleek, the undertaker, and, finally, that odd, depressing discussion with Otto.

Yet if Mollie had been the main impetus toward the formation of a new sort of line, or policy in his relations with the *Clarion,* there were two other contributory factors to the change, notably the case of ex-LACW Hopper and the launching of Councillor Baines' housing scheme, the one following closely upon the other.

It seemed as if Nat, having been forced to take stock of his future, was immediately pitchforked, half unwillingly, into substituting action for abstract thought.

Beryl Hopper was the youngest daughter of John Hopper, who kept a small confectioner's shop at the junction of St. Luke's Road and Beck Street, in the upper part of the town. Mr. Hopper had always been a gentle, inoffensive little man, popular with the children even when he was forced to close for half the week through shortage of supplies. Before the war the Hoppers had been known as a happy, devoted family, and the father, a veteran sidesman at St. Luke's Church, was one of those local nonentities whom everyone liked but nobody missed, once they passed into the hands of Mr. Sleek. Two of his sons were still away in the forces; their mother, a patient soul, had been bedridden for years with rheumatoid arthritis.

Beryl, a fair slim girl of about twenty-two years, was the best known of the family. A prominent member of the local swimming club, she had represented Sandcombe in the Ladies' County Championships before joining the WAAF in 1941. Since then she had spent leaves and week-ends in the town, and her father had made a proud visit to the *Clarion* office when he learned, in a roundabout way, that his daughter had been mentioned in dispatches for "zeal and devotion to duty" at Bomber Command Headquarters. Some of Sandcombe's Thursday Whist Club members, who discussed these things, recollected that Beryl had peroxided her chestnut hair at the age of seventeen and wondered how zealous or devoted she had been to men separated, by distance and the camp boundary wire, from their wives. They had noticed a change since her demobilization a month or two ago.

One Wednesday morning, soon after the convention, the Thursday Whist Club had an opportunity of checking on its communal suspicions. For Beryl came before the petty sessional court, charged with being drunk and incapable in Consort Road, after the dispersal of the young people attending a British Legion dance at St. Luke's hall.

Nat attended the court session, sprawling in the long press bench by the dock. He had sat already through a careless-driving case, two charges of passing Halt signs, one of exceeding the speed limit in a built-up area, five cases of riding cycles without red rear lights and one of committing a nuisance in the public highway. The last one was the only case with a "human interest" angle: the defendant, a sallow carter from the local brickyard, had pleaded "not guilty" and got away with it, having produced two doctors' statements certifying acute bladder trouble. Nat thought he handled the case rather well, and grinned his congratulations as the carter came down from the dock to pay the clerk a mere four shillings costs.

Nat had seen Beryl, whom he knew vaguely, sitting

alone in the seats reserved for witnesses and for defendants awaiting their summons. He thought she might be giving evidence in a case, and forgot about her until Barton, the magistrate's clerk, called her name in sonorous, self-conscious tones.

"Beryl Margery Lynne Hopper."

The girl, who was looking quite ill, rose and walked into the dock. Nat glanced at the charge sheet, pursing his lips when he read. "Drunk and incapable, Consort Road, 18/10/46."

Askew, the county press reporter, who sometimes shared Nat's seat in court, had gone off to wire copy to Paxtonbury, where the careless-driving case would occasion passing interest, since it involved a number of Paxtonbury citizens, so Nat was the only pressman present, and he thought he noticed a swift appeal in Beryl Hopper's eyes as she brushed past him to the stand.

PC Butt, a young, fresh-faced constable, whom Nat did not recognize, gave evidence. Stepping smartly into the witness-box, he reeled off his jargon in a flat, rather unpleasant voice, and all the time kept a pair of bright blue eyes fixed on the downcast head in the dock.

Nat felt, perhaps unjustly, that the young policeman was getting a kick out of the case. Beryl, leaning forward on the handrail, looked rather pretty—not unlike one of the pale figures in a Rossetti picture. It was impossible to imagine anyone so demure being drunk and incapable in Consort Road.

After gabbling through the oath, PC Butt resumed— ". . . on the night of the 18th ultimo, about 12:40 A.M., I was on duty in Consort Road, proceeding in a westerly direction . . ." (Nat, who had forgotten the routine, now recalled that constables never walked, but invariably proceeded—an altogether more dignified mode of locomotion) ". . . when my attention was attracted by a woman's laugh . . . a giggle, Your Worships."

Nat looked at the bench, and felt that Beryl had been unlucky. Miss Julia Gelding was in the chair, and he could tell by her expression that she had already judged the case.

Miss Gelding was the managing director of Gelding

Brothers, a largish drapers' establishment in the High Street, almost opposite the Clarion works. She was one of Sandcombe's most prominent citizens, her family having lived on the two floors above the shop for longer than anyone could remember. For several years now she had been a justice of the peace, and was known to be severe in all cases which seemed to her to involve a loss of civic dignity. Being in the outfitting trade, she depended, to a large extent, upon seasonal patronage, and a case like this did Sandcombe little credit among visitors and the potential purchasers of beachwear, baby linen and locally made sandals. To drive a car through High Street at 45 m.p.h. was one thing—it was an offense, of course, but a colorful one, and one that lent Sandcombe a certain amount of dash and sparkle—but to lie down and retch in the gutter of Consort Road after a dance on hallowed premises was quite another thing. Looking at Miss Gelding's mouth, Nat thought he wouldn't have cared to risk sixpence on Beryl's chances of securing a lenient decision.

PC Butt droned on. ". . . defendant was incoherent and smelled strongly of alcohol. I advised her to go home, but she clung firmly to the base of the privet hedge of number forty-four. When I remonstrated [another constabular prerogative] she sat down on the pavement and began to sing an obscene ditty, sample of which I produce . . ." and PC Butt, decorously lowering his gaze and reaching for his breast-pocket notebook, extracted a slip of typed paper, which he handed to the clerk.

The latter turned, bobbed and passed the slip to the chairman, screwing round his face to get a quick glance at the words in transit. Nat thought Miss Gelding reached out for the paper a trifle too eagerly. He wondered, idly, whether the ditty was of air force vintage, "Roll Me Over in the Clover," or an ATS song, perhaps "Sitting on the grass, polishin' me brass . . ." These service songs were often interchangeable. It might have been either, judging by the swift buttoning movement of Miss Gelding's pale lips. Old Colonel Grimstone-Beech, beside her on the bench, leaned over to the right to scan the page. Everybody said that he was deaf, but presumably he could still read without spectacles, for he remained in this awkward posture for some moments, thoughtfully scratching the thickest portion of his white mustache.

Finally Miss Gelding laid down the paper and looked in the direction of the defendant. Beryl did not look up, but continued to hold on to the rail immediately in front of her. From where he sat Nat could see her knuckles showing white, and the movement of her jaw muscles when she swallowed.

Nat took no notes. "Poor little swab," he thought, but got no farther. The scene in court suddenly struck him as a hideously cruel parody of justice—a sort of twentieth-century parallel of a harlot's penance at St. Paul's Cross in the fifteenth century, or to a formal denunciation in a remote Welsh chapel two generations ago. Beryl, he felt, should have worn a white sheet to match her face, not the taut little two-piece that still preserved its original creases.

What was the matter with the law and with these people? A young girl, loose in civvy street after more than four years in the camps, where drunkenness off duty was merely regarded as an official excuse for minor disciplinary offenses, had gone out and made a fool of herself. So what? Who was worse off? Who had suffered by her action apart from the girl herself? What was that ape in blue talking about? Why was that old harridan on the bench listening to him with such avidity? What, in God's name, was the matter with everyone? Why didn't an intelligent person get up and shout, "Baloney"?

Nat looked round the court, half hoping to see some indication that his view of the case was shared, at least by those in the spectators' gallery. He saw none. The police inspector was watching the way his constable was giving evidence, worrying, probably, more about the man's diction than about the effect of his recital on the magistrates. The clerk was scribbling away at some papers left over from the last case. Another constable, PC Fobb, of the War Reserve, was standing against the door leading to the cells, vacantly contemplating a dusty skylight above Miss Gelding's head, and probably wondering whether it was his turn to clean it. Two witnesses were lounging on the seats, gaping at the dock. One of them, a young motorcyclist, very masculine in huge gauntlets and mackintosh leggings, looked as if he was mentally undressing the defendant. Every now and then his eye sparkled, but not with amusement.

Nat began to feel sick. Then he ridiculed himself for being a fool. How many cases had he heard through in this seat, cases of violence, perversion, exhibitionism, cases that had dragged out a whole string of revolting circumstances before being committed to deposition foolscaps by the clerk and sent off to the quarter sessions and county assizes. Yet before these had never occasioned in him more than a mild disgust, a tired regret that people were what they were and that Society was obliged to use this fantastic machinery to protect itself. But this was different. This girl was a comrade, one of the girls who came into the orderly room with steaming jugs of tea and rain dripping from her shapeless cap. What right had these people to make her feel so wretched? Had any of them ever sat hour after hour in control rooms and checked in battered Lancasters?

Almost immediately Nat knew that he was off on a wrong tack. Of course they had. That had nothing to do with it. PC Butt, who was giving evidence, displayed the Middle East and Liberation medal ribbons on his tunic. He was one of them, too. Then why the hell . . .

"The defendant made as though to embrace me," continued the stolid Butt. "I then conveyed her to the station and she was detained."

"Did she say anything, Constable?" asked the inspector.

"Yes, sir. When I asked where she lived she said, 'You've had it, chum!' "

"Did you charge her?"

"The following morning. I charged and cautioned her, and she made a statement."

PC Butt began to read the statement. It was a long, rambling document, dictated, no doubt, while Beryl still suffered from the effects of a hangover, but Nat pieced together the story, simple and ordinary enough as it was. Beryl, in company with three or four young sparks, had gone out to the dance gaily enough, and slipped into the lounge of the Maltster's Arms, opposite the hall, during the interval. There she had consumed four half-pints of beer, for Ted, the barman at the pub, always served residents in preference to visitors, and there was just enough to go round that evening. When the Maltster's Arms ran dry, the party, including young Eddie Nunn, the cycle agent's son who partnered Beryl, had slipped back to the hall and danced a hectic medley of old-fashioned numbers. Beryl admitted that the whirls of the polka had had the effect of unsettling her beer. Then, after "God Save the King," with one other girl and two boys she had gone out along the seafront in Eddie's car, which they had been unable to start for the return journey. Eddie's friend had won a bottle of gin in the Legion draw, and she had had a drink of this; she didn't know why—just for fun, she supposed. Between that and her waking up in the cell feeling ill she remembered nothing. She was sorry, that was all she could say.

Nat wondered where Eddie had been, and why he had left the girl alone in Consort Road. He remembered a similar spree in which he himself had participated when he was about nineteen. On that occasion a fluffy little girl from Paxtonbury, staying with her aunt in Quay Street, had been left with him singing "Little White Lies" at the top of her voice in High Street, one warm summer's night. But the police had been different then. Old Sergeant Potbury, long since retired, had come along remarking, "This is a bit of orl right!" and helped him get the girl into her aunt's and flee, just as the old lady came downstairs. He didn't see the girl again, but heard, through her cousin, that the aunt had dosed her with strong coffee and then cut up her dance frock with the scissors, as a punishment. Were people different in those days, or was it that everyone was growing old, tired, sadistic, irritable and vicious?

Immediately PC Butt had completed his evidence the clerk, a pompous but well-meaning little man, swiveled his chair and pecked at the defendant, amplifying what he had already told her when the case opened.

"It is my duty to warn you that, should you go into the witness-box and give evidence, you will be liable to cross-examination by the inspector. You may stay where you are and make a statement in mitigation."

Beryl looked up, not knowing the meaning of "mitigation."

The clerk must have divined this, for he added, "Any statement you make there will not be on oath, and the bench will take it for what it is worth."

Not for the first time, thought Nat, the clerk ought to have added "Nothing!" This was a point that had always interested him. Was it better to tell your lies from the dock and remain safe from the tricky let-me-see-if-I-can-catch-you cross-examination of the police, or was it worth the odd chance of convincing the bench on oath and beating the inspector on his own ground? He supposed it depended upon whether you considered yourself innocent or guilty. If you were innocent of the charge, as Beryl admittedly was not, the taking of the oath with steadfast voice and eye sometimes won you a sympathetic hearing, always providing that you were sufficiently glib to turn the inspector's questions back to the police table. On the other hand, if you were conscious of threadbare patches in your story, it was often wise not to expose it to the inspector's probe, for it usually emerged full of gaping rents.

Beryl elected to stay where she was. Miss Gelding, having redigested the typed ditty, laid aside the paper and looked down at her. For a brief instant Nat tried to project his imagination back to early Edwardian days, when Miss Gelding would have been about Beryl's age. Had she ever gone out on a mild spree, say with a young man in a boater and a cummerbund and with a surreptitious bottle of raisin wine in the picnic basket? He decided not. If she went at all she would have been far more likely to lie back in the punt and sing her escort selections from *The Geisha* or *Quaker Girl*. For she was the bastion of the Sandcombe Amateur Operatic Society, and was reputed to have played leads for a generation. She was even billed for the autumn show this year, *The Prodigal Princess* at St. Luke's hall (book early and avoid disappointment), and for which the *Clarion* was printing bills and programs.

"Haven't you *anything* to say?" she asked a little hope-

fully, for if Beryl remained mute there would be no spring-
board for a magisterial homily.

Beryl's lips moved and might have said "No, ma'am,"
"I'm sorry" or even "Wrap up and get weaving!" Nat
didn't know, but he heard Miss Gelding, undeterred, sail
into her homily and glance, appraisingly, in the direction
of Nat's motionless pencil. Miss Gelding, like most prominent Sandcombians, was partial to a good press.

Although Nat made a point of not listening, odd phrases
forced their way into his consciousness. ". . . disgusting behavior . . . wish I could fine you more . . . giving Sandcombe
a bad name . . . might have lost what you prize most . . . lesson to you . . . ," finishing with the quite inaccurate statement that on the next occasion when the defendant came
before the court on such a charge the penalty would be
twice as severe, a promise at which the clerk, a pedantic
man, smothered a cough, for Miss Gelding had already
fined the girl the maximum, and was powerless to fine her
more if she came up for judgment every Wednesday for
the rest of her life.

Nat glanced at his watch and snapped his notebook shut.
He went out through the charge-room door, guessing that
Beryl would try to buttonhole him if he left by the public
entrance. He felt muddled and peevish. Instead of taking
the High Street back to the office, he turned right and went
out along the Promenade.

Under the lash of spray, whipped up by the high tide
which was surging through the jagged gaps in Sandcombe's
sea defenses, his irritation disappeared. He ate a light
lunch in Giocomo's restaurant at the corner of the harbor
and returned, considerably fresher, in time for the afternoon public session of the urban district council. On the
way to the council chamber he dropped in at the shop for
a new notebook.

Marlene, leaning on the counter, patted her hair and
looked coyly at her blood-red nails—nails that, had she
known it, had inspired more than one of Sam's wartime
editorials, and would have long since earned her the sack,
if staff problems had been less pressing.

Marlene rather liked Nat, her attraction dating from the

day when she had danced with him in St. Luke's hall, but Nat never seemed to notice her. He was polite, treating her like a lady, but distant. She knew he was mooning about after that snooty baggage, Mollie Thorpe. Marlene was acutely conscious of Mollie's intellectual superiority and the quality of her clothes—clothes that even Marlene grudgingly admitted couldn't be purchased with the salary Mollie received from the Clarion Press.

"Luvly day it's been," she began, and as Nat did not answer, but picked through the notebooks in the glass case behind the counter, she added, "Time we had some fun, isn't it?"

Nat looked up. "Where's Miss Thorpe?"

What the hell did he see in that woman? She was dumpy, and her hairstyle was years out of date.

Marlene yawned. "Gone out to Surf Bay."

"What for?"

"I dunno. Young Farmers' Union rally or somethin' daft. Said she'd be back this evening."

"All right. Thanks."

He went out again. Marlene resumed a minute inspection of her nails. Hadn't even noticed her. What was there in this dump for a girl who made the best of herself? A lot of silly old men, that dreamy reporter and Bumble, whose hands were always seamed with furrows of printer's ink. He smelled when he perspired, too. She had noticed that at the dance the other night. Pity she had ever left Pompadour's; you did get a bit of class there. A girl was better off in Paxtonbury, where there were two or three smart shops. She looked at Gerald with scarcely concealed distaste as he hurried through the shop and up the stairs to his office. God, this place was dead! Why had the war ended before she had had time to get into the WRNS? There was class in the WRNS. They were a cut above the ATS and WAAF—everybody said so. She might have stood a chance with an officer there. Nesta Payne, her sister's friend, told her . . .

Old Mrs. Frisby came in with an "In Memoriam" notice and diverted Marlene's reflections into more realistic channels. The old fool couldn't decide whether to use the words "Still in our hearts" or "Waiting for us at the Golden Gate." Marlene had known the late Mr. Frisby, and, if she was any judge, his widow would be well advised to use the first lead-in. Charlie Frisby, as she remembered him, had never waited for anything except opening time at the Galleon.

She slipped the notice into an empty cigar box, kept for this purpose, and, giving Mrs. Frisby some change, returned to the contemplation of her nails.

Nat took his seat at the school desk that the town clerk had imported for the use of the press in the Sandcombe council chamber, and glanced round the three-sided table to check off the fourteen members of the council.

Some of the faces were familiar, having appeared there for two decades, but a few, like Baines', were those of new members who had been co-opted during the war. One or two had fought mild elections the previous March, but there had been no changes in representation.

Colonel Grimstone-Beech, JP, the deaf magistrate who had supported Miss Gelding in court that day, now reappeared as chairman of the council. Nobody took much notice of him, but he was a popular chairman because his deafness kept him neutral. He relied implicitly on the offices of Angel, the town clerk, a dark, adroit, dapper man, whom Nat had secretly admired for years, so expert was his handling of this mixed and mediocre bunch.

Angel was a master of compromise. Like Sam, he usually succeeded in maintaining a middle course, but his task was far more difficult than the editor's, for his own peace of mind depended on his ability to get through every committee meeting without making a personal enemy and every public meeting without appearing, to press and public, as the virtual dictator of Sandcombe.

For dictator, in fact, he was. As a solicitor he knew his way blindfolded through the maze of procedure and precedent that controls the actions of every public authority. As town clerk, he was called upon to follow procedure and precedent, but to make it look as if the initial impetus had come from the councillors. He did this with incredible subtlety, putting the right words into hesitant mouths and rounding off halting statements with enthusiastic and expert endorsement. ". . . Precisely what I intended to convey. . . . Exactly the right approach" were phrases that slipped from him at every gathering, and even after a disagreement on the part of rival groups both sides would proclaim, at the inevitable inquest in the saloon bar of the Galleon, that "Angel supported us to the hilt."

Nat had often felt genuinely sorry for the man. Then he discovered that Angel had grown so accustomed to balancing himself on a knife-edge that he would no more have climbed down, one side or the other, than a conscientious fakir would have rolled from his wire rope. Only when Angel perceived a clear majority on a point of policy would he throw in his weight with the winners. He always preferred that councillors should persuade each other to withdraw amendments, rather than wait for them to be put to the vote and defeated. But, despite a constant hedging that nobody but himself seemed to notice, Nat felt that Angel had considerable merit. It needed sound brains to control the Sandcombe District Council, and while Angel's job and salary were safe enough (he was a prominent member of the National Association of Local Government Officials), his office might have been vastly more unpleasant than it was, had he stepped an inch outside neutral territory.

When Nat had left the *Clarion* in 1940 there had been two groups in the council. National politics had nothing to do with this schism. Known Conservatives and prominent Liberals (there were few Socialists in the town, and the party had never been strong enough to fight an election) belonged to both groups. One party favored development, and the other opposed it, but the latter was far too spry to proclaim that fact, and carried on a spirited guerrilla warfare, mostly in committee.

Their Maginot Line in public consisted in the phrase, "The time is not opportune." They were apparently ready to agree to anything, from the building of a new pier to the provision of more litter baskets, if the time for the launching of such projects had been opportune. But it either never was or never would be, for the policy of this section lay in one long, losing battle to reduce the rates, and every half-year they questioned the addition of every halfpenny, referring the most minute details back to committee in the hope that they would get lost in an agenda averaging some hundred and fifty paragraphs a month.

Nat had favored the so-called Progressives when Sam's back was turned, but neither he nor they had progressed very far, for the simple reason that they were far less organized than the opposition. There was no rallying point, no outstanding personality to lead a charge, and most of the motions originating from this scattered body were so ill-planned, and so obviously hitched to the private hobbyhorses of individual members, that they seldom won a clear majority. When they did, they were always whittled down by amendments.

When Nat first heard about Baines he supposed that the Progressives had found a leader, someone to stand up to the rigid cheeseparing of Major Martindale, MC, champion of the Never-opportuners. But he soon discovered that he had jumped to conclusions. Baines and Major Martindale seemed to have called a permanent truce, for report after report, presented by the Roads, Sanitary, Foreshore, Parks and even Finance Committees went through without stirring up anything more than a mild question, generally answered by Vince, the young surveyor. It was clear also that Vince took his cue from Angel, the clerk.

In ten minutes the agenda was cleared.

There had been a time when Nat would have rejoiced at this show of unanimity. It meant far less work on his part. He could snip out interesting portions of the mimeographed agenda, change the tenses of the recommendations, give the copy to Burton on the keyboard and go home to an early supper. But today the speed of the meeting puzzled him. It seemed much too good to be true.

By ten minutes past three there was only one item to be cleared—a formal proposal, in the name of Councillor Baines, that the council should apply to the Ministry of Health for sanction to buy forty acres of land on Hilltop

Moor, for the purposes of erecting one hundred houses. This, Nat supposed, was Baines' much-discussed housing scheme, praised by Gerald and winked at by Mollie on his first day back at the *Clarion*. But why Hilltop Moor? It was more than two miles from the town, and lay at the top of a long, steady gradient. Surely there must be building land nearer the seafront? Yet Baines must have gone into this, or else it was sure to be questioned by other members.

Baines made the proposal, and blew the usual fanfare about homes for the homeless. Nat didn't blame him for that. Fanfares were all part of the game of local politics, and if the man was sincere in pushing the scheme, nobody would begrudge him a certain amount of kudos with the electors. Councillor Morgan, a thin-faced man with small, red-rimmed eyes, seconded. Nat understood that also. Morgan, whose plump niece worked in the binding room of the *Clarion,* had a grocer's shop at the back of the town. He would benefit to an appreciable extent from the erection of a new housing estate half a mile from his shop door. But again, why shouldn't he? Houses were needed, God knows. Nat had himself seen a waiting list of two hundred families in the town clerk's office. Somebody would have to benefit by increased trade, so why not Morgan, who had gone through bad times during the Rhondda coal troubles and had moved southwest in search of a living?

Nat pondered these things as he flicked through the pages of his notebook. He was interested to see what line Major Martindale would take. Nat knew the major as the diehard but energetic Conservative of prewar days. He had taken a strong line in opposition to the Peace Ballot, and was always making speeches about milksop pacifists or the craven's interpretation of a fighting Christianity.

Major Martindale supported the motion. He went further. He remarked that, in his opinion, no more suitable site could be found. It was high, healthy and bracing. There was nothing like high ground for health. Nat searched his memory for the exact location of the major's detached home. It was one of the first houses on the Ridge, down by the eastern end of the Promenade—probably about twenty feet above sea level.

No one else spoke. Evidently the need for a new housing estate was so patent to all that further discussion seemed unnecessary. This was a good sign. Or was it?

"There will, of course, be the usual government inquiry, but I don't anticipate any hitches," volunteered Angel.

Some of the councillors nodded, but Baines, with a swift glance at Nat, grunted, "If them departments sit on the scheme, chivy 'em up on the phone, Mr. Clerk! Our people won't wait!"

Angel assured Mr. Baines that he would do all the "chivying" necessary, and the chairman stirred in his sleep and muttered, "That's all the public business."

It was a hint to Nat and the few members of the public in the gallery. They rose and went out. Nat returned to the office, but not by the direct route. He went along the seafront and back over the Flats without arriving at any conclusions. He decided to use his new intimacy with Mollie to extract more information from her. Baines . . . the Moor . . . concord in the council . . . high, healthy acres. . . . Mollie ought to know a thing or two about that. If not, why the wink?

SEVEN

It was about five when Nat reached the office. He passed Gerald on the stairs. Gerald, looking more studious than ever, tucked a couple of files under his arm and told him that Sam would be unlikely to come in again for his usual scrutiny of the inside pages. The Big Machine had formerly printed eight pages in four machine runs, two on Wednesday and the others on Thursday afternoon. The Wednesday pages contained the routine advertisements and a page of district news, mostly contributed by the secretaries of local clubs and organizations. Some of Nat's news also went in, if it was set in time, but the more important items were reserved for the second workings and appeared on the back page.

The front page, of course, was a static affair, and did not vary by so much as a column rule from month to month. It was only unlocked when one of the regular advertisers died or sold his business to a man with another name and brighter ideas about advertising.

Gerald liked to call the inside pages "the supplement," but wartime paper shortage had reduced the *Clarion* to six pages. The true supplement dated from prewar days, when the term applied to a folded sheet, printed on both sides, that was inserted between the outside pages by the journeymen and the binding-room staff every Thursday afternoon and evening.

"Don't suppose the Old Man'll be in to read the supplement," said Gerald. "He went home early, feeling rather dicky."

"He's got an engagement in his diary at seven," replied Nat.

"He'll skip that, if he's any sense. It's a Free Church affair!"

Gerald had small patience with Sam's religious activities, and had often told him so. "What's it bring us in? Two-fifty oratorio programs twice a year!"

Sam had turned on him with quiet menace. "I don't intend to neglect God's work for my own, my boy." Whereupon Gerald had shrugged and afterward complained to Nat, but he won no ally here, for Nat had found Gerald's fidgeting very tiresome of late, and preferred to check over on his own or with Mollie.

He went upstairs into his office, throwing down the folded council agenda and his notebook, and filling the dented aluminum kettle for tea. Mollie was still away on the Surf Bay job, whatever it was. So he sat down in the leather chair and rolled a sheet of thin foolscap into the typewriter.

There was a soft tap on the works door. Nat looked up, a little irritated.

"Come in."

The door was pushed open, with more caution than any of the employees would have used, and a stout, elderly man, with white hair and Victorian side-whiskers, edged into the office. Nat recognized Wainer, once the town surveyor, who had retired and settled down in Sandcombe several years before the war. He had always liked Wainer —a prim, clean, helpful man, with red cheeks that matched his white mane and gave him a vaguely Pickwickian appearance. Nat noticed that he had aged appreciably during the war, and was carrying some rolled-up plans, neatly fastened with rubber bands. He stood up and shook the former surveyor's plump, capable hand.

"What can I do for you, Mr. Wainer?"

The pensioner came farther in, first turning to shut the door very quietly. It seemed to Nat that the old fellow was acting furtively.

"You remember me, Mr. Nathaniel?"

"Of course." How could he forget? Wainer and Sam were the only two people in Sandcombe who used his full Christian name. It was about the only thing that the two men had in common. "Were you in council this afternoon?"

Wainer shook his white head. "Ah no. No, no, no. I wouldn't go there, not now."

"Why not? You're a ratepayer."

"Mr. Vince, the new surveyor, might resent it. Besides, I'm afraid I've lost touch. It's been a long time. Eight years now."

Mr. Vince, Wainer's successor, was the keen, flashily dressed young man who had answered most of the council meeting questions. Nat thought him a little too keen. He had been genuinely sorry to see Wainer accept the inscribed dining-room clock, which the councillors had given him, and retire to his semidetached villa in Brunswick Terrace.

He noticed now that Wainer had seated himself, but was pretending to look out of the window. He seemed both anxious to speak and loathe to begin.

"You were there . . . this afternoon . . . ?"

Nat nodded.

"What did they decide—about the houses, I mean?"

Nat told him. Before he had said very much Wainer was fidgeting with his plans. One of the rubber bands peeled off and the roll fanned out, like a child's trumpet.

When Nat had finished, Wainer looked straight at him, for the first time since he had entered the room.

"It's very wrong of them," he said, so quietly that Nat could not have sworn to the words used.

"What's wrong about it?"

Wainer looked startled. "You don't know?"

"I'm vaguely suspicious. It's too unanimous. But I don't know that it's wrong. We've got to build somewhere, and the sooner the better."

Wainer's diffidence seemed to drop from him like a loose garment. His deep-set eyes smoldered, and he beat Mollie's table with his bundle of plans.

"It's all worked out, Mr. Nathaniel. I've never heard of such a thing. *This* is the plan we ought to have. It was blueprinted in 1920. There was the same shout for houses then. This isn't just a housing estate. It's town and foreshore development on our land. But no one's mentioned it, no one's even mentioned it. I tried to interest Major Martindale, but he fobbed me off. 'Out of date!' he said. It's not out of date, Mr. Nathaniel, not one bit out of date.

It's as good now as it ever was. Only . . ." He dried up, suddenly embarrassed by his own vehemence.

"Only what, Mr. Wainer?"

Mr. Wainer folded one lip over the other, as though determined to set a physical check on renewed outbursts. "You'd better see the plan," he said.

Nat took the smooth roll and spread it out on his desk, pushing his wire trays to the floor. He had never seen the blueprint before. It was entitled "Proposed Layout of the Flats Area. Housing and Foreshore Amenities, August 1920." Underneath was a faint facsimile of Wainer's signature.

It was a neat, elegant plan, sketched in broad outline, but with sufficient detail to make it something more than a first draft. It embraced the whole eastern end of the Promenade and the reclaimed sandhills and gorse patches beyond. The houses—eighty two-story dwellings and fifteen bungalows—were shown behind the existing track that wound an eastward course parallel to the sea, about two hundred yards above high-water mark. The area between track and sea had been earmarked for a children's yachting pool, an open-air swimming bath, and a large café, with flagged terraces and a sun loggia. Beyond the path were two plots appropriate for putting greens.

Nat's interest was immediately caught and held. He had often wondered why the council had never considered developing this locality, but he had not even heard of this plan.

"Has this ever been before the council?" he asked Wainer.

"Only through the committee stage. It was thrown out in October, 1920. They got up a petition about it."

"Who did?"

"Colonel Grimstone-Beech, Major Martindale and the retired people who live on the Ridge."

"Why? Why a petition?"

Wainer smiled, partly out of satisfaction at having captured the journalist's interest, but more from the memory of that autumn evening twenty-six years ago, when an irate, bustling Grimstone-Beech, his mustache iron gray in those days, had marched into the council chamber and laid the petition on the chairman's desk. He had looked hard at the chairman, then old George Trayherne, and rapped out, "This proposal is an outrage! An outrage, sir! The signatories dare you to proceed with it! We shall fight you, sir. We shall fight you all the way to Westminster!" Grimstone-Beech had been a little deaf even in those days, and his voice carried out into the council yard.

The colonel's running fight never materialized. It was not necessary, for George Trayherne was no Afghan tribesman. As far as he was concerned, what the colonel said went. The Foreshore Committee threw the plan out by nine votes to two. Both proposer and seconder had since left the town, the one in disgust, the other with arthritis, a complaint reputed to be on the increase in Sandcombe.

Nat took down the 1920 *Clarion* files, but there was no mention of the plan there. Why should there be? Reporters were never allowed in the committee rooms. Nat said, "If the colonel objected to the plan then, Major Martindale and the rest of that mob would object to it now. I can see why. The proposed housing estate is too near the Ridge."

"That good-class property's on higher ground," said Wainer. "Nothing could interfere with the view."

"They could see the washing from their bedroom windows. But that doesn't explain Baines' attitude. He's just the sort to seize on a class prejudice like this and use it as cheap election propaganda."

Wainer looked hard at the floor.

"Baines has got a bus service," he said.

In that moment Nat saw it all, so clearly, so unmistakably that he almost blushed for his witlessness during the past few months. Mollie's wink! Baines' appeal for a write-up in the "Round About Town" column. His big printing orders. Colonel Grimstone-Beech's sleepy acquiescence. The grocer Morgan's support. Major Martindale nodding heavy eyebrows, eyebrows that were said to have cowed several hundred square yards of the Northwest Frontier in the nineteen hundreds. All this and the curious silence at the council that afternoon.

It was rigged. There could be no doubt about that. The whole thing was a slipshod intrigue, yawned over and winked at in committee, dribbled out to the ratepayers in hints and promises until that afternoon. Why build on the Flats, within view of the big houses on the Ridge, when two miles up the Paxtonbury Road there was a perfectly good patch of land served by Baines' buses and provisioned by one of his supporter's shops?

Nat went through the councillors one by one. Only three could fail to benefit, in one way or another, from the proposed site; two of the three were far too old to care, the other was a nonentity left over from the co-opted batch in 1939.

For a moment Nat felt wildly indignant. Then a steadying thought occurred to him. He turned to Wainer to discover the old gentleman regarding him attentively, even a little pathetically.

"Suppose it's all true, suppose it is a piece of jiggery pokery. It can't get very far, if it's as bad as we think it is. They've got to apply to the ministry for sanction to borrow the money. There's bound to be a public inquiry, like the ones we had over the town sewage and the Promenade gardens, remember? The government inspector would see through a thing like this in no time."

Wainer dropped his eyes to the floor again. After a minute or two he said, "You've been away. You don't seem to realize what's happening in places like this. The local council have twice the power they used to have in my day. They're getting more and more delegated to them. The government will institute an inquiry, of course, but they'll be influenced a good deal by the clerk and the initial vote. What would you do in the inspector's position? He's ignorant of the locality. Here's a constitutionally elected council, unanimously deciding on a building plot. There are no objections lodged, and not likely to be any. . . ."

"We could object, couldn't we?"

"I couldn't. I'm the original surveyor. This is my plan. They'd only think I was indulging in professional jealousy."

"Then Mr. Vane, the editor. If it's put to him . . ."

Wainer shook his head. "I put it to him, months ago.

He told me to give the younger blood a chance."

Nat grinned. It must have cost Sam a good deal to say that. But at least it proved that the Old Man had been sounded, probably by Baines, and asked to support the adopted scheme.

Wainer cut into his reflections.

"*You* might lodge an objection," he said, "but that couldn't do much good on its own. The opposition would have to acquire a representational aspect. I know these inspectors; they're so tired of objectors whose opposition is personal or irrelevant. There are some people who make a habit of objecting to everything on principle—silly people. . . ."

"Cranks?" said Nat.

"Well, yes, cranks, I suppose."

"I see what you mean, Mr. Wainer."

Nat got up and went over to the window. It was already dusk. If Sam was coming in to check over the inside pages, he would arrive at any moment. Wainer had better go. If Sam were to be approached on this matter—and Nat realized that to take any effective action he would have to confide in Sam at this stage—it would do no good if Sam discovered that the former surveyor had gone from editor to subeditor in search of support.

"You'd better go out the front way, Mr. Wainer. Let me turn this over for a day or two. I'll think of something. Are you on the phone?"

"No, Mr. Nathaniel. It worried my wife. I had it taken out. I'll leave the plan, if you like."

"Please. Wait until I get into touch with you. Don't go to anyone else yet. One other thing. Do you mind if I print these plans?"

"No, I suppose not," said Wainer without much enthusiasm. Then, as he shuffled to the door, he turned and smiled. "Thank you for listening, Mr. Nat."

As though slightly embarrassed by his first use of the shortened name, Wainer pulled on his worn kid gloves and quickly let himself out through the shop door.

When he had gone Nat sat down on the window seat, and remained in thought for nearly half an hour. He decided that this was too big a thing to be merely a personal intrigue. It was intentional, perhaps, on the part of Baines, and even of Morgan, the grocer; but not so with the others —the men like Grimstone-Beech and Martindale, or Sam and the young surveyor. Most of these people were a long way from being rogues. Some were just disinterested townspeople—people who always swam downstream when faced with a major decision. By this time even Baines and Morgan must have persuaded themselves that the scheme up on the hill was the best scheme for Sandcombe. Town politics were like that. You had to make up your mind on an issue, and somebody offered a ready-made solution. You took it, because you were too lazy or too ill-informed in town affairs to think up an alternative. Men like Baines, who knew what they wanted, were never short of followers, and where, as in this case, a scheme suited the personal interests of several minor groups, he was bound to get his way if he managed to keep cool in committee. Moreover, there were several men round that council who hated scenes, and Baines was the sort of councillor who could stir up a deal of unpleasantness if he wished. Unpleasantness like that interfered with the social side of council work, and created a bad atmosphere in the town. If these people, then, were faced with a cut-and-dried scheme designed to satisfy the growing demand for houses among ratepayers, most of whom were too desperate to be fussy, it was twenty to one that they would vote for that scheme, particularly as no other, least of all Wainer's, had been laid before them for approval.

Nat knew better than anyone, including Gerald, that Sam Vane was not an intentionally bad journalist, not a man who would deliberately put personal advantage above the well-being of the community he served; but Sam was like so many people in towns like Sandcombe: he had long since acquired the habit of squaring his conscience with his personal inclinations. If someone, therefore, went boldly up to the Old Man and said "This is a frame-up. Baines is only interested in bus fares," then surely a man who was admittedly proud of the influence he wielded might be inclined to reconsider the matter?

At this point Mollie came in, and Nat noticed that she was wearing what was, for Sandcombe, a very daring hat—a tilted, three-cornered affair, that sat wickedly an inch and a half above the right eye. She smiled, and he realized how glad he was to see her.

"Switch off the light. Just for a moment."

She flicked up the switch and came over and kissed him warmly, as though she enjoyed doing it; but when he tried to hold her a moment she glided out of his arms and returned to the switch again.

"You shouldn't wear clothes like that at a Young Farmers' rally," he said.

"I should. After the plowing-match I went on to a wedding. A big one. Two popular farming families united. How's that for the heading?"

"I've used it a dozen times. Want any tea? The kettle's nearly boiling."

"No, thanks. I've had gin. That's wrong, isn't it? Gin at a farmer's wedding, I mean. It ought to be mead, or sack, or at least cider, don't you think?"

Nat grinned.

"I think you're a wee bit squiffy."

"A tiny bit. I'll hold my breath and turn to the wall, if Sam comes in."

The kettle was rattling on the gas ring. She got up and began to make Nat's tea. He felt a rush of affection for the girl, admiring the natural grace with which she moved, the quality and cut of her clothes, the warmth and ease of their relationship in this stuffy little room, still smelling of leather, apple cores and printing ink. He knew that if she left, if she married someone and stopped coming here every morning, he would tire of the *Clarion* in a week. He would take his chance anywhere sooner than stay on, grinding out columns of tripe on the old typewriter, answering Sam's petulant questions and Gerald's pompous ones, taking down shorthand notes about Mr. Sleek's deceased "duties," writing up advance notices of Miss Gelding's operatic ventures, working out local tide tables and combing through old periodicals to fill the humor column.

For a moment he thought he would tell her all of this.

Then he saw Wainer's plan and changed his mind. Deliberately sipping his tea, he said, "I've rumbled Baines, Mollie."

She refilled the kettle from the corroded tap near the door.

"Well?"

He told her about Wainer's visit and some of his own reflections after Wainer had gone.

"What are you going to do about it?"

"Tell Sam."

"He's already been told, hasn't he?"

"He didn't understand; he couldn't have."

She laughed. "Oh Nat! Dear, funny old Nat. You're so incredibly naïve."

"Sam's got to see. What else can I do?"

"Why do anything?"

He got up and went over to his desk, where she was sitting.

"Look, Mollie. I don't mind if you think I'm naïve. Sentimental even—'holy grailish,' you once said, didn't you? I don't mind that, from you. I suppose I rather like it. But it won't do to go on joking about this—not as long as we're working here, anyway. Everybody's being led up the garden path about this scheme. We've got to do something. Otherwise . . ."

"Otherwise what?"

"Otherwise it's all pointless—everything we write and read and talk about and feel; just pointless. Everything that people like you and I believe in. Oh, I know it's fashionable not to believe in anything, but so it always happens after a war. That won't last—never does. I still believe in people. If I didn't, I'd go crazy. I'm sorry; it's just how I'm built. I've told you all this before."

"I know, Nat." There was no laughter in her voice. "I suppose that's what makes you so lovable. But, seriously, dear, think for a minute, and for God's sake use some gump! You talk of going to Sam. That's the craziest thing I've ever heard. He'll not only push you on one side, and queer your pitch before you can lift a finger, but, if you keep on at him, he'll sack you. That's all there is to it. And that mightn't be such a bad idea either."

EIGHT

When Beryl Hopper had paid her fine and left the court she walked home, slowly and reluctantly, for she was aware that the police had informed her father where she had spent the night. Her mouth was very dry and her head continued to ache. She felt slightly sick.

The initial shame she had felt when she came out of the whitewashed cells and into the courtroom had gone. It was replaced by a burning sense of resentment—resentment against the police, against Eddie Nunn, who had shinned off and left her the night before, but, more especially, a burning resentment against the old cow on the bench. Fragments of hackneyed hut conversations came back to her, the talk of '42 and '43 in the camps, when the girls in uniform had often discussed factory workers and the civvies generally.

She remembered Floss Marker, a meteorologist who slept in the next bed, picking up a remark made by Cpl. Marsh, the NCO i/c the billet. Marsh had been shooting a line about her intentions, on being demobbed, of going back to her old job in a Liverpool solicitor's office, "I'm going to ask double," she had said, "double or they've had it!"

Floss had taken a long pull at her cigarette, "It'll be you that'll have it, Jean. Do you think they'll give a damn where you've been and what you've done? They don't give a damn now, with the war still on. It'll be ancient history by the time you get out."

Floss was right. Had that old battle-axe on the bench taken her service into consideration? Had she hell! Hadn't even mentioned it. She ought to have got herself a mouthpiece—someone like the Camp Welfare Officer, who could jabber about momentary impulses and maladjustments to civilian life. . . .

But what would the Old Man say?

Beryl wondered whether he had gone upstairs and told

Ma. She suspected not. Surely to God he'd have that much sense. Ma would fret and fret, and the Old Man would bind and bind. Every time she wanted to leave the house of an evening in future she would have to say where she was going. Every time she came in she would have to describe where she had been, whom she had met.

God, this town! Why hadn't she signed on? Who cared if you had one too many at a camp dance?

She remembered four of them getting Floss back to billets after a spree at the Crown and Scepter, when the squadron was moving overseas. Floss had been singing too —a variation of "Mountains of Mourne," with the dirty bits implied but unuttered at the end of every verse. Just inside the wire the five of them had run smack into the Squadron-Leader Admin. He had grinned and suddenly decided to make a right-angled turn toward the perimeter. They got back to the hut OK and Floss had wept while they took off her clothes.

But here . . . all this bloody fuss. . . .

She reached home and went slowly through the untidy shop to the living room at the back. No one was there. She stuck her head into the kitchen. Her father was sitting on a wooden chair beside the gas stove, boiling some milk. She went in and sat on the edge of the table. He looked up and then away. His face was so drawn that Beryl suddenly felt more sorry for him than for herself.

She said, "Told Ma?"

He shook his head.

"I'm sorry, Pa; it wasn't anything really . . . just a bit o' rotten luck that I came over queer. If on'y Eddy had stayed on and explained to that swine of a copper. . . ."

Mr. Hopper swallowed and stood up to turn down the gas.

"What did they give you?" She noticed that his voice was hoarse, the same as when he had one of his chesty colds round about January.

"Ten bob. I've paid it. It's not that; we've just got to keep it from Ma. She'll take it awful."

"How can you keep it from her?"

"No one'll be mean enough to tell her."

"There's the papers!"

The papers! Beryl suddenly remembered Nat and the sympathetic look he had given her when she brushed past the press bench. Nat Hearn! He was an ex-RAF type, too, and the only pressman present. She vaguely remembered him reporting her swimming galas before the war. He was a good sort; everybody said so. She'd fix it.

The milk frothed over the saucepan as she jumped down from the table and drifted out of the kitchen.

"Where are you off to now?" he said.

"*Clarion* office," she told him.

He poured out the milk and stirred his wife's mid-morning drink. Then, forcing his mouth to grin, he creaked up the narrow stairs to her room. Beryl walked slowly down to the High Street and into the *Clarion* shop.

She knew enough about the *Clarion* to go away again as soon as she learned that Nat was not on the premises. She called back in the afternoon, and again in the early evening.

On the last occasion she met Burton, the keyboard operator, smoking in the yard. Burton was a punctual workman, but he believed in being fair to himself as well as to Gerald and Sam. He took his full half hour for tea on the evenings when he worked over, and although he had insufficient time to cycle home, he always stayed out of the works, sitting on Bumble's three-wheeled trolley and enjoying a pipe. He remained here until he heard St. Luke's clock strike the half hour.

Burton said Nat had been up in the office for some time, closeted with a caller, he didn't know who. It was growing dusk as Beryl climbed the steps and entered the works with Burton following and jerking a casual thumb toward the dusty speaking tube that connected the foreman's desk with the editorial office. Beryl blew, gave her name and passed upstairs. Burton had sufficient curiosity to glance after the girl, before sitting down on his soiled cushions to keyboard "Sandcombe's Doubtful Goal," a handwritten sheet of copy from the honorary football correspondent.

Inside the editorial Beryl stopped short when she saw Mollie, but Nat waved his hand.

"She's all right—on our side!"

It was a good beginning, and Beryl suddenly felt cheered, losing her awkwardness and plunging right into her story. Nat, who knew it, let her run on for Mollie's sake.

"I don't give two straws myself," Beryl told them, "and as for the Old Man—well, he's always been a bit stuffy on account of being a sidesman at the church. But Mum— well, that's diff'rent. She has a lousy time anyway, and if it gets back to her . . ."

Nat interrupted, for the first time.

"She's bound to find out, isn't she?"

"No. She don't see many people, and those she does wouldn't tell her. Dad'n me would keep our traps shut, naturally. It's on'y the *Clarion;* she reads it right through every Friday, adverts an' all. She's glad of it, lying up most o' the day."

Nat pondered, and Mollie noticed, for the first time, that he had a funny little habit of blowing out his cheeks and letting the air hiss slowly through closed lips when he was making an effort to concentrate. For a moment it was so quiet that she could hear the ticking of the cheap office clock and the clank of a pedal cycle with a loose mudguard bowling down High Street hill.

Finally Nat rose and stretched his long legs.

"I don't have the final say in these things," he began, "I thought everybody knew that."

"You could skip it, and Mr. Vane wouldn't miss a single court case," replied Beryl. She was surprised at the excitement she felt, as though this lanky ex-RAF type was deciding whether or not to sign a gallows reprieve—not hers, but someone's who mattered to her very much, like Mum.

"I could do that," he told her, "and I will do it . . . but if he hears about the case I'll have to have it out with him. It depends."

Mollie spoke unexpectedly.

"Oh, skip the wretched thing, like she says, Nat!"

He turned on her, a little irritably.

"It isn't as easy as all that. You ought to know as much."

Mollie subsided.

"I don't mind, if you'll . . . you'll just do what you can, Mr. Nat," said Beryl.

Nat looked at her and grinned. For the second time that evening someone had used his shortened name for the first time. Did it mean anything? Were people beginning to recognize that he was the real editor? The thought flattered him, just enough to make him determine to do his utmost to keep Beryl's case out of the paper.

"You'd better go out by the shop door," he told her; "it won't do to run into Sam. He always comes in at the back. Come on, I'll show you down. By the way, were you at Nethermarsh when it was an OTU? Rotten dump! Sort of air force Belsen. I was there in '41 summer. It was before the new CO . . ."

They went out talking, and Mollie heard them go downstairs into the closed shop, and draw the bolts to let the girl out into the High Street. She got up to pull the drab office curtains across, just as Sam, followed by Miss Gelding, came into the room from the works. Sam said something, but Mollie pretended not to hear, and cut across the landing to meet Nat on the stairs.

"He's in there now, and that Gelding woman's with him," she whispered.

Nat looked annoyed. He paused with his hand on the wobbly banister.

"Her! What the hell? I wonder if she's been getting at him about the damned case?"

"Better go in; I'll hang around, too."

Nat felt irritated that Miss Gelding was there. He was in the mood to tackle Sam about Wainer's plan as well as the case of Beryl Hopper; but Miss Gelding, who beamed at him when he entered the room, precluded the possibility of an editorial conference, however brief. Sam looked tired and out of sorts. In spite of his own preoccupations, Nat could not help noticing how much the old fellow seemed to have aged in the last few months.

"I'm on my way to the Christian Endeavor meeting, Nathaniel," he barked. "I just came in to ensure that Miss Gelding got a good advance notice this week."

"Advance notice . . . ?"

"Come now—the opera—they've advertised for the past three weeks."

Nat switched his mind to *The Prodigal Princess,* forthcoming autumn show of the Sandcombe Amateur Operatic Society. He had noticed announcements on the bills, and had said to Mollie, "What, that again!" *The Prodigal Princess* was an old favorite with the society, for its leading role was Princess Mathilde, a Ruritanian soprano sufficiently mature, even in the script, to sustain Miss Gelding's determined efforts. Julia Gelding always produced for the amateurs, and usually cast herself in the lead. Nat had seen her as Iolanthe, Miss Hook of Holland, Yum-Yum (three times), the Quaker Girl (twice) and even Rose Marie. During the war the activities of the society had been suspended, which was unfair to Miss Gelding, for it was one thing to weather the storm year by year, but quite another to ride out a first night after six years in dry dock. By adroitly coercing the committee into choosing *The Prodigal Princess,* however, she had postponed her farewell performance for another twelve months. Mathilde might be any age. Prince Otto fell in love with her voice, not with her beauty.

Mollie foraged among the proofs on the table.

"There's a write-up already set, Mr. Vane," she told him.

Sam ran a disapproving eye down the column.

"It's too short. No longer than the write-up for the fire brigade dance," was his verdict.

Nat shrugged. "They've advertised as well," he said, quite aware of Sam's testy grunt at receiving what seemed to him an implied protest in front of a valued customer.

"You'll have to make it longer," he said.

"I can't do that without telling the story."

"Then tell the story, Nathaniel. I want it to be a good puff."

Miss Gelding, sensing a little unpleasantness, tactfully intervened.

"It's quite all right, Mr. Hearn; the show isn't for a fortnight. Give us a bigger advance notice next week."

It was unlike Miss Gelding to act as a peacemaker, and both Nat and Mollie were well aware that she made the effort only because she knew Nat would be reporting the show as critic on Wednesday week. She knew that Nat knew this also, and threw in a quick smile. Nat recalled that she had an ill-fitting set of false teeth. He had first noticed them during the second act of *The Gondoliers* in 1935.

"I'm afraid it'll have to be next week, Miss Gelding," said Nat, with quiet malice. "That write-up's already printed."

Sam spluttered a little. "How long have you been going to press before I so much as see the proofs?" he demanded.

Mollie cut in, and Sam thought he did not like her tone.

"Skinner was ready to run an hour ago," she said; "it would only have meant more overtime if we'd held him up."

Because this was not strictly true, and because Mollie must have known that the machine run was barely five minutes old, Nat had to suppress a grin.

Miss Gelding began to steer Sam toward the door.

"Come, Mr. Vane, we mustn't be late. . . ."

But on the threshold another thought occurred to the editor. It was as though he wanted to make an effort to assert himself in front of Miss Gelding, and show her that he still was occupying the editor's chair. Something sullen and near mutinous in the manner of Mollie and Nat had annoyed him. He spun round.

"We'll say no more about the write-up. But that case today—the young woman Miss Gelding was telling me about—display it, Nathaniel; I want it prominent. I'm writing a leader on it."

If Nat had heeded Mollie's quick glance he would have said nothing and let Sam go, but he did not. He stood up quickly, and crushed out his cigarette, rather too dramatically, Mollie thought.

"Mr. Vane . . . I've got to speak to you about that case."

Sam, who had half turned to follow Miss Gelding onto the landing, paused. He was checked by Nat's tone, without quite knowing why. For a second or two he was inclined to grunt "Nonsense!" and go on his way, but he saw, out of the corner of his eye, that Nat had already half crossed the room, as though he would grab the editor by the arm if necessary. Miss Gelding was halfway downstairs, and so Sam called, "Please go up to the Free Church hall, Miss Gelding; I won't be a moment," and turned back into the room, closing the door.

"Well? What are you trying to say?"

Mollie noticed, unhappily, that Nat's glance dropped when Sam stared balefully into his corner of the room. This old superiority of the less intelligent man—she had never really understood it. Was it that Nat, like all men who tried, obstinately, to behave with reason, was never quite sure of the line he ought to take, whereas a selfish individual, like Sam, never wavered from the course of self-interest?

"I'm in a hurry," said Sam.

Mollie felt that she could not bear the silence for another moment.

"We've had the girl up here," she told him. "Nat and I feel . . . we think you ought to leave it out!"

Then Nat broke in, before Sam could recover from his surprise.

"It's not fair to the parents, Mr. Vane. The girl's been punished enough, God knows. Publicity will only come back on the mother."

"The mother?" Sam felt himself growing excessively angry. "The mother should have kept her in at night."

"The mother's a bedridden invalid," retorted Nat, biting back the words "you bloody old prig," but somehow contriving to imply as much without uttering them.

Sam felt this, and took hold of himself, pacing across the room with hands clasped behind his back in order to give himself time to think out the most effective method of crushing the little mutiny without losing dignity. He glanced quickly from Mollie to Nat and back again.

"I've sensed something like this for a long time," he said, in a more level voice. "There seems to be an impression in here—and Gerald's not altogether outside it—that I've retired from active participation in the *Clarion* since my illness. I think this had better stop now, don't you? Before you and Miss Thorpe find yourselves dismissed, I mean. I'll deal with Gerald myself. . . ."

Nat blazed out, gaining confidence at the sound of his own voice.

"I don't care what you think, Mr. Vane. Gerald has nothing to do with this, or Miss Thorpe either. I heard that case. That Gelding woman isn't fit to be a magistrate, she's one hundred percent out of touch with life today. You can't judge these things on prewar standards. That girl is fundamentally a good kid, and people like that Gelding menace were damned glad of her a year ago. That isn't the point, anyhow; she doesn't care two straws what people here think of her, but she came to me on account of her mother, and I think . . ."

It was Sam's turn to cut in. Mollie noticed that the old fellow had gone slightly purple, as though suddenly assailed by oppressive heat. He was so angry that he had difficulty in speaking.

"You think! What does it matter what you think? You're paid to write what I think, and I'll tell you what I think about this . . . this glaring example of public indecency! I think the war's being blamed for every misdemeanor that comes under review. I think women who behave like this should be hounded from the society of decent people. Old-fashioned, you say? Well, I'm proud to be old-fashioned and to take my stand for decency and circumspection. As long as I've been in that chair I've fought for the things that used to be held sacred—a standard of public morality. . . ."

For a moment Mollie forgot Nat, forgot Beryl, forgot everything except the scorching contempt she had always felt for this man. She jumped off the edge of the table.

"Oh, for Heaven's sake, stop that cant!"

Sam was so taken aback by this totally unexpected attack that his denunciation spluttered into a rasping cough. Mollie took full advantage of the check.

"Why don't you admit it? I wouldn't mind if you'd admit it. But to stand there fooling yourself, week after week, year after year, can't you see how sickening it is? If this girl were a good customer you'd burn before you hung out her dirty washing, but because she's a wretched little nobody you use her for ammunition. And why? You don't give a damn about public morality or any of that other drivel. You know as well as I do that the sort of stand you intend taking will help to sell your dreary little rag and keep you in with the stuffed shirts you depend on for printing orders!"

In the brief silence that followed Nat could hear Sam wheezing. He stood there in the center of the room almost an object for pity, like a tired old boiler stoked far above its maximum pressure, and liable to split into fragments before somebody could rush across and turn the safety-valve screws. They waited for the explosion—an explosion that would tear the room wide open and vomit them both into the street to look for new jobs without references.

No explosion came. Sam's left hand flicked up to his waistcoat and began to massage, gently, just above the ponderous watch chain with the four dangling seals. Mollie sat down again with the air of having said all she had to say.

"Skip it," said Nat, quietly but quite inadequately. "I'm sorry I mentioned the matter!"

Sam turned for the door, without looking left or right. Reaching it, he gripped the handle and, having steadied himself, said, in a very low voice, "I'm not sorry, Nathaniel. No, no. Far from it. It's shown me how things are about the place. You, Miss Thorpe . . . you'd better go now. I don't want you here again. I've never liked you, never. I'll write to your father. We'll go into it all tomorrow, Nathaniel, with Gerald."

He pulled open the door and shuffled onto the dark landing. Halfway across the threshold he turned and spoke over his shoulder, his voice suddenly rising almost to a shriek.

"That case . . . you put it in . . . every word of it. Main news page! You hear me . . . !"

They heard him stumbling downstairs, far too agitated to remember to turn on the landing light.

Neither of them spoke for a moment. Then Nat said,

"Hell! He's in a state. I've never seen him so wobbly on his pins, never!"

Mollie opened a drawer and began to take out some of her things—a mirror, a powder compact, an English-French dictionary, odds and ends that had accumulated there over the past three years. She stuffed them all into her capacious brown handbag.

"Why didn't you tackle him about Wainer's plan and Baines' bus service while you were about it?" she asked.

"I'm coming with you, Mollie, if you'd like me to."

She stopped packing and looked up.

"Nat . . . I was so afraid . . ."

"Afraid?" He crossed over to the desk and, bending, softly kissed the top of her head. "Afraid of losing me?"

She caught his hand, and he was surprised by the intensity of the grip.

"Oh, partly, I suppose; but not only that. I was afraid that if you didn't make a break now, at this moment, you never would, and you'd be stuck here always, and become —well—feeble. I don't know what I'd do if you got feeble, Nat."

"I'm afraid I am a bit feeble, Mollie. You'll have to put up with that."

"I don't think you are. It's only because you're a kind person. If Sam had been young and strong, or even well, you'd have stood up to him. I could see that just now. You just hate hurting people. I suppose it's a good qualification for a husband."

"You'll marry me, then?"

"I think Father would prefer it, and, strictly speaking, so would I!"

He laughed and stretched himself.

"Good. Well, now what? Do I see the *Clarion* out, or do we disappear into the night hand in hand, luggage sent on?"

"Where do we go anyway? London?"

"Heaven knows. You got us the sack, I didn't!"

She stood up and caught his face in both her hands.

"Let's lock the door and work it out," she said, kissing him on the mouth.

Nat began to cross the room, but he did not get as far

as the door. There was a sudden patter of feet on the works stairs, and Bumble hurried in pale as his soiled apron, and very much out of breath.

"The Old Man," he shouted; "he's just bought it—in St. Luke's Road!"

Nat stared. "Bought it? Accident?"

Bumble shook his head vigorously.

"No, Nat . . . collapse. . . . Old Brody fetched me'n Burton. . . . The ambulance is there, but he's had it, I could see that. . . . He looked awful!"

Bumble sat down, much distressed, for all his dislike of Sam and his unconscious elation at being first with the news. He had only seen one dead man before—his grandfather, who had been more than half dead for years before he finally nodded off while dozing on the porch.

Nat ran down the steps and out through the yard gate, Mollie following him more slowly. Bumble trailed down behind her, but he did not approach the little group a hundred yards up St. Luke's Hill. He hung about on the outskirts, and saw the St. John Ambulance duty squad strap a bulky form to the stretcher and slide it into the waiting vehicle. People were collecting already, a policeman appeared as Dr. Payntor, whose surgery was just opposite, straightened himself and replaced some instruments in his bag. It was all over in a few moments.

Mollie went back into the works, where Skinner had shut down the machine.

"We'd better have something in about it," she told the foreman.

Skinner grunted. He could hardly realize that Sam Vane was dead. He had worked for him since he was younger than Bumble.

"Nat'll do something for the front page. We've got a block of 'im. In the file cabinet it is. You'd better look it out."

As she turned to the heavy cabinet behind the typecases, Nat came in. He looked puzzled and a little vacant. She said something to him, but he did not appear to hear her. He went upstairs to the office. She decided to leave him alone for an hour.

NINE

They saw little of each other during the next four days.

Sam had died on Thursday night. The funeral took place on Monday, and Mollie did not attend. She was the only member of the staff not present.

Nat gave his former employer a good spread in the *Clarion* that Friday—a big photograph with reversed column rules round it and a banner headline, the first news headline ever seen on the front page; to make room for it Gelding Bros.' advert and two others were lifted. The headline read LOSS TO SANDCOMBE: VETERAN EDITOR'S SUDDEN PASSING.

Underneath, in heavy type, was a readable summary of Sam's life, made up almost exclusively of facts, with little or no comment. On one of the inside pages, however, there were two formal tributes, one headed "A Dear Brother Moves On," by the Secretary of the Free Church Union, the other a racier pen portrait written by the Hon. Secretary of the Sandcombe Philatelic Society. This was headed "Our Founder's Death: Sandcombe's Philatelists Lament."

Apart from these and other tributes, brought in by post or word of mouth, Nat was a little disappointed at the absence of any notable stir in the town's life. The funeral cortège was neither so large nor so select as one might reasonably have expected. Outside the house in Cliff Terrace, when the hearse was about to start its descent to the churchyard, Gratton's butcher boy passed whistling "Roamin' in the Gloamin'." Bumble, crushed into the fourth cab with Skinner, Burton and Marlene, looked at the boy with disfavor. Nobody quite knew what was happening to the *Clarion*. There had been a number of disquieting rumors, and Bumble felt it was nothing to whistle about.

Mr. Sleek organized the funeral, and Nat, who had been instructed to take the names of "others present" at the lych-gate, thought he excelled himself in quiet display. He formed up the family mourners two by two outside the yard, the preliminary service having been conducted at the Methodist Chapel half an hour earlier. He paired off Gerald and Mrs. Vane. The widow was almost invisible under a heavy veil that bellied in the sea breeze and twice wrapped itself round Gerald's head. Gerald tried to look as if he did not mind his neat parting being disarranged.

There were no other immediate mourners, Sam's family having scattered and his wife being an only child, whose parents had died so long ago that they were laid in the original part of the churchyard years before the Rev. Galahad Ormsby had negotiated the purchase of Dodger's field, adjoining.

Behind the widow and son came Nat, walking with Miss Morgan from the binding room, and behind them the staff, paired off in order of seniority, Bumble last, and walking, to his secret delight, with Marlene's gloved hand tucked under his arm. This familiarity was permitted because Marlene was enjoying herself, and felt somewhat indulgent.

Behind the staff came the public, walking as they liked. Miss Gelding was there, a little tearful, for Sam had always treated her with a consideration that amounted to deference. Several church members were there also, loitering outside the chapel until the cortège left after the service. The local police inspector turned out in uniform, and so did Company Officer Martin, of the local NFS. The silver buttons of these two sparkled in the afternoon sunshine as they walked impressively in step.

The town Clerk and town surveyor were there too, together with one or two councillors. Baines was unable to attend, but sent Nat a card. The previous night one of his vehicles had been engaged in a collision on Gallows Head Hill, and he was out superintending the breakdown gang.

That, together with a dozen churchyard regulars, who were present at almost every public funeral, was the complete turnout. There were twenty-seven wreaths, eleven sprays and a bunch of violets past their prime.

Sleek's four henchmen doubled round the shuffling crocodile as soon as it entered the yard and piled the floral tributes on the freshly turned earth, stepping back and casting down their eyes just as the head of the column came into view.

Sleek himself, conspicuous in the van, was balancing his stovepipe hat in the crook of his arm, and bobbing between the yews as he tried to set a course along the firmer patches of the path, for the clay was sticking to his boots. He made a mental note to speak to the sexton about these paths. It took him an hour to clean up after each afternoon's work.

Nat forgot to notice whether Sleek was bald.

After the committal everyone mounted the little platform and gazed down on the lid of the polished oak coffin, set squarely in the grave, which had been lined with moss. Gerald gripped his mother's arm, and then eased her down the soft bank and out to the waiting cab, people making way for them in respectful silence.

Looking down into the hole, Nat found himself thinking odd thoughts—about the sort of man Sam might have been and the pleasant, useful life he might have had, if he had even begun to give himself a chance. He must have come to Sandcombe in the pride of his youth, strong, eager and ambitious, and in those days Sandcombe, although a smaller town, was a far prettier one. There was only the older part of the town, the sea, the wind and the heath behind the beechwoods. Sam had acquired the *Clarion* before he was thirty. He could have forged it into a lively, jolly little paper and made scores of good friends. If only he hadn't cared about money so much or, supposing he did, if only he had enjoyed a pint or two and not judged everything and everybody by the Old Testament standards of a militant, mid-Victorian piety, then there might have been genuine regret at this pitiful little ceremony, instead of dutiful attendances and a certain amount of morbid curiosity.

What had made Sam what he was? Power? The power to praise or condemn in his weekly rag? Lack of security? The fear of growing old and helpless without money? Lack of culture, for Sam had seldom read anything beyond the *Methodist Recorder* and a penny newspaper? Nat decided that it might be all or any of these things. He only knew, with certainty, that Sam had never known much happiness, and that he never remembered hearing him laugh. Perhaps, if he had been younger—young enough to serve in either of the wars—Sam might have come home to Sandcombe seeing things differently. Nat could feel no regret at his sudden death, within a few minutes of the only important quarrel they had ever had. He knew that at least one person in the town would secretly rejoice about it all —young Beryl Hopper, whose case had been almost miraculously omitted from the last week's *Clarion*. He had seen her since, when she told him that her mother was still in ignorance about her appearance in court. Beryl had decided to reenlist in the WAAF. Thinking of this, Nat was reminded, for a moment, of the family that had learned of Scrooge's death with joy, because they owed the old man money.

And now what? He and Mollie would be leaving, he supposed. What would happen to the *Clarion?* Gerald would keep on the printing works, but what about the paper? Would Gerald get someone in to run it, or would he sell it for what he could get and concentrate henceforth on jobbing? He fancied that Gerald had looked very anxious from the time he was told of his father's fatal collapse in St. Luke's Road.

Here Mr. Sleek respectfully jogged his elbow, and Nat found that they were the only two left at the graveside. As they moved off, together, toward the last cab, Sleek said, "This new ground's getting full, Mr. Hearn. We shall have to be looking for some more."

TEN

The day after the funeral Nat was turning out the drawers of his desk, when Gerald and Mrs. Vane, the latter still in mourning, came in from the shop landing.

Mollie had not been to the office since Sam's death, but Nat had been up to her home and had dinner with her and her father, a quiet, gentle little man to whom he had taken instant liking. When Mr. Thorpe had retired to his little library, Nat and Mollie had sat for a long time in front of the fire. They had not spoken much, and beyond deciding to spend a fortnight in town, as a preliminary to looking for jobs and rooms, they had not discussed the future. Nat had told her about his financial position— £850 in the bank as the result of prewar savings, a small legacy, money he had saved after being commissioned and his gratuity. Mollie had a tiny income of her own—shares bringing in just under three pounds a week. Her father lived on his pension from the bank. They decided, like most young people who feel a desperate need for one another, that this was more than enough for the present and a good deal better start than most couples received nowadays. Nat had said he would tell Gerald about leaving in the morning.

But Gerald, who looked even more worried than on the day of the funeral, gave him no opportunity. He sat his mother in Sam's leather chair and crossed over to the works' door, slipping the catch.

"We want to talk, Nat," he said, "just you, Mother and I. I don't want any of the men butting in."

They settled themselves, and Gerald offered Nat a cigarette—something he had never done in the past. Nat took it, wondering.

He noticed that Mrs. Vane was ill at ease. She was a pale, plain woman, with thin lips and masses of gray hair bunched untidily under a black straw hat. She looked as though she had been crying a good deal. He had never known whether she cared much for Sam, or whether it was one of those humdrum partnerships that never seem to mean anything at all until dissolved by the death of man or wife. On the few occasions that Nat had been up to the house she had treated him as if he were the man calling with the fish or to inspect the drains. He had always felt her to be a woman whose insignificant personality had long since been swamped and overborne by her husband. How little one knew about anyone, even after years of association. She sat there like a big crow, nervously plucking at a strand of black cotton that trailed from one of her gloves.

"We've been over at Thornton's, the solicitor's, Nat," began Gerald.

Nat nodded, sympathetically. He felt rather sorry for Gerald, left here with no wife—with nobody but this dismal woman and the works.

"He read us the will. It was pretty grim. There's hardly any capital at all."

Nat was surprised. He would have wagered that Sam had a good bit tucked away somewhere. He had been notoriously secretive, almost furtive, about his money affairs. Nat had seen him checking the petty cash in the tin box under the counter, and tearing off the slip of paper he was writing on when anyone approached too closely.

"Surely this place is freehold?" he said.

Gerald nodded. "It's not the place ... we can run on here donkeys' years. No one can get any new buildings put up anyway. It's the machinery. I told you about it; there's hardly a piece of plant in the works under fifty years of age. What are we going to do about renewals?"

"What about insurance?"

"Mother got two small endowments; they don't come to more than two hundred and fifty pounds, and anyway they belong to her. There's about one hundred and forty pounds in the current account and none on deposit."

"The house is yours, I suppose?"

"We're not going to sell that!" said Mrs. Vane tartly, and Nat saw Gerald grimace.

"The point is ..." he began, and then, when he seemed

to dry up, his mother cut in, suddenly gaining assurance.

"We should like to take you into partnership, Nathaniel," she said, looking hard at him.

Nat's obvious surprise gave Gerald the chance to recover himself.

"That's it, Nat—equal partners, the three of us. I've got a bit of my own, and I'm willing to sink it. You raise as much as me for down payments on plant replacements, and we'll call it a deal. You'll be getting a third share in an old established business at a figure a good bit less than it's worth in the open market. You're not without money, are you?"

Gerald ended on a note of despair, for he had misread Nat's distant expression. Thoughts set in motion by Mrs. Vane's pronouncement had begun to race through Nat's brain. A partnership! To run this paper as his own! To whip those dismal advertisements from the front page, replace them with a display of short news items, establish a standard of dramatic criticism, write a real leader every Friday, comment on council decisions, build up a sports section instead of relying upon weekly driblets from club secretaries, take on another reporter perhaps, expand the circulation as far as the borders of Paxtonbury, deliver by van, cut down the long funeral reports, go in for a page of pictures, run small competitions, put a readers' postbag on one of the inside pages . . . there was no limit to what a man could do if he had some say in his own destiny, even a Sandcombe destiny; this was the pipe dream of every tired journalist in Fleet Street.

"I've got eight hundred and fifty pounds," he told Gerald simply.

Gerald smote his knee. "More than enough with mine," he said, and Mrs. Vane smiled—a thin, wintry smile that looked as though it hurt a little.

Nat felt that he could not sit still. He got up and walked to the window, trying to think calmly and logically. There was Mollie . . . She wanted to go away; but this altered things. It meant that they could have their say here and now, a bigger say than they would ever get on a daily or a weekly in a city. Had he better stall the Vanes and consult her? No, she would only try to talk him out of it. He did not want to be talked out of it; he wanted to do it. He knew, without a flicker of doubt anywhere, that he wanted to do it, badly. He turned to Gerald.

"What sort of partnership do you contemplate? I mean, how is the place to be parceled up?"

Gerald, thoroughly at ease now, rubbed his plump hands together.

"That's easy. We go on as we are. I run the works, you run the paper. Mother takes a third share of the profits and a minimum of say, three hundred pounds a year? How does that suit?"

"That's all right; but a paper, even a local like ours, has to have some sort of policy."

"As the editor, Nat, that's your headache. Brighten it up a bit. I shan't mind, so long as we sell more. Paper must come back into circulation. We can slam in two more pages of ads and a feature or two. We've always got on together, Nat. We won't fall out over policy. What do you say, Mother?"

Mrs. Vane considered, as though she were digging down into her memory for something pleasant that somebody had once said about Nat long, long ago. Whatever it was, it eluded her, for she only said, "I'm sure Samuel always liked your writing, Nathaniel. He must have—he never complained to me."

Nat fought back a grin, and suddenly wished that Mollie had heard Mrs. Vane say that. Obviously neither she nor Gerald had heard anything about the row that preceded Sam's death. But how should they? He must himself have been the last person to speak to the Old Man; after, he hurried out in pursuit of Miss Gelding just before his collapse.

"Well?" asked Gerald, his anxious look returning for a moment.

"I'll do it," said Nat. "Get Thornton to draw up a draft agreement right away."

Gerald jumped to his feet and caught Nat's hand.

"Good man! Good man! You'll never regret it, old boy —never."

"We'll go across to Mr. Thornton right away," added Mrs. Vane, looking as though she couldn't relax until she saw Nat's signature on the official sheet of parchment.

Nat thought of Mollie again.

"Tomorrow," he said, "I . . . er . . . I've one or two things to do first."

"Right. At ten A.M.," said Gerald, and shook hands again. Nat thought that he had never seen Gerald look so young and eager.

ELEVEN

Nat was never able to find out how Mollie had got wind of his change of plans before he was able to see her and tell the story himself.

After Gerald had gone across to Thornton to arrange the initial partnership meeting, Nat had difficulty in leaving the office, three callers coming into the shop in quick succession. He set out for Mollie's house in the early afternoon, but before he had gone far he came to the conclusion that confession was not going to be easy.

Mollie's attitude toward the Clarion Press had never been cordial; lately it seemed to have been growing increasingly bitter, right up to the moment of her outburst in the office. It had occurred to him, on thinking the matter over, that perhaps she felt responsible in some measure for Sam's collapse. It was Mollie who had provoked Sam's fatal rage that night. Perhaps this feeling had kept her away from the place since his death. Nat decided against this, for he remembered that she had since been able to discuss Sam quite dispassionately, and had even shocked him a little the evening before the funeral by saying, in that quiet, mellow voice of hers, "It's no good, Nat; I'm not coming up to the churchyard. It would be the sort of thing he'd do. I still think he was a dreadful man, and the fact that he's dead doesn't sweeten my memories of him. Besides, I've nothing suitable to wear."

He had not argued with her, for he could well see the logic of her views. Now that Sam was gone, however, Nat found considerable difficulty in stoking up any resentment about the man. The worst he could think of his fifteen years' association with the *Clarion* was that its editor had been inclined to be old-fashioned in his methods and testy in his approach, particularly just before the time of going to press. That was not enough to account for

Mollie's attitude and, he reasoned, she had had only a few years of such memories to match his fifteen.

He knew, of course, that his decision to stay on in Sandcombe would irritate her, but, as things were, or would be, with himself as editor-partner and Gerald under complete control, he felt that she would soon come round to his way of thinking.

He had a good deal to learn about Mollie Thorpe.

He walked out over the Dunes that afternoon, and, turning left at the mouth of the Beck, followed it upstream to the spur of the beechwoods. On the way he occupied himself with mapping out the opening phrases of his confession. None of them sounded very convincing. All had an air of self-excuse, as though he was an LAC again, trying to explain to the flight sergeant why he had missed 8 A.M. parade, or a young reporter trying to convince Sam why he had failed to sit through the Methodist Choral Club's rendering of Handel's *Messiah*.

Nat reflected, during this walk, that most of his adult life had been spent in doing things he was not inclined to do, or in dodging them and then talking himself out of trouble with those in authority over him. Well, Gerald's offer had put paid to all that.

It was nearly five o'clock when he turned into the little gravel drive that led up to Mollie's house. He rang the bell and heard it jangle away to a tinkle. Nobody came to the door. He rang again, and then went round to the back. The back door was locked. He squinted through the letter box and caught a glimpse of the Paxtonbury evening paper lying on the mat. This meant that no one had been home since 4 P.M., the hour of delivery. He could see also that Mollie's fawn coat was gone from the hall stand. So was her father's black trilby hat. Everyone was out, and reluctantly he went back to the office, racking his brains as to where Mollie and her father could have gone.

He did not have to ponder very long. Marlene handed him a sealed envelope as he lounged in through the shop.

"Miss Thorpe left that for you. She was on her way to the station."

Since it had gone around that Nat and Mollie were

practically engaged, Marlene's attitude toward Nat had been a studied mixture of sulkiness, defiance and disdain.

He took the letter and went upstairs. Sitting in Sam's chair he tore open the envelope and read:

My dear Nat,

The news reached me. Things do, pretty quickly, in these parts. I don't mind you being such a fool with your money and your future, but, in view of our "arrangement," I feel pretty sick about it all. It might have helped if you'd talked it over first. I don't suppose you would have changed your mind; I'm resigned to your pigheadedness. What I mean is that it mightn't have hurt so much.

There was the inevitable feminine postscript. It ran:

I stampeded Daddy into coming up to town with me. *He's* coming for a few days.

Nat folded the letter and put it in his correspondence drawer. Years of habit had schooled him into keeping all notes and letters that came into his possession, not for the information they contained, but because of the little scribbles of shorthand he was always writing on the back.

His first reaction was one of intense irritation at Mollie having found out about it before he could tell her himself. His second was a feeling of frustrated anger directed against all women—women who tried to run men's lives and then put the man in the wrong when he made an independent wriggle or two. Then he began to wonder if she intended staying in London for good. He took the letter out again and reread the postcript. Did it mean that she was staying three weeks, six months or five years? Or was it purposely vague in order to keep him guessing? That was the sort of thing most women in his limited experience would have done. But Mollie had always seemed too adult to indulge in that sort of caprice. It was why he had been so attracted by her. She had the mind of a sensible man, the face and figure of an attractive woman.

Nat broke off, suddenly realizing that he did not possess as much as a snapshot of her. He told himself that this wasn't likely to matter. If things went as he planned, he would be too busy in the next few weeks to moon over a photograph.

He was conscious of an urgent need for a man's company, and drifted out of the office and down High Street to the Galleon lounge. There he was relieved to find Otto de Vere, and Otto in a receptive mood. He was having woman troubles himself.

They discussed each other's affairs over four bitters and four whiskies. Otto's wife, from whom he had been separated for years, was demanding money with menaces. Otto's mistress, the raddled woman who shared his house on the cliff, had not spoken for three days. She was going to have a baby, and kept pestering Otto to make arrangements to get rid of it. Nat found that his comparatively minor troubles were swallowed up in Otto's complications, which made them ridiculously insignificant.

"I didn't know you wanted a kid, Otto," he said, regarding the tired old roué with tolerant amusement.

Otto sighed.

"I don't, old boy. God forbid. But it's far less trouble to have it."

"Less trouble for you?"

"No, no, less trouble for everybody. These things are risky. I keep on telling her that. And all she can say is 'So is the real thing, and you lose your figure.' What the hell can you do with a woman like that? What's the matter with us? Why, in God's name, do we ever get into these absolutely voluntary toils? Tell me that now!"

"My old CO used to say it was chemistry," mused Nat, upon whom four pints of draft on an empty stomach were having a mildly mellowing effect, "pure chemistry."

"I'll tell you what I'm going to do, old boy," continued Otto, who had been drinking for some time before Nat's arrival. "If that child of mine's a boy, I'll have him doctored, so help me I will. And he'll live to bless me for it."

It turned out quite a pleasant evening. They both went back to Otto's place and rooted out some brandy. Between long recitals of Otto's amorous adventures in Chile after the First World War, Nat told him about the future of the *Clarion*.

They finished the bottle drinking the health of the paper, damnation to Miss Gelding's operatic endeavors, perdition to Baines' ideas of local government and a final toast to Sam's chances of getting a subeditor's post on the *Celestial Recorder*. This toast was Otto's idea, and Nat thought it original.

Nat had little opportunity to reflect upon his personal affairs during the next few days. Time passed very quickly. There was a good deal to be done.

He went over to Thornton's chambers as arranged and sat under the stacks of tin deed boxes and ribbon-tied documents while Thornton, a stout, fussy, middle-aged man, junior partner of the firm of Snow & Thornton, hovered over the signatories of the deed like a thrush putting the finishing touches to a neatly constructed nest. Gerald beamed when he was handed the flamboyant quill pen. Nat noticed that he signed with a self-conscious flourish, quite unlike his usual crabbed signature. Mrs. Vane looked very grave, as though she was putting her name to a questionable death warrant.

Then they shook hands all round, congratulating themselves and thanking Mr. Thornton, who kept wheezing "Capital!" and filling the office with the not unpleasant odor of the special cough lozenge he favored. Nat thought it smelled like camphor.

The deed itself was even better than he had hoped. He read through the draft very carefully before the others arrived, and found that he appeared to have complete control of the paper and a considerable voice in the handling of the staff—a matter to which a separate clause had been devoted at his request.

He parted from Gerald and Mrs. Vane at the foot of the stairs and went over to Barclay's Bank in High Street, in order to transfer the major part of his capital into the *Clarion*'s account. Gatwood, the chief cashier, wrote out the firm's balance in hand on a slip of paper and pushed it across the counter. There was nearly one thousand pounds in the current account, most of it paid in by Gerald on the previous day.

Later they had the staff up in the office, and Gerald made a little speech, formally presenting Nat as the new partner-editor and adding one or two comments aimed at strengthening morale. Nat thought him extraordinarily like a brand-new adjutant taking over a new unit in the presence of a dozen hard-bitten NCOs. The former reporter felt a little embarrassed when Gerald said, "Now that Mr. Hearn has joined the executive, I must ask you all to be a little more careful when addressing him, particularly in front of customers. It doesn't do to make use of the Christian name, you know! Sounds rather cheap, if you see what I mean."

The men, all of whom had called the new partner "Nat" for the past fifteen years, said nothing. There was no one present who was unfamiliar with Gerald and Gerald's mannerisms.

There was, however, one incident which might have proved disruptive, had it not been summarily disposed of by Gerald.

He had asked if anyone had anything to say, adding, "It mustn't be said that I do all the talking."

Burton, the phlegmatic keyboard operator, gave a preliminary cough.

"Well?" asked Gerald patiently.

"It's just this, Mr. Gerald," mumbled Burton, who appeared to be speaking not because he wanted to but simply because he owed it to himself. "Mr. Carstairs has been onto me to join the union . . ."

Gerald gave a long and discouraging sniff.

"Mr. Carstairs is a troublemaker, Burton. I've told you that before. I'm afraid I must stress that my policy as regards unions is identical with that of the late Mr. Vane. I won't tolerate a union man. That's flat."

Gerald's tone implied that he had very decided opinions upon the matter, as indeed he had. Nat looked a little uneasy, but said nothing.

Burton was not deterred.

"Mr. Carstairs pointed out that union rates were a good deal more . . ."

Gerald, noting that the remainder of the staff were showing considerable interest in Burton's remarks, slapped his thigh, like a plump oriental despot dismissing an importunate vizier.

"Come now, Burton, this is final. We should be sorry to lose you, but if you go over to Carstairs I'm afraid we shall have to." He turned to the staff in general. "Now, men— and you, ladies, as well"—this to the stolid Miss Morgan, whose hands were still sticky from the binding-room glue, and the somewhat bored Marlene—"if we pull together we shall get along a good deal better than in the past. My father—well, I don't mind admitting that his methods were a little old-fashioned; we shall not be so out of date in future. Mr. Hearn and I have decided, for instance, to replace some of the plant, and I leave tomorrow to supply our requirements from London."

This announcement created a mild stir, which was by no means lost upon Gerald. Nat realized how much the man had expanded, despite his financial worries, since Sam had died. He was like a head prefect mounting the housemaster's rostrum and enjoying his first taste of authority. The pained look that Gerald had habitually worn was gone. In its place was a brisk, almost bouncing confidence, a twentieth-century challenge to everything that was mellow, musty and sere in the offices and works. Nat felt that within a few hours Gerald might be relied upon to start a major offensive, hurling old ledgers and files into a vast pile in the yard, and applying the ceremonial torch with his own hand. It was not an altogether bad sign, he felt. Gerald might not prove an obstacle to a new *Clarion;* he might even be persuaded to support the policy Nat had been planning since he made his decision the day of the funeral.

These plans, having matured for forty-eight hours, were ready to be put into operation the moment Gerald's visit to London gave Nat a clear field for a single publishing day. They had cost him some thought. His first intention had been to launch an assault on a wide front, trusting that he could win a substantial measure of local support by the simple boldness of his attack.

But then he had changed his mind. The blueprints of the Flats Development Scheme had gone away to Paxtonbury in order that a series of blocks could be made. They would not be to hand in time for this week's paper. Lacking their official backing, Nat felt it wiser to concentrate on a more personal issue—Miss Gelding's opera, for instance, following up with a full-scale exposure of the council's building scheme the following week, or perhaps the week after.

It was difficult to plan very far in advance. So much depended on local reactions. In the meantime there were many minor issues that called for attention, and there was no sense in using all one's ammunition in a single bombardment.

Contemplating these moves Nat began to feel somewhat like the Mikado. "He had a little list."

Nat and Gerald had one insignificant clash, but it could hardly be called a tiff, for Gerald gave in almost without a struggle.

Soon after the dismissal of the staff that afternoon, Bumble drifted back into the editorial and hung about looking rather diffident until Gerald asked him, somewhat irritably, what he sought. Bumble spoke up manfully.

"I was wondering, Mr. Gerald. Could I go in with Mr. Nat?"

Gerald stared, not fully comprehending. Bumble looked particularly inky and tow-headed, and although he had a cold in the head he seemed reluctant to use a handkerchief that was almost as black as his apron.

"Go in with Mr. Nat?" queried Gerald.

"As a junior reporter," added Bumble, without much hope.

Nat intervened.

"That's a good idea, Gerald. We need someone for routine stuff. It takes up far too much of my time as it is."

"But there's Miss Thorpe . . ." protested Gerald.

"She appears to have left us without notice," grunted Nat.

Gerald shrugged. "If you really want someone, I should have a nice grammar school lad—young Aubrey Baines, for instance," he hedged.

Nat smiled grimly. "I couldn't teach young Aubrey anything," he said, "he'd soon start teaching me! Bumble's stuck to his shorthand in evening classes. Why not give him a chance?"

"I can do sixty words a minute," added Bumble piously.

"Well, it's your funeral," replied Gerald; "you'd better try him out." And, turning to Bumble, he snapped, "See you come to work in your best suit on Monday."

After Gerald had gone, Bumble hung on, watching Nat out of the corner of his eye. Presently he said, "I haven't got a best suit. Mum's 'ad me blasted coupongs."

Nat chuckled. "What do you wear in church?" he asked.

"I don't go no more," said Bumble. "I blow the organ for the Methodists. They pay more. No one can't see me pumping it, so I wear working clothes."

Nat gave him three pounds and a sheet of demobilization coupons that Mollie had spared.

"Get a clean pair of flannels and a sports coat with those," he said, and Bumble took the money, gratefully.

"It's easy enough to pick up, isn't it?" he asked.

Nat considered, forcing his mind back to the boy who still hovered in the doorway.

"It is if you'll listen to me," he bantered. "Concentrate on detail. Never despise detail, Bumble. From now on its your meat and drink, your bread, butter and bacon ration. You are the sorrowing friend at funerals, the joyous well-wisher at weddings, the critical enthusiast at school sports, the eager yes-man to the bores who will try and waste your time in the streets. Remember this and you will be a big local success. We'll devote a whole column to you in the *Clarion* obituary when Sleek finally lays you to rest in the churchyard on the hill."

"Will I do fires and accidents?" asked Bumble hopefully.

"Not for years and years," said Nat. "You'd drop us into a libel action in less than a fortnight. Run along now. I'm up to the neck in it."

Bumble ran along, with joy in his heart.

Gerald left on Monday morning, promising to be back on Saturday, the day after publishing day. He would make preliminary overtures and inspect some good secondhand plant that had been advertised in the London area. Then they could go up together in about a fortnight.

Nat said nothing about his plans beyond casually informing his partner that he intended to bring out a *Clarion* with front page news, redistributing the advertisements on the inside pages. Gerald nodded enthusiastically.

"I'm with you, old boy—what we lose in ad revenue we shall pick up in prestige and circulation."

Nat wished Gerald good luck at the station. Then he went back to the office and fired his first shot. It took the form of a letter headed "Sandcombe Expands—Upward!" The letter was a simple affair. Slipped unobtrusively into the correspondence column, it nestled between a reader's bitter comment on the constant fouling of footpaths by Pekinese dogs and an appeal from Miss Startwright for Girls' Life Brigade funds. It ran:

SIR,

May I trespass upon the hospitality of your column [*Clarion* correspondents habitually "trespassed," and Nat felt that he might as well keep in the groove the better to throw Baines off the scent] to point out the abysmal folly of our town council in choosing a site nearly two miles out of Sandcombe, and situated at the top of a steep hill, for the newly planned houses?

I would like to know, as a ratepayer of long standing, why this site was chosen when a far better one is ready to hand. I refer, of course, to the Flats, where development was envisaged as long ago as 1920.

Why has nobody mentioned the original plan? Have the electors been consulted in the matter? As no voice was raised at last week's council meeting, I appeal to you, sir, to give your readers an opportunity of considering this alternative site before it is too late.

> I remain, sir,
> Faithfully,
> SOLOMON EAGLE

After the nom-de-plume Nat wrote, "Correspondent's name and address submitted as act of good faith, but withheld in accordance with his own request."

It took him a long moment to resist the temptation of signing the letter "Editor," but now that he was definitely established as a partner, instinctive caution was taking the place of his original urge toward iconoclasm. Nat also felt that the early stages of the campaign should be conducted under the cloak of anonymity. There would be time enough for a showdown if Baines rose to the bait. So he took Burton into his confidence, and got him to keyboard the letter after working hours. He did not trust Skinner and the others. They had too much native conservatism. He felt cheered when the phlegmatic Burton grunted his approval.

"Time we pushed the boat out," was all he said, but it satisfied Nat as to the old printer's loyalty.

Then Nat went off to St. Luke's Parish Hall, handing his complimentary ticket in at the boxoffice and worming his way into a stall just as the curtain rose on the first night of *The Prodigal Princess*. They gave him a program, but he put it into his jacket pocket unread. There was no one on the stage whom he did not recognize, wig and greasepaint notwithstanding.

TWELVE

The chorus work was fairly good. By this time a dozen of the younger members had drifted back from the forces, and some of them appeared to have gained considerable experience in the amateur societies in the camps. Their volume, particularly that of the men, was excellent, and they looked well enough in their mid-Victorian costumes.

It was not until the opera was fifteen minutes old, when Miss Gelding sailed through a screen of Habsburg hussars, sending their dolmans and sabretaches flying and crowding the warriors into the wings, that Nat recognized the familiar trend.

The Princess Mathilde had been unfortunate in her choice of leading man, securing little Ivor Morgan, brother of the mountainous Miss Morgan of the *Clarion*'s binding department.

Ivor was excessively short, even by the standards of operatic tenors, but what he lacked in height he made up for in self-possession. He had a kind of bouncing perkiness that sent him prancing about the inadequately braced Viennese café like a blue-and-silver Ping-Pong ball, clanking his saber against the flower tubs and looking more like a kingfisher pursuing darting minnows than an upstart hussar planning to elope with the emperor's daughter.

Princess Mathilde did her best to steady him, even going so far as to pin him against her generous bust on more than one occasion, but he always contrived to wriggle free, hop onto the table and point frenziedly through the latticed windows to the Dolomites, where, he alleged, his dear old peasant parents would strew the cabin floor with nice new rushes immediately the satin shoes of Princess Mathilde honored the threshold.

This sort of thing went on throughout most of the first act, occasionally varied by the sudden appearance of a cloud of hussars, each arming a beribboned serving wench.

All seemed to share the secret of the forthcoming elopement, for they constantly raised empty drinking mugs and drank to the health of the runaways and damnation to the doddering emperor and his scheming prime minister.

The latter made a dramatic appearance just before the first-act curtain. Walking somewhat stiffly, for his knee breeches were rather tight about the thighs, he called up two jailers, complete with manacles and bade them rivet the gyves to Ivor's ankles. Twelve sabers flashed from their scabbards, and as many sweeping brooms were threateningly raised, but Ivor stayed center just long enough to forbid bloodshed, and was led away upstage left, still in possession of his drinking mug, which young Oliver Marshall, playing No. 2 Jailer, had forgotten to confiscate.

The fetters had the effect of slowing down the curtain, and Nat thought it rather a pity that they had not been clamped on earlier in the plot. He reflected, however, that they might be worth their weight in papier-mâché during the second act.

Princess Mathilde, after indulging in a paroxysm of grief, sufficiently violent to tilt her blond wig an inch or so, went into conference with Stephen, the portly café proprietor, who did not seem to begrudge the loss of a drinking mug and agreed to collaborate. Then, as the honeymoon in the Dolomites seemed likely to be postponed indefinitely, the hussars called for more wine and settled down to make a night of it.

During the lengthy interval Nat went round behind the stage, and stood in the prompt corner watching a sweating team of stagehands transform the café into a roomy dungeon, with apparent access to the battlements.

All was not well behind the scenes. The property manager had mislaid Princess Mathilde's rope ladder, without which Ivor would be doomed to spend the rest of his life padlocked to the wall, and a feverish search was in progress.

Nat was buffeted into the narrow, gas-lit passage that ran along behind the principals' dressing rooms.

Everybody, from Miss Gelding down to the callboy, was looking for the rope ladder, and the chances of finding it were steadily diminishing as crinolines cascaded from the walls and hampers were turned upside down on dressing room floors.

Miss Gelding, sweating freely through her rouge, was rating Ernie Potter, the stage manager, a truculent young barman not long home from the Middle East.

"If you had a *plan,* if only you had a *plan!*" she shouted at him.

Ernie was showing signs of strain after a long voyage with Miss Gelding on the bridge. He flung down a brass candelabra he was holding, combining a fierce clatter with a fine, theatrical gesture.

"That's the bloody limit!" he shouted. "The absolute, outside bloody limit!"

"Don't you dare to swear at me!" screamed Princess Mathilde. "I won't have it, do you hear me? I won't *have it!*"

"Then you can find another bloody stage manager," said Ernie, brushing aside a pair of would-be peacemakers and stalking onto the stage.

Miss Gelding burst into tears, and was led away to be coaxed into her hussar pantaloons, for she was due to enter the jail as a bogus sergeant of the guard, and the pantaloon-donning had held up the show for twelve minutes during the dress rehearsal the previous night.

Ernie was followed onto the stage by a dark girl in slacks who should have been helping Gunter at the switchboard, but had been much attracted by the stage manager's saturnine masculinity during rehearsals.

"Oh, *come on,* Ernie," she wheedled, "don't let the old girl get you down! Mind out, clumsy!"—this to Gunter, who was squeezing past with a section of battlement. "What do you think I'm made of? Scotch mist?"

Nat wandered down the wooden steps and round toward the front of the house again. The atmosphere behind scenes was not unfamiliar to him. Amateur shows were always more or less like that, and were often none the worse for it. Those taking part were entitled to the luxury of a little phony temperament. It made them feel professional. But somehow tonight was different. This flare-up was not the ordinary amateur's tiff, forgotten in the excitement of the final curtain and joked about at annual dinners years afterward. Nat felt that there was tyranny behind the scenery—the tyranny of a woman who sensed that the scepter of the society was loose in her hand, and might be wrested from her before the next show.

It wasn't as if she was any good, or ever had been. Her performance tonight, her casting and production (for she always insisted on doing everything unaided), were among the worst he had ever seen. He went back into the hall rather sadly. There was sufficient talent and enthusiasm to present a really good production in Sandcombe, if only people like Miss Gelding and her imitators would keep away from it, and not seek to create a monopoly of amateur entertainment. Ernie and one or two of the chorus might have provoked mutiny before this, had it not been for the utter lack of critical standards in the town. For that lack the *Clarion* was largely responsible. He himself had written dozens of fulsome notices. It was a somber thought.

Nat did not pay a great deal of attention to the second act. The trouble backstage had had its effect. Some of the entrances were ragged, and Ernie or his deputy had been obliged to manufacture a makeshift rope ladder out of hamper cording. There was unpleasant laughter in the audience when Princess Mathilde, as sergeant of the guard, produced the ladder from under her sky-blue tunic. It was manifestly clear that, had Ivor essayed an escape by this means, the castle moat would instantly have put an end to all hopes of a morganatic marriage in the house of Habsburg.

Miss Gelding went off key, but there was nothing new about that; Ivor, now shorn of his fetters, bobbed about the battlements just out of her reach. The finale, with a whole jailful of hussars and transformed serving wenches, was a riot of color and song. It appeared to Nat as though the entrance of one more hussar, even a little drummer boy, would bring the entire castle down about the company's ears. Electrician Gunter and the girl in slacks, clinging to the rear of the portcullis with the tenacity of a besieged garrison who could expect no mercy, evidently had the same idea. The girl called lustily for Ernie, who was drinking beer in Ivor's dressing room. But Ernie, if he heard, heeded not.

The audience responded generously to the fifteen curtains; the clapping closed in loud bravos when three spruce young men walked down the center gangway to hand three separate bouquets over the footlights to Miss Gelding. The young men were mere stewards, and unaware that the bouquets had been paid for out of Gelding Bros.' petty cash.

While Miss Gelding was making a pretty little curtain speech, Nat slipped from the hall. He heard her say "... we've had our little troubles behind, of course, but *then* ..." before he threaded his way through the car park and down the hill to the *Clarion* office, where he let himself in by the yard door.

He was half inclined to enjoy himself with *The Prodigal Princess,* build up a notice of light-hearted ridicule and treat the whole affair as a good joke, but after the opening paragraph it occurred to him that this sort of treatment might defeat its end, for most of the readers would conclude that he was merely amusing himself at the society's expense. Then again, it would be unfair to condemn the society as a whole, for here and there he had detected performances that might have been excellent if the players had been properly produced, instead of being carefully placed as stage background for the two leads. Besides, it was important not to alienate local sympathy from the new paper. Something told him that he would need all the support he could get in the next few weeks. He had better tell the truth about the politics of the opera and concentrate on Miss Gelding and Ivor Morgan.

After one or two false starts, unusual for Nat, who seldom made more than one attempt at a criticism, he wrote:

HERE WE ARE AGAIN!
MUSICAL ANNUAL STILLBORN IN PARISH HALL.
PRODIGAL PRINCESS EXHUMED.

On Wednesday night, and for three successive nights in St. Luke's Parish Hall, the Sandcombe Amateur Operatic

Society exhumed an outdated operetta and played it to appreciative audiences. Mercifully, the proceeds will be devoted to the funds of the Cliffside Convalescent Home.

It is evident that the society is badly in need of new blood. Several returned service players were in the cast, but every one of them figured in the chorus. This is a pity. Any one of them could handle the leading roles more convincingly than they are played at present.

There are a number of questions we would like to ask about this year's opera. In the first place, why *The Prodigal Princess?* This operetta was first produced in 1878. Subsequently it has been seen twice in Sandcombe, once in 1929 and again in 1934. It is a bad operetta, which only a good production could make bearable. Miss Gelding's production was a shoddy one.

Now this, in itself, is excusable. The society, only recently re-formed, is struggling against many physical handicaps, inexperienced members and scenic difficulties, to mention only two postwar troubles, but Wednesday's production was worse than shoddy. It was built round a single individual—Miss Julia Gelding, who, as a veteran amateur, ought to have known better.

We suggest that the piece was chosen with this in mind. It would be difficult to build a Gilbert and Sullivan operetta round a single lead. *The Prodigal Princess* has only one major role. That is partly why it is a bad work, quite unsuitable for amateurs, who should concentrate on teamwork to compensate for their obvious lack of stars.

Another question. Why was it necessary to cast Mr. Ivor Morgan, notwithstanding his excellent voice, in the ridiculously unsuitable role of the ambitious trooper? Realism is not essential for an operetta, but the least a producer can do when he looks round for a hussar is to find somebody who looks as though he could sit a horse. This cannot be said of Mr. Morgan, for all his dash and flourish.

A third question. Why was the chorus limited to a dozen rehearsals? The chorus work, even so, was far superior to that of the principals, with one or two exceptions; but we have it on excellent authority—that of the caretaker of the institute where rehearsals were called—that the room was cleared for chorus work on eleven occasions only, whereas the principals have been called on thirty-two occasions during the past six weeks. This is not production. It is sheer exhibitionism.

By and large, *The Prodigal Princess* does its producer and her company little credit. It would be easy to make excuses, and we freely admit that Wednesday night's audience appeared to enjoy the entertainment. But this does not mean that it was a good, or even a moderately successful effort. There can be no standard of taste among patrons while the present state of affairs exists within the society. Fresh leadership is essential.

We left St. Luke's hall on Wednesday with a heavy heart, heavy because we were weak enough to reflect on what might have been. In an age when the public is inclined more and more toward "canned" entertainment, when the radio and cinema are destroying the creative faculties of a naturally creative people, here was a fine chance lost.

There is one good thing about this week's operetta. It will provide a sum of something like £200 to a needy convalescent home. Should it end there? We feel that it should not. It ought to be possible to raise money *and* to present first-class amateur entertainment at one and the same time. With things as they are within the society this is quite impossible.

Nat signed the article with his initials.

On Thursday afternoon he attended a special meeting of the Parochial Church Council, to which the press received a written invitation.

The meeting was called by the vicar for the purpose of discussing the allocation of a town memorial legacy, a sum of £1000, tax free, left by Rear Admiral Boucher, who had died in the last year of the war, soon after receiving news that his only son, also serving in the navy, had been killed off Corsica.

The old rear admiral, who had other urgent matters claiming his attention during the last few weeks of his life, had not made things very clear in the will, but the executors had ruled that, within the meaning of a codicil, inserted within a few days of the old man's death, the vicar was charged with the responsibility of spending the money in any way he deemed advisable, providing that it commemorated, in one way or another, the Sandcombe men who had lost their lives in the war. There was a vague sentence in the codicil which implied that the memorial, whatever it was, should "benefit" the ex-servicemen who returned home, and the vicar, who was even more puzzled than the executors, decided to clear the air by calling a church council meeting, to which members of the press and public were invited. The meeting could then share his responsibility by deciding what form the memorial should take.

Nat had worked closely to schedule throughout the week, and saw the inside pages to bed soon after midday on Thursday, leaving him a clear margin of two hours before the front pages were assembled on the stone. He decided to cover the meeting and squeeze a half column into the back page of the current issue.

The Rev. Galahad Ormsby, who presided, was a pleasant man, but a bad vicar. For years he had been dominated by Mr. Norton, his senior churchwarden. Nat had known this for long enough, as indeed everybody in Sandcombe knew it, for if ever any matter cropped up at a committee meeting involving church property or policy, the committeemen invariably said, "No good writing to Vicar, write direct to Norton!"

Norton was a tough customer. He had an intimidatingly deep voice, and thick, tufty eyebrows which arched in an alarming manner when he was piqued or challenged. Nat remembered him tackling a wretched CMS missionary at a foreign field rally just before the war. The missionary had complained of the unsuitability of New Guinea's climate for South Sea Island mission graduates, who invariably died soon after setting foot in Papua. It was all rather tiresome, he explained. Replacements were needed more rapidly than they could be trained, and training was an expensive business.

During question time Norton stood up and expressed himself forcibly upon the folly of wasting so much money so regularly. He pointed out that here at home mission funds were hard to collect. If the missionary had no better way of spending St. Luke's annual contribution than to squander it on a succession of Papuan funerals, then the CMS had better strike the parish off its subscription list, and the church council would set about buying its long overdue electric organ!

Nat had admired Norton for his forthrightness. The missionary had been so astonished by the attack that he was rendered inarticulate.

Now, no sooner had the church council meeting been formally opened by the vicar's announcement concerning the legacy, than Norton stood up and moved a resolution to the effect that the sum be put to the parish organ fund.

The vicar was gratified, but somewhat embarrassed. Fudge, one of the sidesmen, who did not like Norton, chiefly on account of the latter's uninterrupted series of successes in the tomato class at the parish fruit, flower and vegetable shows, expressed the view that ex-servicemen could hardly be said to "benefit" by the installation of a new organ in St. Luke's, particularly in view of the fact that not one in a hundred of returned ex-servicemen ever took the trouble to attend divine service.

"So much the worse for them," countered Norton. "Perhaps they'll come now—to hear the organ."

This was unanswerable. Fudge muttered something about "fantastic notions" and subsided, folding his arms as an indication that he had no intention of raising either of them when the matter was put to the vote.

Miss Bonnington, who represented the Ladies' Working Party, said that she could conceive of no better use for the money. The organ needed renewing, for the present one failed to do Mr. Dobson, LRAM, full justice, and everybody knew that Mr. Dobson was young and brilliant (she almost said single), and would soon be leaving unless a better organ was installed.

The vicar was not so sure. He thought that perhaps half the money should go toward the organ and the remainder be spent on wallets, which could be presented to all ex-servicemen in the parish when they gathered together to bless the new organ.

Mr. Fudge, who seemed to be in a querulous mood, cried, "What about the Home Guard?"

The vicar asked what about them.

"They were in uniform," said Mr. Fudge, with vivid memories of falling into the golf-links pond during Sunday maneuvers in 1942, "and there won't be enough money to go round."

"There is one ex-serviceman present," ventured the vicar, with a nervous glance at Norton, whose eyebrows already showed ominous signs of lifting. "Perhaps he would like to express an opinion."

Nat fidgeted. He was not addicted to speaking in public. During his years of local reporting he had seen so many people make fools of themselves while engaging in this thankless pursuit, that he seldom opened his mouth at any gathering he attended. But he saw the eyes of the meeting turned upon him, and Miss Bonnington piped up, "Come now, Mr. Hearn. What do *you* think we ought to do with the money?"

Nat cleared his throat.

"I couldn't say. You'd better ask an assembly of ex-service people. But I don't think you ought to spend even a part of it on an organ."

He sat down again, and pretended to be absorbed in his notes.

Norton jumped up.

"Unless there are alternative suggestions, I move that the matter be put to the vote here and now."

"Have you any real objections, Mr. Hearn?" asked the vicar, and again the eyes of all present turned on Nat.

The journalist felt himself growing angry. It was disturbing to reflect how little it took to make him angry since the night Sam had died.

"Yes, I have, Mr. Ormsby."

"What are they?" growled Norton, but Fudge nodded approvingly.

"Well, to begin with, there are many ex-servicemen in the Nonconformist Churches. They'll have to change their faith to hear the organ. Apart from that, I don't believe that the admiral intended the money to be spent parochially. He wasn't a churchgoer himself."

"He directed the vicar to administer the money," said Norton, who could see the chances of his new organ disappearing under such arguments.

"He named the vicar as he might have named the chairman of the council. He was selected as a responsible person, not as a churchman."

"Come now, don't let's quarrel over this matter," interposed Mr. Ormsby. "We can settle it amicably, if we keep our tempers."

"Settle it by putting my resolution to the vote," demanded Norton.

"It hasn't yet a seconder," said the vicar, playing for time.

"I'll second it," said Miss Bonnington. "I'm sure the dear boys would love an organ."

"Proposed and seconded . . ." said the vicar, again looking at the journalist.

"I'll move an amendment," interrupted Nat. "Postpone decision until a real public meeting of ex-servicemen can be called. Put the matter to them, and see that the meeting is advertised."

"In the *Clarion,* of course," retorted Norton.

"Now, now," said the vicar. "Any seconder?"

Fudge cast his mind back to the August flower show and thought of Norton's three first prizes. He recalled that Norton's son-in-law had been one of the judges.

"I'll second the amendment," he said, and looked hard at Holman Hunt's "Light of the World," which hung immediately behind the vicar's bald head.

The amendment was put to the vote and defeated. Norton's resolution was carried by twelve votes to three. The third opposition vote was an error. Mr. Hopper, Beryl's father, had contributed nothing to the discussion, but happened to be scratching the back of his neck when the vicar asked "Any against?" Notwithstanding this, Norton never forgave him.

Nat went back to the office and called for his two proofs, one referring to Baines' scheme and the other dealing with the opera. He read them through for literals, made one or two minor adjustments and then wrote a full report of the church council meeting. At the foot of the last page he bracketed the note: "See editorial."

By 6:30 P.M. Bumble was hurrying downstairs with two closely typed sheets for Burton to set. It was an editorial comment, and carried the heading: "Church Militant— You Fight, We Expand!"

THIRTEEN

About 7:45 A.M. on Friday morning, Doris Copp, Miss Gelding's elderly maid, took in her mistress's morning tea, drew the curtains and laid the Paxtonbury *Herald* and Sandcombe *Clarion* on the little table beside her bed.

She then withdrew, but had only descended a dozen stairs when she was startled almost out of her wits by a piercing scream, coming from the bedroom. Hurrying back, she found Miss Gelding on the verge of hysteria. She was stabbing her finger at the front page of the *Clarion,* hitting it in the spot where her time-honored advertisement usually appeared. In place of the advertisement there was the half-column notice devoted to *The Prodigal Princess.*

Doris Copp did not link the scream with the newspaper until long after her mistress had dressed, refused everything but tea and aspirin, and marched out of the house and down to the *Clarion* office. But Doris guessed it had something to do with Miss Gelding's principal preoccupation over the last few weeks, for she pottered about the cold scullery mumbling "All this playactin'. It fair gives me the sick!" Almost all Miss Gelding's activities gave Doris "the sick," but none more consistently than her mistress's theatrical interests.

At the top end of the town, near the hump backed bridge over the Beck, Baines was closeted in his box of an office, a glass-partitioned affair which commanded a sweeping view of all sectors of the bus depot.

On a busy morning he looked rather like a plump general directing a battle. He issued orders and rebukes through a homemade loudspeaker, and a small but active staff of greasy other ranks darted in and out of the glass box bringing news from the firing line.

Baines was wondering what he ought to charge Mr.

Martin, an elderly customer, for a thirdhand Buick. The Buick had been in his oil store since the outbreak of war, axles jacked up and chassis stripped. Foster, a garagehand, had been over to the military car depot a fortnight before. He knew a man there, and came back after dark with an interesting assortment of spare parts. Together they soon got the Buick running again. Secondhand cars were fetching good prices these days, and deliveries were growing worse every month. Baines thought four hundred and fifty pounds a fair price. He made a marginal note to this effect on his charge sheet and reflected, with quiet satisfaction, that he had turned down the scrap-iron merchant's twenty pound offer for the car a week after war broke out. That Buick had once been a good car. He could not bear to part with it for a mere twenty pounds.

Out of the corner of his eye he saw Foster discussing something with Garnett, one of the bus conductors. Foster was holding a newspaper in his hand and grinning as he displayed it to the other employee. They were out of range of the loudspeaker, and so Baines flung open one of his little windows and bawled, "Funny enough ter keep a busload o' people waitin', Garnett?"

Garnett started, looked at his watch and hurried across to the petrol pumps, where his bus was waiting. Foster was unabashed. He looked Baines in the eye. The two men understood one another. Baines never bullied Foster, but sometimes wished he could get rid of him without a fuss. Push him over the cliffs, for instance. It was a pity the fellow was so expert locating trouble under the bonnets of his employer's vehicles.

Foster sauntered over. "Something to interest you, boss," he said, and passed a grubby *Clarion* through the window.

Baines glanced down the column and read, frowning and sucking his teeth as he neared the final paragraph.

He looked up and caught sight of Foster, looking in at him. The fellow had a grin on his sallow face, as though he knew precisely what the councillor was thinking.

"Come in an' keep a dekko on this cash," said Baines shortly. "I'm gonner look into this. Someone's 'avin' me on."

He put on his brown tweed jacket, tried and failed to fasten the lowest button, clamped the black bowler on his huge skull and set off toward the High Street.

Norton read the brief editorial headed "Church Militant —You Fight, We Expand!" in his greenhouse, where he usually spent his mornings. He sat down for a cup of cocoa about 10:30, and his wife brought out the *Clarion* with the drink.

Norton did not usually read editorials, but he arrived at this one via Nat's tailpiece at the foot of the report of the church council meeting on page six.

Norton turned grimly to the place indicated, and ran his eye down the column. He did not understand it all. There were one or two phrases the full meaning of which was not clear to him. But he was sufficiently perturbed to take off his brown overalls and put on raincoat and cap. His wife met him in the hall. "Where you off, Sam?" she asked, puzzled by the break in her husband's routine.

"Out," he said.

Throughout twenty-eight years of married life, Mrs. Norton had received this simple answer to the same question. Norton was not disposed to give much away, even to his wife.

He went up St. Luke's Hill to the vicarage, which adjoined the sham Gothic church. Mrs. Ormsby let him into her husband's study without preliminaries. He was one of the few entitled to call upon the vicar at any time he felt inclined.

The Rev. Galahad was writing a sermon, coat off, sleeves rolled up. It took the form of a rather involved parable conned from the passage about David's lament over Saul and Jonathan. It began: "Why were these men, whom today we should call bellicose desert chieftains, 'lovely and beautiful in their lives'?" It went on to explain how the standard of values among ordinary folk inhabiting Palestine at that particular period put a moral premium on prowess in the field. The arts of peace were not prized. Now in the Zionist Palestine of today we had a rather curious parallel. . . .

Mr. Ormsby had a journalist's nose for the topical twist. He was a little vexed at being disturbed by Norton, who did not even knock on the study door. He knew that a visit from Norton at this hour meant trouble. And the vicar was a genuine man of peace, even at the price of a new organ, the installation of which, he felt, would only add more laurels to the already overloaded brow of his senior church-warden.

"What is it, Norton? Church heating again?"

Norton said nothing, but handed the vicar his copy of the *Clarion*. He knew that Mr. Ormsby did not read the local papers.

Ormsby read the leading article with some misgivings. He had not felt altogether happy about the result of yesterday's meeting, but had hoped that it would blow over, as almost everything did blow over in Sandcombe if you left it alone and patted all shoulders within easy reach.

"A bit stiff, a little unkind," was his comment.

"What are you going to do about it, vicar?" asked Norton, his tone implying that if the vicar was going to take it lying down he, Norton, had manlier intentions.

"Well ... er ... that needs thought," temporized the vicar, morally certain that his sermon, which had promised to be a good one, would now be stillborn.

"No, sir," said Norton, his mouth squaring like that of a Cromwellian trooper about to cut down a galloping Cavalier. "We can retaliate at once. Cancel our Church Services column."

The vicar scratched his nose. Churches were hard enough to fill these days without deleting the standard advertisements from the local paper. Yet perhaps Norton was right; some form of reply was necessary.

He was about to suggest a telephoned protest and a threat to delete the Church Services, but Norton, having said all he had come to say, was preparing to go.

"I'll go back and write the letter now," he said. "*I* can see what's happening, if no one else can. That young man's feeling his feet."

He went out, and the vicar heard him shut the front door. Mr. Ormsby sat down again and looked, unhappily, at the neatly written manuscript spread on his oval table. Then his eye fell on a sixpenny Stephen Leacock, resting on top of Peake's *Commentary of the Bible*. He picked it up and turned the pages. When in doubt the Rev. Galahad Ormsby always reverted to Stephen Leacock.

He was still chuckling when the tinny gong sounded for lunch.

While Miss Gelding and Councillor Baines, in person, together with Norton's hand-delivered letter, were converging upon the *Clarion* office, other people in various parts of Sandcombe were cocking eyebrows at the latest edition.

Neither the opera report nor the editorial occasioned as much comment as the fact that here, for the first time in local history, was front-page news. The brief letter, sandwiched in between the pavement-fouling protest and the Girls' Life Brigade appeal, almost escaped notice altogether.

The opera report caused a certain stir among members of the cast, but no one else read it. The editorial went largely unnoticed, because Sandcombe *Clarion* subscribers were so used to Sam's heavy touch that the majority of readers mistook the headline for some sort of church rallying cry.

In fact that first week the circulation neither rose nor declined. Only those townspeople who had known Sam intimately, or were on particularly friendly terms with Nat, examined the paper minutely.

Up in his redbrick eyrie on the cliffs, Otto, slumped in his favorite leather chair, and wrapped in the dressing gown which he wore most of the day, savored the editorial and gave the opera notice an approving nod.

Foreman Skinner, who seldom read what he printed each week, was bullied into reading the opera notice by his wife, who, having read it twice, asked him to explain "who that lanky scarecrow of a reporter was a-gettin' at?" Skinner read the column and shook his head, sorrowfully. "She's a regular advertiser," he said, nodding vaguely Geldingward. "It won't do no good to get 'er over'eated."

In his bungalow on the Paxtonbury Road, old Mr. Wainer, the former surveyor, moistened his lips over the Baines letter, but felt a tremor of apprehension when he recalled that his blueprints had already been sent to the blockmaker for next week's issue. Perhaps he had been indiscreet? It wouldn't do to upset the council too much. After all, there was his pension, upon which he was entirely dependent. Still, somebody ought to have mentioned the Flats Development Scheme. . . .

Bumble, who took a paper home on Tuesday evening and read it over his supper, enjoyed Nat's comment on the opera, chiefly because Miss Gelding had once threatened him with the birch when he was hauled up at a juvenile court for throwing a firework into her shop doorway. He also disliked Norton, who, in his capacity as churchwarden, had organized a system of fines for late attendances on the part of St. Luke's choirboys. Bumble had been a choirboy for some years before the Methodists bought him off to blow their organ in the North Road Chapel. It was a lonelier job than choir-singing at St. Luke's, but more lucrative, for it brought in extras for weddings and funerals—a far better proposition than Mr. Norton's tightfisted flat rate.

So Bumble, his mouth full of bread and cheese and pickles, muttered "Good ol' Nat!" and made a mental note to be at work early on Friday morning and see the fun.

The fun was clearly due to commence. At 10 A.M. on Friday Nat went down to the back door of the Galleon and fortified himself with two pints of illegally served bitter. He came into the office in the wake of Miss Gelding, who had swept past Marlene, completely ignoring her "Mr. Nat's out, m'm."

Nat climbed the stairs and followed her into the office, shutting the door behind him. She heard the bang and veered round, all gun ports open.

"You!"

Nat decided to treat her indulgently. He felt glad that Gerald had not yet returned. It might have proved distracting to handle Gerald and Miss Gelding at the same time, with Baines and Norton due at any moment.

"Please sit down, Miss Gelding."

He noticed that her face was very red—partly rage, no doubt, and injured vanity, but high blood pressure had something to do with it as well. She ought to take warning from Sam's death, or perhaps she would go off one night in the middle of an aria. What a headline. "Prominent JP Falls Dead in Footlights"; "Swan Song of Amateur Soprano."

Miss Gelding at once launched into an avalanche of recrimination. She was already on the verge of hysterical tears. Nat felt that she ought to be nursed a little, and so he heard her out.

"How could you be so cheap, so cruel? The houses! Look at our houses! Packed every night, a dozen curtain calls . . . flowers. . . . It wasn't as if *we* got anything out of it . . . we aren't professionals. . . . The work and the worry of it all. . . . If you only knew, if you only stood behind those scenes a single night . . ."

It took her about three or four minutes to blow herself out. Then, when she realized that he was making no reply, she checked herself abruptly.

"Well, Mr. Hearn? What have you to say? How can you possibly justify yourself?"

Nat cleared his throat and laid aside the late editor's ebony paper knife he had been fingering.

"I'm sorry, Miss Gelding. I didn't mean to be cheap. Or cruel either. But you asked for it, you really did, you know. Somebody had to hand it out to you sooner or later."

She blazed up again. "How dare you? How dare you say that? The *Clarion* has always been so kind, so encouraging. . . ."

"Yes, Miss Gelding. That's what I mean."

"When Mr. Vane was alive . . ."

He looked straight at her, and there was a note of irritation in his voice.

"Mr. Vane's dead, Miss Gelding. I'm a partner here, and I'm also the editor. As long as I'm not libelous, I can say what I please. You sent me a complimentary ticket as a critic, I take it?"

"If I'd dreamed you would have used it for this . . ."

"Now listen, Miss Gelding. I don't suppose that this will do any good, but I've got to say it, and you've got to listen, either now or at some other time in the paper. Will you please let me say something?"

The hint of future criticism in print checked her temper for a moment.

"I came here for an explanation," she said, "and I won't leave without one."

"Good. Then I'll tell you why I wrote that notice. It wasn't only because the show was genuinely bad—one of the worst you've ever put on. It was because you and one or two others won't allow the standard to become any better. You've never had an operatic society in Sandcombe, only a mutual admiration society, bent on enjoying itself at all costs. For years you've told yourselves that you stood for local culture and for art. But for years you've done nothing of the sort. People about here have seen so many shows like yours that they've got round to believing it's the real thing. They've never had anything outside the cinema to compare with it, and as long as you cling to office they never will. You've never given any of the younger members a chance, either in leads or in production."

"You know nothing about it," she cried; "there's not one of them with any experience . . ."

"What chance do they ever have of getting any?"

"They could start a group of their own if they wanted."

"Nonsense. You'd have priority all the way. You book the hall. Where would they rehearse in winter? Where is their orchestra coming from? Or their scenery even? It was to expose things like this, Miss Gelding, that I bought an interest in the *Clarion*. Having done so, I'm going to have my say, you can be sure of that."

"I shall take legal advice straight away."

"Don't waste your money. Every word of that notice is fair comment. I didn't plan this attack. . . ."

She swooped on the word. "*Planned!* Then you admit it! The whole thing is a disgusting intrigue to get me out of the way."

Nat thought for a moment, and she had the satisfaction

of imagining that she had scored a point. But he was thinking only of how much he should tell her. Finally he said, "Yes, Miss Gelding, it is a sort of intrigue, I suppose. Your notice was part of a bigger plan. I'm going to try bringing out a paper that really says something. I'm going to write what I honestly believe to be true, and see what happens. It's never been tried here. It's going to be fun."

"Fun!" She jumped up and brandished her umbrella. "I'll show you how much fun it will be! Wait until it touches your pocket. You'll laugh on the wrong side of your face then, young man. Our firm has advertised for years—ever since the *Clarion* was founded. We'll never advertise with you again while I'm a director."

Nat knew that this was coming. He knew, also, that it was her final shot. What did she imagine he would do? Stagger back like one of her operatic characters, shielding his eyes and shouting "No, no!" or fall on his knees and plead for forgiveness. He felt a sudden contempt for the woman. She was so typical of all that had bored and irritated him for years. He stood up, crossed the office and opened the door.

"That's a fair exchange, Miss Gelding, and I'll jump at it. Freedom from having to write yards of cant at the price of a four-inch double-column ad once a week. If that's all you have to say, you'd better go. I'm finding it very difficult not to be rude."

For a moment he thought that she was going to cry. But pride checked the tears; she got up and hurried across the room. At the door she paused a second, as though she was going to say something more, but she evidently thought better of it, and stormed past him and out onto the landing.

It was a good exit—far better than any he had ever seen her make on the stage of St. Luke's hall. But at the head of the stairs, unfortunately, she almost cannoned into Councillor Baines, who was coming up from the shop, closely followed by Gerald, still wearing his "going-to-London" pinstripe.

Baines swerved, grinned and cried jocosely, " 'Old 'ard, Miss Gelding, 'old 'ard!" She did not even look at him, or at Gerald either. Recovering herself, she sailed down the stairs and through the shop, slamming the glass-fronted door with such violence that Sam's crêpe-decked photograph, which Marlene had been ordered to put in the window, fell flat on its face among a pile of leather-bound ledgers marked "Slightly soiled; at sacrifice!"

Marlene, who witnessed the exit, afterward described the fall of the late editor's portrait as "rather spooky, don't you think?"

Baines walked into the office alone, Gerald having hurried downstairs again in vain pursuit of Miss Gelding.

The garage proprietor gave Nat a knowing and sympathetic wink.

"I'm alwus 'avin' trouble with the ol' girl," he confided. "She keeps writing to Roads Committee about the slopin' pavement outside 'er shop. Wants us to strip the ol' bloody street for 'er!"

Gerald hurried back. He was a little pale. For a few seconds he forgot that Baines was there.

"Good God, Nat!" he began breathlessly. "I knew there'd be a scene like that. What the devil's got into you? Did you think that old war-horse would take a slating lying down?"

Nat realized that Gerald must have seen a *Clarion,* and wondered how and when? He could hardly have been back in Sandcombe an hour. He was not to know that Gerald, waiting for the early train at Paxtonbury junction, had run into the bunch of Sandcombians who traveled up on the workmen's train to Paxtonbury each morning. Gerald had begged a copy from Mr. Bowdler, promising to replace it with a new one when he passed the shop on his way home that evening. Gerald had fifteen miles in a stopping train to digest the *Clarion's* pages, and had missed little or nothing.

He had read the letter first, having glanced with pride at the front-page display, without absorbing the headlines.

He always read the inside of papers first because he was a confirmed picker-up of bargains advertised in the small ads column. Habit compelled him to run an eye down the list of perambulators, beach huts and wringers for sale. At the foot of this column he found the letter and frowned over it.

But the letter itself did not cause him much concern, for he assumed that it had crept in unnoticed. Letters to the *Clarion* had a habit of doing that. Sam had once inadvertently published a violent attack upon himself in this manner and then, when the fact was pointed out to him, wisely taken the credit for such a show of fair-mindedness. He made up for it later by sacking the proofreader.

Gerald decided to speak to Nat about it. It would not do to upset a customer like Baines.

He then turned back to the front page and read the operatic notice. It made him feel quite sick. Surely there were grounds for a libel action here? Gerald knew little of the law of libel. He had always left that worry to Sam and Nat, trusting the latter to tone down his father's copy when it outran discretion. But here was Nat himself writing as Sam had never written, not even when he had attacked the Licensed Victuallers' Association's application for a new public house in the High Street. Sam had always encouraged local culture. This notice seemed to Gerald next door to scurrility.

It was then that Gerald remembered something which made his stomach contract a little. He recalled Nat's odd remark on the day they had invited him to be a partner. What had he said? "But a paper, even a local paper, has to have a policy. . . ." What had the fellow meant by that? *A policy?* What was this policy when applied to the Sandcombe *Clarion?* A stupid, cranky crusade or something? Well, if he intended filling the paper with this sort of nonsense he would soon find himself up against strong opposition from within. There were two Vanes to one Hearn in the firm, and Nat could promptly be outvoted on the question of "policy," if it arose.

The thought comforted him a little, but not for long. By the time the train had run into Four Firs Halt, Gerald had rummaged his memory for the general outline of the partnership agreement. If he remembered correctly, Nat had been given sole charge of the newspaper. Ah, but there was the little clause which Gerald had insisted upon, something about ". . . following a policy calculated to improve the general success of the business." Gerald felt momentarily relieved again. But almost at once he began to wonder how that phrase would be construed by an arbitrator. Was it possible that the Nat Hearn who wrote this operatic notice, yes, and the Nat who must have looked the other way when a local busybody sent in the protest against Baines—was it possible that he might regard this sort of copy as being in the best interests of the firm?

Gerald, who fortunately had the carriage to himself, nibbled unhappily at his thumbnail and wished that the train would not stop for so long at so many halts. In an effort to calm himself he turned back to the paper again, and this time he read the leader article. By the time he had finished it he was lightly perspiring, though the morning was fresh and his feet had been stone cold all the way down from London. He came to the conclusion that Nat must have gone stark, staring mad. The opera, Baines and the church, all in one week! What might he not do next week and the week after?

Gerald folded the paper and thrust it into his overcoat pocket. He lit a cigarette and let it go out. He put his feet up on the seat opposite and tried to think back over the past, searching for some clue or hint that would help him to discover the reason why his wretched partner should stir up so much trouble for so little reason. He found none, and reflected, rather miserably, that he had never really known Nat at all. They had been adolescents together in the firm all those years ago. They had both resented Sam's bullying. They had been grown men together up to the time when Nat joined the RAF. They had seen one another a dozen times a day for years, but they had never been friends. Sam had somehow managed to keep them apart. Only since his death had they come near to knowing one another, and during those few days it seemed to Gerald that he had taken the initiative, he had been the dominant factor of the new partnership.

Underneath his alarm and irritation Gerald felt genuinely unhappy. Almost unconsciously he had been building on the hope of having a friend at last, a friend tied to

Gerald's first and only love, the business, a friend who would come into his office and drink morning coffee with him and look at his efficiency charts. They could have done so much together, tried out so many new lines and experiments—sound, sensible experiments. They could have been complements of each other, he, Gerald, initiating the ideas, Nat following them up with his typewriter and local contacts.

And now this, done behind his back, a stupid, outrageously dangerous policy (damn that word) carried into effect within minutes of his setting off on his first trip to London on the firm's behalf! All that shaking of hands, all those expressions of mutual goodwill, with even his mother, who had never trusted anyone after finding out Sam, lulled into a sense of limited serenity about the future. And then *this*.

The mood of self-pity soon passed.

By the time the train had crept into Sandcombe station Gerald was himself again. He had resolved to settle the matter immediately. There was to be no temporizing, no argument, no compromise. It must stop now, before Skinner and the men were put onto preparing a second series of spiteful attacks on customers. Nat must have no second chance of making inroads into the goodwill of the Clarion Press. Then and there Gerald made a vow never again to leave this partner alone on publishing day.

In this frame of mind he passed through the barrier gates and out into Station Square. He felt better already. The damage done by this week's *Clarion* was not irreparable. It could be mended by tact and a show of humanity. Gerald fancied himself saying "High spirits, Miss Gelding ... my partner's a good fellow at heart, but a little irresponsible ... needs a steadying influence ... happened to be away on business ... new machinery, you know. ... Why, *of course*, Miss Gelding, we shall reserve a column for your reply next week. Nothing like a good healthy controversy, providing that both sides get fair play. ..."

And to the vicar and his bully, Norton, "My partner wrote solely as an ex-serviceman. Very unfair of him. I've rapped his knuckles about it, I can tell you. He's like most of these young fellows home from the war, Mr. Norton. They've acquired barrack-room manners, I'm afraid. We'll soon have him toeing the line again, old chap."

And to Baines? Well, fortunately the Baines letter wasn't signed. Perhaps it could be written off as a proofreading error. It would not be the first in the history of the *Clarion*. As he said this to himself Gerald gave a little start, for he observed Baines in person, stalking *Clarion*-wards, and with a *Clarion* held firmly in his pudgy hand.

They met as they turned into High Street, and Baines greeted Gerald sourly.

"What's goin' on down there?" he asked, jerking his huge head toward the top of the hill, where the *Clarion* premises jutted from the junction of St. Luke's Road. Then, as he saw Gerald's case, and realized that the man had only that moment arrived back in the town, "You won't 'ave seen this stab in the back, I s'pose?"

Gerald smiled, rather primly.

"As a matter of fact I have, Mr. Baines. I read it in the train. It's all a mistake, I'm sure. Nat will explain the matter to our joint satisfaction. You know we're one hundred percent in favor of your building scheme."

"You didn't oughter let these smart alicks get past yer like that," grumbled Baines, but his tone showed that he was slightly mollified, and Gerald glowed. Already his plan of healing showed signs of succeeding.

They turned into the shop and climbed the stairs, Baines panting slightly after their fast hill climb.

It was at that moment that Miss Gelding crashed out of the editorial and met them on the landing. At the sight of the JP's expression all Gerald's new-found confidence evaporated instantly.

After his initial wail when he came back up the stairs again, Gerald sat down on the window seat. He would have preferred his father's chair, but it was already occupied by Nat, who did not appear to be the least put out by Miss Gelding's dramatic exit. He waved Gerald's recriminations aside.

"Mr. Baines doesn't want to hear about her; he'd better tell us what he is after himself."

Gerald's worst fears were confirmed by Nat's casual tone. It sounded as though the journalist was pretending to be bored, and using boredom to cloak a pleasant excitement. Baines did not seem to notice this. Miss Gelding had done something toward restoring his customary geniality.

The councillor yawned, and Nat, who had a frontal view, caught a fleeting glimpse of gold-filled teeth and coated tongue.

"I'm not complainin'," said Baines. "You can't be expected to see everything that goes into the rag. I don't see 'arf wot goes on in me own garrige nowadays. But I reckon you ought to know about it. Someone's bin gettin' at yer."

"Getting at us?" This from Nat, and Gerald felt certain that the idiot was secretly amused. He compressed his lips and said nothing.

Baines threw down his paper, folded in such a way as to display the letter commencing "Sir, May I trespass on the hospitality of your column . . ."

"That letter. It's aimed at me. Know who wrote it?"

Nat nodded.

"You do?" Baines rubbed his red hands. "Well, that's okay. Who was it? I'll fix 'im soon enough."

"I . . . er . . . I don't know that I should say, Mr. Baines. It's not always wise to disclose . . ."

Here Gerald broke in, harshly. In the midst of his agitation he realized that he had not breakfasted, and it was now past eleven o'clock. The long train journey, the worry, the scene with Miss Gelding—all had contributed toward his irritability.

"Don't fool around, Nat. We've had enough of this. Who was it?"

Nat stood up.

"It was me!" he said.

He had played for effect, and was not disappointed. Gerald, who had risen, almost reeled. Baines' broad features flushed sunset red. Gerald's hand flew to his lapel and began jerking like an express piston. Nat, very conscious of the stir, nonchalantly extracted his cigarette case, but he noticed that his fingers trembled a little as they groped under the elastic band.

Baines was the first to recover voice. He spoke deliberately, his eyes fixed on the journalist.

"You mean you writ the blarsted letter yerself?"

Baines' grammar, never very sound, always broke bounds
when he was angry. He had never been angrier, not even
when he ran into one of the mechanics coming out of his
wife's bedroom after a night shift many years ago.

Nat nodded. "That's it. I wrote the letter myself!"

"This is fantastic," said Gerald, after having sought a
more expressive word.

"Is it? I don't think it is. Baines' building scheme is fantastic, if you like. The council's endorsement of it is more
fantastic still. But I can't see why there should be all this
fuss when someone makes a mild protest. What's fantastic
about that?"

Before Gerald could speak again Baines began to roar.

"A stab in the back!" he shouted. "That's what it is, a
stab in the back—from a quarter I least expected." He
whirled round on Gerald. "We've always bin pals, 'aven't
we, ever since I stood fer council? I looked after *you* all
right. Brought ev'ry penny o' me work into this office.
More'n that, too. Look at the times I've stood up in council an' give the paper a boost. The Old Man wouldn't 've
done it to me. Not 'im! 'Ee noo which side 'is bread was
buttered. An' don't you sit there lettin' on *you* don't know
nothin' about it. You planned it between you, I know yer
did. Then you slink orf ter London an' let 'im write it,
so's ter cover up your printing side!"

This totally unexpected line of attack annoyed Nat, and
he interrupted Gerald's indignant protest.

"That isn't true, Baines. Mr. Vane knew nothing about
this. I've been digging into it for weeks. I could have said
a great deal more, and I daresay that in time I will."

"You dare, just you dare, young feller-me-lad! Make an
enemy o' me an' I'll bust yer, you see if I don't!"

Nat sat down again and folded his hands. He realized
that no good could come of prolonging this scene. It was
a great pity that Gerald and Baines had come in together.
He said, "It's no good standing there threatening, Baines.
They can hear you down in the shop, and I daresay out in

the High Street. You're only making a bloody fool of yourself. Go home and think it over."

Gerald found his tongue.

"I won't have you talking to Mr. Baines like that on my premises! Haven't you done harm enough for one morning?" He turned, piteously, to Baines. "Can't you *see,* I had nothing to do with it?"

Baines could, but was past caring. He only knew that in the lean, determined-looking man sitting before him, with his long legs thrust through the aperture that had for so long screened Sam's fat, short and familiar legs, he had encountered a check that might prove extremely irritating, perhaps even dangerous, in the months ahead.

With the trained eye of a local politician, Baines conjured up a swift sequence of possible events—a newspaper campaign, gossip in the Working Men's Club and in the pubs, spasmodic interruptions from the public gallery during his council speeches, anonymous letters thrust under his garage door, a bloc of objectors forming when the Ministry of Health sent down its inspector to hear the case for the council's application to borrow money, a whole string of annoying and, so far as he could see, totally unnecessary setbacks that would make a tedious countercampaign certain, with all its attendant worries, hard work and risks. If the opposition had come from a council member, Baines would have known just how to deal with it. He would have pointed a threatening finger at the objector and growled, "There's a man you've elected, and he's against 'ouses for ex-servicemen!" But this Hearn fellow was himself an ex-serviceman, and such a charge would seem ridiculous. Besides, he had a newspaper, and the only control Baines could exercise over what went in and what stayed out of that newspaper was by way of the distribution of his not inconsiderable printing orders, but for the moment this was the only card Baines held, and he decided to slam it down. He looked hard at Gerald, the weak link in the partnership.

"You come out against me in this," he said, "and you'll lose every penny o' my work! Every penny, see?"

Gerald began another protest. All this seemed to him horribly unfair. "Mr. Baines . . ." he began.

But the councillor went on, "Not on'y that. I got influence. You oughta know that by now. I'm on the Gen'ral Purposes Committee, ain't I? Chairman of it. Well, then, you go against progressive policy, an' then see wot 'appens when you try an' tender for council printing."

Nat pulled open a drawer of the desk and took from it a new, stiff-covered notebook. He flicked it open.

"I told you I'd had my eye on this matter, Mr. Baines. I've been collecting data for weeks. It's all in here—all the speeches and figures right back to 1920. Everything about housing in the urban area, both your scheme and the original one. I've been piecing it together. It's not finished yet. I'm being as thorough as I can. I even know what your bus service takes in and out of the season. I've worked out what it might take if you run services up to the new houses, when they're built. I can well understand you pushing that scheme. I don't suppose you even realize that what you're doing is wrong. I'm sorry, Baines. I thought you were going to be a good councillor. If you drop this, I'll always back you on any really progressive scheme, but you ought to know this—from now on, no matter what Mr. Vane says to the contrary, the policy of this paper isn't going to be controlled by the price of billheads and timesheets. It's a separate concern, and I think it's important that you should realize it. In order to make it quite clear I'll write a leader about it next week, and I'll name you and Miss Gelding as the people who tried to buy me off."

Nat held up his notebook for a moment and then put it back into the drawer, turning the key and slipping it into the breast pocket of his sports jacket.

Baines moved toward the door. His color had subsided a little, and he looked as though he had mastered his rage, accepting battle on even terms.

Gerald moved hurriedly across to escort him down to the shop, but Baines spun round and stopped him with an impatient gesture.

"You'd better get 'im to leave me alone," he said quietly.

"You'n 'im are partners, aren't you? You share aht end o' the year? Well, then, if you know what's good for you, use yer pull and see it works. I'm not stayin' 'ere to be threatened, young feller-me-lad. You'll 'ear from me in doo course!"

And with that Baines went out, leaving the partners alone.

For a few moments neither of them spoke. Gerald had gone back to the window. He seemed to be brooding. Nat picked up the paper knife again and balanced it, waiting for Gerald to open the debate.

After a while Gerald said, "Are you determined to follow this sort of policy?"

"Yes."

"It's not just a sort of lark, for this week?"

"No, Gerald."

"That's why you wanted control of the paper, I suppose?"

"You asked me to come in; you were very pressing, you know."

"You damned fool! Do you think I dreamed that you wanted to land us in this mess?"

"What mess? Miss Gelding a little ruffled and Baines a bit apprehensive about his phony building scheme?"

"We depend on these people, you idiot. We aren't the *Daily Express*. We can't afford to crusade. We've hardly any capital."

"We'll get capital. Once they are used to it, the people here will like the paper. The circulation will go up. We shall get a name for saying what we think. That can only help to advertise the firm."

Gerald snorted, genuinely contemptuous of the man's naïve ignorance of small-town psychology.

"Sensationalism never advertised anyone. Down here people like things to go on being the same, forever and ever. You've made three sets of enemies in a single week. Suppose you do that every Friday? Twelve a month, thirty-six a quarter. Hell! by the end of the year we shan't have a friend in the town; and no friends, no customers. What does the paper bring us in, anyway? About eight hundred pounds a year net, if so much. The printing connection is worth three times that amount, and if you have your way we shall soon be glad to get a visiting-card order. Can't you see that a town of this size can't stand internal criticism? D'you think my father didn't know that?"

"Your father left the firm practically bankrupt, Gerald."

"He'd never get any new machinery. If he had done, we'd have cleaned up a packet during the war. But at least we got most of the local trade in the printing line, and if we reorganized now there's nothing we couldn't do, if we put our minds to it. Where is your policy going to lead us? Tell me that?"

"I've told you, Gerald. I think that our policy will bring in new customers. But that isn't important at the moment. What is important is that I can't sit here any longer and write fulsome nonsense. I can't, and I'm not going to try. I had a skinful when your father was the boss."

"All right, then; let me buy you out. I could do it in two years, and I'd get a stooge in to run the paper meantime."

Nat braced himself for a final effort. He realized, more clearly than ever, now that they appeared to be in direct opposition to one another, that he did not, and had at no time, disliked Gerald. But neither did he fear him as he had feared Sam. With or without Gerald he was committed to a sensationally progressive policy. Such a policy, however, might become very difficult to pursue if Gerald came out against him.

"Before we begin shouting at one another," he said, "what is your honest opinion, your personal opinion, of Baines and Gelding?"

Gerald thought for a minute. "How will that help us?" he said guardedly.

"I must know."

"Very well, I'll tell you. In my opinion Miss Gelding's a vain old fool, and Baines is only interested in lining his pocket. But what the hell does that matter? They're both old and paying customers, and that comes first with me."

"What about their influence on the community?"

"I'm not interested in their influence on the community. I wouldn't tell everyone that, but you asked for my opinion."

"That's your last word?"

"Absolutely my last word!"

Nat drew in his legs and stood up. He walked across to the window, still holding Sam's paper knife.

Gerald looked across at the empty chair, but he no longer wanted to occupy it. It was as if the initiative had passed to Nat once more, and he had an uncomfortable feeling that the journalist had somehow contrived to grow several inches since they had parted earlier in the week. He wondered, unhappily, why publication of a single issue of the *Clarion,* compiled without restraint after years of Sam's uncertain supervision, could produce so powerful a change in the man. But there it was, clear and unmistakable, a cockiness and aggressive confidence which had managed to bowl a man like Baines from the room before his eyes.

Nat continued to stare down on the High Street. When he spoke again it seemed to Gerald that his partner's voice came from a great way off—from the top of the cliffs or from the thin spire of St. Luke's Church on the hill.

"Will you listen to me uninterruptedly for a few minutes before we finally fall out on this issue?" asked Nat.

"You'd better say what you've got to say," said Gerald sulkily.

"Right. Now listen, Gerald; I'll try not to shoot a line, and I'll only say what I really feel about this business. It's not just that Baines and Miss Gelding have offered themselves as Aunt Sallies this week. They merely happen to be topical illustrations of my point. I admit that it was because of them that I accepted your offer of a partnership, but the whole thing is much bigger than that."

"They were a damned long time getting under your skin," grumbled Gerald.

"They always got under my skin," said Nat. "I spent the whole of my youth in this office. At least ninety-five percent of the words I turned out here were so much junk—mostly harmless junk, I admit, but none the less junk. Then I went away, and while I was away I was foolish enough to imagine that things would be different when we started again. We always think that; God knows why, but we do. Well, they weren't different at all. If anything, they were worse, for on top of all the old hypocrisy and jobbery that always went on in places like this, there was a sort of postwar graft manipulated by comparatively new people like Baines. I might, of course, have started looking somewhere else for a living, but you gave me a chance of doing something useful in a place where I knew my way around. I accepted your offer solely for that purpose, but now, the first week I get to work, I find that the strongest opposition comes from my own partner."

Nat paused for a moment. Gerald growled, "All right; what do you propose we do about it?"

"We seem to have arrived at a deadlock," said Nat, "and I can only say this. I don't care whether you support me or not. I'm going on until my money is used up, and if I lose yours in the process—which I think is extremely unlikely—it's just too bad."

The first part of Nat's speech had sounded so reasonable, that Gerald had to resist an impulse to nod sympathetically. It was mention of his money that brought him back to earth. Gerald worshiped money, but in a different way from his father. To Sam, the actual acquiring of money had been the driving force, but to Gerald money was a means to an end—the end being his idea of "position" in Sandcombe. Without money he could never expect people to look up to him, he could never expect his customers to employ the word "Mister" when addressing him. Nearly all of them still continued, after all these years, to call him "Gerald" or "Vane."

When Nat had finished, Gerald discovered that most of his frightened temper and pent-up irritation had ebbed away. In its place was an ice-cold resolve to combat this man, whose behavior, during his brief absence, had threatened to bankrupt the firm, and who was now calmly announcing his plans for renewed excesses.

Nat had expected Gerald to stage a similar exit to those of Baines and Miss Gelding. He was disappointed. Gerald rose and said, with unexpected dignity, "Is that *your* last word, Nat?" and when Nat nodded, "All right, then, it's war. You can't expect me to stand by and see this place wantonly smashed, after all the years of hard work I've put into it. I wouldn't have let my father do that if I could have stopped it. You can do what you please for as long as you can, but I'll fight you every inch of the way. I'll fight you to the last bloody ditch!"

Then he went out and down the stairs, leaving Nat to reflect that this was the first occasion he had ever heard Gerald employ such a word.

FOURTEEN

The week that followed Gerald's declaration and the publication of the first new *Clarion* was a confused period for the *Clarion* staff and their new editor.

Soon after Gerald's departure Norton's letter was brought up from the shop by Marlene. Nat opened and read it on the spot. It was simple and very much to the point, like most of Norton's pronouncements. It ran:

> Sir,
>
> Please note that from Saturday next onward we shall not require the space allotted us for the publication of Church Services each week. This applies to all announcements in respect of St. Luke's Parish.

It was signed "Faithfully, Chas. S. Norton," and in brackets "For and on behalf of the Parochial Church Council at St. Luke's, Sandcombe."

Nat gave the necessary instructions downstairs, and watched a gloomy Skinner lift the notices from the static inside page. The foreman muttered that before the week was out there would be other gaps in the form. He was right. Baines' regular advert beginning "Visit the car hospital..." was canceled by phone, and Miss Gelding's four-inch double column was thrown into the box that same morning. The battle was on, and these were the first casualties. Others followed. Councillor Morgan, a small advertiser, canceled his space the following Monday. Obviously Baines had lost no time in getting into touch with him and acquainting him of the editor's opposition. Morgan, with his grocer's shop some way out of the town, had been Baines' most dogged supporter in the new housing scheme.

There were, in addition, faint signs of mutiny from inside the firm. Soon after the new *Clarion* had gone on sale at the news agents, Miss Gwyneth Morgan—a cousin of the grocer and the sister of Ivor, who had played opposite Miss Gelding in *The Prodigal Princess* the previous week—came up from the binding room, where she occupied the position of supervisor, and demanded to know of Nat "What our Ivor has done to be held up to public mockery?"

Nat was more gentle with her than he had been with Miss Gelding. If Gerald was going to make trouble an editor would need support from the staff, and little could be gained by upsetting the ponderous Miss Morgan.

"Ask your brother to come in and see me," he told her. "I think I can satisfy him that the notices I published will do amateur theatrical work in Sandcombe more good than he imagines."

Ivor came in, but was surprisingly noncommittal. Nat told him all that he had told Miss Gelding, but the little Welshman had nothing to say in reply, and Nat was left with the uncomfortable feeling that Ivor had been tampered with by the opposition, and, through his sister, was probably acting as a scout for the Gelding faction.

Looking back on that week, Nat was always ready to admit that Gerald handled the opening stages of his campaign with the uncanny skill often exhibited by the humiliated possessor of a one-track mind. There was a cold and efficient deliberation about the way Gerald went to work, moving up and down the town, calling here, phoning there, sealing up an escape hatch in one direction, turning a screw in another.

Not once, until the strike of the following Tuesday afternoon, did he come near the office. Nat made out the wages check and paid the men and girls. Bumble was called in and told that he would have to do most of the general reporting the following week. Bumble was delighted. He gave Marlene a good deal of trouble selecting his notebooks and pencils; he was not going to be fobbed off with a pad of scrap paper and a sharpened stub.

Gerald's first action was thoroughly characteristic. It concerned money. When he left Nat he went straight home to Cliff Terrace and emerged almost immediately, with his mother. The pair made straight for the local branch of Barclay's Bank, and by Monday morning Nat was made aware of the fact. A phone call from the manager informed him that in future no checks could be accepted without two signatures. Gerald must have persuaded his mother to countermand existing arrangements for check-drawing. Therefore, from now on the Clarion Press account was sealed, and Nat realized that he would have to depend on his own slim resources. These amounted to something over £50. The wage bill next Friday would swallow up most of that. Unless he could draw on further capital, he had less than enough for one more week. He decided to do his best with the limited time at his disposal. In the meantime he must try to borrow on the security of his own shares in the business.

He rang Thornton, the solicitor, on five separate occasions during Monday, and called at his office twice. Each time Mr. Thornton was not at home. Gerald had obviously been there first. Nat hesitated to go to the bank, for it did not seem likely that the manager, having suspended withdrawals from their joint account, would assist him with a personal overdraft.

There was only one thing for it—a private loan—and the only man Nat considered likely to advance him money without security was Otto, the detective writer up on the cliff.

He called upon Otto on Monday evening. The author, still in his woolen dressing gown, opened the door himself and led the way into his study overlooking the bay. Nat noticed that the man looked more than usually dissipated.

"How are you doing?" asked Otto, pouring him a drink. Nat told him, withholding nothing.

"Sticky," was the novelist's comment, "decidedly sticky. What are you going to do for rhino?"

"That depends on you," said Nat bluntly. "I want you to lend me two hundred and fifty pounds. The only securities I can offer are my shares in the firm. They're worth the eight hundred pounds I put in less than a fortnight ago. They can't take that away from me, whatever happens. It's already in black and white, and the partnership deed signed and settled."

Otto's expression did not change, but Nat had a feeling

that he had not been attending to him very closely. The house seemed very quiet, and the study looked as if it had not been swept for weeks. He also noticed that Otto had not shaved for forty-eight hours. He had evidently been on the bottle for days.

"How long do you think two hundred and fifty pounds will last you?" he asked.

"At least five weeks. By that time I shall know where I stand, legally and logically," replied Nat.

With a sudden movement Otto got up, hunched his dressing gown around him and moved over to the window, where he remained standing with his back to the room, his frayed dressing gown cord trailing on the floor.

"Tell you something," said Otto, after an uncomfortable silence.

"Yes," said Nat, fearing the worst, and keeping his eyes fixed on a large ink stain which starred the back of Otto's dressing gown.

"I'm finished. Washed up," said Otto. "Haven't got a bean in the world—not a bean."

"You're tight," said Nat lightly. "You've been tight for days."

"That's right. S'true, all the same," rejoined Otto, still keeping his eyes fixed on the bay as though, for the first time in their long acquaintance, he was ashamed of his appearance. "Remember that business I told you about the night the Old Man was buried? Came to a head last Sunday. Pam's left me. Walked out Monday morning. Can go to hell, for all I care. That's not all either. Wife's solicitors pressing me for money. 'Way behind with my payments. I owe the kid's school fees. This place is mortgaged up to the hilt. Haven't written anything for months. See what I mean?"

Nat saw, and was not unduly surprised. He knew that Otto had been going from bad to worse in recent months. What he did not know was that Otto was three books behind schedule with both his publishers, and in his present state of health could never hope to catch up, not even with the Dictaphone he was said to have used in his prime. As far as a loan was concerned, Otto was definitely out.

"What do you intend to do?" asked Nat, forgetting his own difficulties in the realization that Otto's were infinitely more pressing.

"I don't know," said Otto, and suddenly, to Nat's intense surprise and embarrassment, he burst into tears.

The spectacle invited Nat's contempt rather than his pity, but perhaps this was because he had always kept Otto in the back of his mind as an indirect form of insurance. The sudden revelation that the man was not only powerless to help him, but powerless to help himself, was more than he could bear after the nervous strain of the past few days. He felt an overwhelming desire to escape from this drab room and from the sound of Otto's alcoholic sobs. He hesitated for a few moments, then patted Otto awkwardly on the shoulder and went out to the back of the house to look for Grudger, Otto's handyman. He found the old fellow in the pantry, where he was unstopping a choked drain.

"You'd better go in and see to Mr. de Vere," he told him. "I think he needs you."

Grudger grunted, but did not relinquish his hold upon the cane rods which he was thrusting through the drainpipe. Apparently the drain had a superior claim upon his attention. He was accustomed to his employer's periodic remorse.

Nat left by the back door and passed round to the front of the house on his way down the drive. Through the uncurtained window he could see Otto still slumped over the table. The spectacle left him profoundly depressed.

FIFTEEN

On Tuesday morning Nat sketched out a skeleton paper. So far he had no replacement for Miss Gelding's four-inch double-column advert, and the space left by Baines' withdrawal had also to be filled.

The Church Services and Morgan's small advert were too insignificant as space fillers to be taken into account, but the general news that week appeared to be rather short; so Nat decided to drop the idea of a middle-page supplement and make the edition an eight- instead of a ten-page paper, as originally planned. The paper position, although easier, was still difficult, and he could use the newsprint saved in future issues.

He also gave instructions to use one of two standby features, one dealing with cookery and another with film notes. He could always get plenty of these features. They were sent free of charge by the publicity firms from whom they originated.

He planned to use the entire front page for what he designated his "Declaration." It was to contain a full-length piece, giving all the facts, as far as he knew them, of the council's housing scheme. He had worked on this article most of Sunday. It was a brief, chronological survey of the successive housing committees' deliberations over two decades, together with a précis of Wainer's plan, inset in heavier type, toward the foot of the two-column spread. The article was headed: "Your Future Homes; the Facts," and underneath, "If You Are Satisfied With This, So Are We!" Nat liked the sub-heading. It had a touch of irony about it, and he thought that might appeal to the type of ratepayer who invariably grumbled about all councillors, good, bad and dormant.

The Declaration was six columns wide, and the housing article occupied two of these. Two more were reserved for Wainer's plans, the blocks having arrived in good time for the schedule. They helped to clarify that part of the article which might have seemed too technical without adequate illustration.

In the fifth column there were to be two reports, one headed: "Their Opinion" and the other "The Organ-grinders." The first contained a selection of the personal views of men who had voted for the Hilltop Housing Scheme. The interviews had taken place some time before Nat had announced his opposition. Baines' own view was there, and so was Major Martindale's. None of the councillors had referred to the original scheme, and Nat intended to print their opinions just as they had been dictated at the time.

The second half of the fifth column dealt with ex-servicemen's comments on the Parochial Church Council's organ-fund decision. It was simply a follow-up from the previous week's editorial.

Nat husbanded a generous proportion of his ammunition for the sixth column, which was to contain a simple statement of his aims and an outline of the future policy of the paper. It was stale news as far as Baines, Gerald and Miss Gelding were concerned, but in reading it through, changing an adjective here, inserting a colon or a comma there, Nat felt that it was among the best things he had ever done. Without being plaintive, it was a strong appeal for local support. It concluded: "If you want this sort of local paper you can have it; but remember that we cannot print it without your active support."

He wondered, uncertainly, if this article would rally active support in the town. Most of the congratulations he had received at street corners, or in the bar of the Galleon, had been either furtive or flippant. He told himself that this was because he had made the initial mistake of using the soft pedal. He was beginning to realize that it would have been more effective if he had printed the issue he was planning now last Friday.

Notes and copy dealing with minor matters, all needing attention, were beginning to accumulate in his wire basket. More than once he found himself wishing that Mollie would walk in. During the last few days he had been hardening his heart against Mollie. She could have been such help in so many different ways. Bumble covered the routine jobs, and seemed to be doing quite well, but Bumble was no good as a confidant.

It was not until that afternoon that Nat found an unexpected ally.

Having satisfied himself that the Declaration page was as good as he could make it, Nat went off to attend a special court for a housebreaking case which he could not afford to leave to the inexperienced Bumble. From Thornton's bow windows down the High Street Gerald and Mrs. Vane watched him go. Then the two of them, followed by Mr. Thornton himself, went downstairs, across the street and into the *Clarion* building. They climbed the stairs to the editorial office. Gerald had a plan.

It was a simple plan, and Gerald felt sure that it would work. So did Mr. Thornton, who, by this time, was almost convinced that the plan was his own. Mrs. Vane was not so sure. Schoooled in Sam's steamroller methods, it seemed to her at once too subtle and too undignified. For Gerald had decided to place himself in the hands of his staff.

It had cost Gerald a good deal to arrive at this decision. He was not the sort of man to go cap in hand to employees. All his life he had been striving to introduce what he termed "business methods of address" into the Clarion Press, and his failures in this direction had weighed heavily upon him in the past. After his father's death he had resolved to try again, even if his insistence meant dismissing one or two of the more recalcitrant members of the staff— men like old Skinner, for instance, in whom the habit of surly independence was ingrained. But Gerald had the makings of a realist as well as those of a bureaucrat, and now that the business as a whole was in danger he was not going to let punctilio stand in the way of a victory. He was disinclined to rely on lobbying, preferring frontal attack.

So he took his place at Nat's vacant desk with the air of a commander in chief about to sign an order for general advance, well aware that such an order would involve casualties. The dead, in this case, would be some of

Gerald's cherished principles—sacred principles of how an efficient business should be run.

"Send for Bumble!" he began and, picking up the speaking tube, proceeded to execute his own order. Had he known how much that young man was enjoying his new occupation he might have sent for somebody else—Skinner, for instance, whom he had already, to use his own expression, "sounded."

Bumble popped an unusually well-greased head through the works door, and frowned when he recognized the now-familiar conference atmosphere.

"Tell Skinner to shut down and assemble the staff in here," snapped Gerald, a little more authoritatively than was necessary.

Bumble hesitated. "Shut down, Mr. Gerald? It's only 'arf-past three."

Gerald pursed his lips. "I didn't ask you the time," he said. "I asked you to get the men in here at once. Jump to it."

Bumble closed the door and jumped, emerging into the works rather breathlessly. He crossed to the platen and passed Gerald's message to Skinner. The latter did not seem very surprised—a fact which puzzled Bumble. The foreman crossed to the power switch and stilled the clattering machinery.

The other compositors looked up from their work. Skinner's method of summoning an assembly was limited to a general nod toward the office. Bumble, with his eyes still on the foreman, noticed that nobody seemed surprised at the summons. He concluded, quite accurately, that Skinner had been doing a little lobbying himself.

Bennett, one of the other compositors, went out into the binding room to summon Miss Morgan and her small staff. They collected Marlene on the way up. The shop assistant had the forethought to bolt the shop door before leaving the counter.

By this time Bumble, who was not unaware of the trouble which Nat's policy had caused during the last few days, began to grow alarmed. He was genuinely fond of Nat, and it seemed to him that there was altogether too much concerted action about this oddly timed conference in the editorial office. Why had he not been consulted? Was he not practically a sub-editor now? He sidled over to Burton, the only man who appeared reluctant to abandon his work.

"What's cooking?" he asked the keyboard operator. "Gerald and old Mother Vane are up there with that solicitor bloke. Is Nat coming?"

Burton's mouth came as near to a smile as Bumble could remember; he said, "What do *you* think?"

Bumble hesitated a moment, resolving to take a chance on Burton's loyalty. He knew that the silent keyboard operator preferred Nat to Gerald.

"Don't you reckon that we ought to let him know? He's at court."

Burton thought for a moment. Then, without speaking, he extracted a stub of pencil from the pocket of his waistcoat and wrote something on a piece of spiked advertising copy.

"Give that to the railway carrier," he told Bumble. "Ask him to drop it in at the court on his way back to the station."

Bumble took the note and went into the yard, where the carrier, who had just delivered newsprint, was trundling his barrow through the yard gates into St. Luke's Road. He gave him the note and instructions, and returned to join the keyboard operator. Then the pair of them crossed the works and made their way up the wooden steps into an office crowded almost to capacity.

Gerald had already begun to speak, but broke off as the newcomers entered.

"Hurry up, you two; now I've got to begin again," he said.

The staff were ranged in a wide arc at the back of the office, pivoted on Skinner, who had taken his stand near the works door. Mrs. Vane and Thornton had moved over to the window seat, and the lawyer had tucked his fat calves under the little desk that had been Mollie's. Bumble and Burton noticed that everyone, including Gerald, looked a trifle self-conscious in their workaday clothes. The men had not troubled to remove their aprons, and one of them—Bennett—was fidgeting with a torn pocket. Bumble glanced at Marlene, but she was studying her red finger-nails and failed to notice his look of interrogation. Skinner was scratching his ear, and his ink-stained fingers left a smear on the back of his neck. Miss Morgan, who weighed close on fifteen stone, was still breathing heavily. She hated that stair climb. It always distressed her.

Gerald began to speak again. Some of the men noticed that on this occasion there was no condescension in his tone.

"I've called you together this afternoon because I badly need your advice—the advice of all of you," he began. Mr. Thornton apparently approved this frank opening, for he nodded several times at a knot in the uncarpeted floor. "I daresay that you've already discussed among yourselves the things that have been happening round here since my fa-ther's death. I don't know whether you approve or disap-prove. So far I have only spoken to Skinner, who, I may say, sides with me in the matter. The fact is, that Mr. Hearn" (even at this stage Gerald could not bring himself to cancel his earlier instructions and call Nat by his Christian name) "has been seeking to make certain changes—gravely dis-turbing changes—and my opinion is—I intend to be per-fectly frank in the matter—that if he perseveres with this sort of nonsense you will all find yourselves out of a job in a very short space of time!"

Here he paused a moment for effect, and was not dis-appointed. A subdued murmur ran to and fro along the arc; but Gerald had no intention of allowing the confer-ence to degenerate into a discussion. So he quickly went on, "I have been into the position with the firm's solicitor, Mr. Thornton" (here Thornton gave an almost imper-ceptible bow), "and as a lawyer he has no hesitation in telling me that the tone of last week's *Clarion,* if con-tinued, can only lead to the bankruptcy court. Now, while that is primarily my concern, it does not need very much imagination on your part to see that a failure on the part of the firm will involve every one of us in this room. Be-fore I go further, perhaps one or two of the senior hands—

you, Skinner, and you, Bennett—would like to tell us how you feel about it all?"

"I'll tell you what I feel," said Skinner, without preamble. "I reckon that the things he's bin writing lately are plain daft and can only land us in trouble. Sooner or later we're going to find ourselves up against a libel suit."

Gerald shot Skinner an approving glance.

"I think that was very sensibly put, Skinner," he almost purred. "What about you Bennett?"

The compositor thus addressed gave a long sniff. This was partly to show his disdain for the *Clarion*'s recent outspokenness, but also because his nose happened to be running. Bennett's nose always ran from mid-September until early May. He had a perpetual cold, and was famous up and down among the High Street chemists for the variety of cures he attempted.

"I think that the stuff Nat's writing is barmy, Mr. Gerald," he said. "I talked it over yesterday with Bert Hole here and my missus in the pub, and we reckon he'll have a go at everyone before he's through."

Bert Hole, who stood beside Bennett, sucked his breath sharply through parted lips. It was a Sandcombe way of saying "That's true."

Gerald looked quite elated. Bennett's pronouncement was more than he had hoped for.

"And you, Miss Morgan?" he asked. "How does the binding room feel about it?"

"He was very rude about our Ivor last week," was Miss Morgan's sole contribution to the discussion, but Gerald, who had hitherto failed to connect the operatic notices with the family pride of the Morgans, judged it to be more than enough, as apparently did Mr. Thornton, for he again favored the knot on the floor with a series of vigorous nods.

Gerald paused for a moment. He wanted to be absolutely sure.

"What about you others?" he inquired, looking from one end of the arc to the other, where Bumble and Burton were standing near the landing door. "Is there any comment that anyone else would like to make, before I tell you what I propose that we should do?"

At this juncture Mr. Thornton interrupted. "I think I'd better take over from here, Gerald," he said paternally.

Gerald looked a little piqued. He had not observed his mother give Mr. Thornton's ankle an encouraging poke with the ferrule of her umbrella.

"Very well," he said, "tell them what we propose, Mr. Thornton."

"I think that you would all be wise to take, shall we say, a week's well-earned holiday," said Mr. Thornton, in the voice of a school governor winding up a highly successful prize-giving.

There was a short pause. Then Skinner voiced the suspicions of all.

"What about our wages?" he asked, amid a general murmur of approval.

Mr. Thornton smiled expansively.

"I think I am safe in saying that Mr. Gerald would see you did not suffer on that account," he replied.

"I'll pay everyone out of my own pocket," said Gerald, and, his jubilation outstripping his caution for a moment, added, "and when things mend I shan't forget your loyalty. There'll be a rise for everyone." A split second later caution drew level with jubilation again, and he hastily continued, "as soon as we can afford it, of course."

Burton spoke slowly and with great deliberation.

"I'd like to know," he said, fixing a pious eye upon the portrait of the late Mr. Vane hanging by the door, "I'd like to know whether Nat knows about this offer o' yours, and whether 'e's been consulted in the matter."

This was something of a bombshell, and everyone began to feel uncomfortable again. Everyone, that is, with the exception of Bumble, who fairly beamed upon the keyboard operator. But there was another surprise at hand. The landing door swung open to reveal Nat, who looked into the office with much the same expression as Peter the Great must have employed when he exposed the conspiracy of his fifty guardsmen. He took full advantage of the situation.

"I can tell you that, Burton old man," he said. "He knows *all* about it, and, quite frankly, he doesn't care a damn one way or the other. You can stay or you can go, which ever you like. If you stay, I can promise that you won't lose your jobs, any of you; if I have to run the paper myself, I'm going on running it as long as I possibly can."

"Good for you," grunted Burton, now looking almost happy.

Gerald stood up. His face was very white.

"So you've taken to eavesdropping, I see," he shouted, though even he thought that this was a little feeble for the occasion.

"That's better, at any rate, than holding a partners' meeting in my absence," rejoined Nat, and he came into the room, closing the door behind him.

A good deal of shuffling and collar-jerking followed.

Some of the men, notably Bennett and Hole, looked like little boys surprised in raiding a hen roost. Bumble, who was beginning to feel that this was quite the most exciting thing that had ever happened in Sandcombe outside of the Granada cinema, where he was a constant and uncritical patron, moved across to Nat and piped up, "Me'n Burton's with you, Nat!" but immediately regretted the remark, for it made him feel rather silly.

Skinner came to the rescue of all parties, addressing Nat frankly, but without rancor.

"Pack it in, Nat," he advised. "You'll on'y land all of us in the soup."

The remark restored a sense of reality to the room. Everyone relaxed a little.

Mr. Thornton wearing his most benevolent expression, now rose from behind Mollie's desk.

"I'm sure that we can arrive at some satisfactory compromise," he began.

Nat spun round. Skinner and the others never remembered him in this sort of mood before. Nat's good temper had always been taken for granted in the Clarion works.

"You'd better shut up and clear out, Thornton," he said. "I took a shorthand note of your comments just now, and I'm not at all sure that they wouldn't land you in trouble if I published them."

Thornton, who had been reared in an atmosphere of summons and countersummons, was genuinely alarmed.

"Anything I said was purely in the nature of friendly advice to a client and quite without prej—"

"Clear out," growled Nat, "and that applies to all of you who have been taken in by his claptrap. Go on. I want to get on with my work."

"That's precisely what we intend to do," said Gerald shrilly. "Believe me, you haven't heard the last of this yet. Come along, men!"

With the air of leading a strategic but perfectly well-ordered retreat he marched through the works door, leaving Mr. Thornton to extricate Mrs. Vane from the window seat, where she was virtually cut off and in danger of being abandoned to the enemy.

The others filed out without a word. Only Burton and Bumble remained.

Nat looked at these two, and they saw that his flash of temper had given way to a broad grin.

"Thanks for letting me know," he said. "We'll talk it over directly. In the meantime you'd better go down, both of you, and keep your ears open."

They went out after the others, and a moment later Nat heard voices raised in argument. He sat down at his typewriter and forced himself to begin reading back the long court case. He was surprised to find himself trembling.

SIXTEEN

On Wednesday morning the *Clarion* staff mustered four. Nat, Burton, Bumble and Marlene put in an appearance.

The arrival of Marlene in the shop at 9 A.M. caused Bumble momentary delight. He felt that the circumstances might help to promote "an understanding," but he was cruelly disappointed, for it turned out that Marlene had no intention of joining the *Clarion* Rump, but had merely called to collect some of her things from the cloakroom.

Marlene was one of those young women who carry a good many "things" around with them. She had left the shop on Tuesday night loaded like a Congo explorer. The ladies' "cloakroom" at the *Clarion*—a tiny, box-like apartment halfway up the stairs—looked very bare when Marlene had removed her more prized belongings the previous evening, but she was obliged to return in the morning for the leftovers.

Bumble caught her on the stairs. She was carrying an attaché case, a sponge bag, two pots of face cream and a flowered overall with more sex appeal than any overall deserved.

"Where you orf?" he asked.

"Where'd you think I'm off? Timbuktew? I'm leaving, o' course, like all the others, and if you had any gump you'd leave too."

Bumble's face fell.

"You can't leave, Marlene. Who's goin' to look after the shop? We must have the shop open, mustn't we?"

"Must we? I'm sure I don't know. I'm not getting meself mixed up in that silly business no more. It's dangerous, my Aunt Carol says, an' not on'y that, it's *common!*"

Marlene implied that she might have braved the danger, but to ask her to share an adventure that was common was altogether too much. She pushed past Bumble at the foot of the stairs.

"You'd better lock the shop door after me," she said. "I'm not going all through the works; it's mucky."

"But look here," pleaded Bumble, hurrying along beside her. "Nat wants 'elp bad. You aren't standing in with that other crowd, are you? You couldn't. They got no guts."

Marlene winced, and Bumble perceived at once that he had employed a wrong word.

"I'm sure I don't know what you mean," said Marlene, fumbling with a bottom bolt of the shop door. "I'm not 'standing in' with anyone. I'm leaving here right now."

"What, for good?" cried the stricken Bumble, who thought that he had never seen her look so desirable. Her struggle with the bolt had caused a heavy lock of corn-colored hair to fall across her face. She was like Veronica Lake, only better, and not so soppy with it, he thought.

"Yes, for good," said Marlene, straightening up and wrenching back the door. "I'm sick of it all. No one's got no manners down here. I'm going after a hairdressing job in Lilian's in Paxtonbury. There's a bit of class there. José Thompson can get me taken on as an improver. Said so."

With that Marlene hurried into High Street, ignoring Bumble's crestfallen "Well, g'bye!"

He trudged back into the works and told Nat. The editor did not appear overwhelmed. "Well, good riddance," he said, "she always was a stupid little bitch. Nuisance though; who's going to look after the shop?"

"Not me," grunted Bumble, a little piqued at Nat's remark, "we'd better put a notice on the door."

Bumble himself scribbled a notice: "Shop Closed for Repairs. Enquiries at Works Door," and fastened it up with drawing pins. All that morning would-be purchasers of stationery, textbooks and postcards got a brief glimpse of a real printing works.

Then Nat set about organizing his manpower. Skinner and three journeymen had left. So had Miss Morgan and her two girls. Gerald's department could be closed down; the three remaining members of the staff would have to concentrate on essentials—the keyboard, the caster and the flatbed. Neither Bumble nor Nat could operate the flatbed, and Burton only indifferently. Nat made a decision.

There could be no more jobbing and no copy for the paper. The material already set would have to suffice. It could be squeezed into six pages, although a fold would be necessary, for he had calculated on eight and started printing on a double sheet. They could only hope that nothing sensational in the way of local events took place between then and Friday morning.

Bumble, therefore, was set to watch the casting of the news and features. Burton began to print the inside pages on the flatbed. Nat acted as general odd-job man, folding papers and answering the door and the phone. It was vitally important that customers should not get the impression which Gerald would probably be spreading—namely, that the *Clarion* had temporarily closed down.

Before long, however, Nat concluded that it was easy enough to be defiant in front of Gerald and the staff, but not so easy to bring out a six-page paper with only one man and a boy. All that morning he bitterly regretted his lack of technical knowledge. He had to rely on Burton for everything. The keyboard operator had said little to explain his loyalty. "If you're out after that bleeder Baines, I'm with you," was his sole comment. Up to that moment Nat had always taken Burton for granted. He was just "one of the men"; less talkative than the others and inclined to be surly, perhaps, but, to Nat's mind, without much character. He now discovered that the old printer had a distinctly interesting personality, a banked-up hatred of sham and deceit, and a contempt for the lack of spirit shown by other members of the staff, who saw nothing in Nat's efforts but the discomfort of being levered out of their ruts. Nat did not know that Burton had once tried to organize them into demanding a higher rate of wages from Sam. Probably his failure on that occasion partly explained the keyboard operator's actions at the conference the previous day.

For two hours the works were silent except for the rhythmic clumpety-clump of the big machine and the metallic clang of Bumble's caster—sounds against which their ears had long been immunized.

From time to time Bumble emerged from the caster

room, munching bread and cheese. He shouted a question at Burton, received an answer and wandered back again. Nat went on folding the inside pages.

Soon his back began to ache from the unaccustomed exercise of stooping, swishing his left hand across the fold and jerking upright again to grab the next sheet. It was a monotonous job. His mind began to drift back to the past, odd reporting calls he remembered in prewar days, evenings in the NAAFI, girls he had met at station dances and Mollie.

He wondered if Mollie knew what had happened. He had heard that her father was back in town. Perhaps he had written and told her. Why hadn't he called on her father? Pride? A determination to let her stew in her own juice? But it was he who was stewing, not Mollie. What was he going to do after this week's edition had come out? Who could he turn to for help? The labor exchange, or an ex-service organization, or the chamber of commerce? They might get him some men, if Skinner and the others still kept up this ridiculous strike. But if he got men, how was he going to pay them?

Who could have thought Gerald had so much influence over them all? They had always laughed at him behind his back. But perhaps Sandcombe, as a whole, was laughing now behind the new editor's back? Was there any evidence that his last issue had made the slightest impression on the town, apart from stirring up a packet of trouble among customers and staff?

Old Wainer, the surveyor, had been in, inquiring unhappily about his plans. The old fellow was obviously scared stiff. He was like everyone else; he didn't want any trouble. But if everyone in Sandcombe went on merely avoiding trouble, what would happen? People like Baines and the Gelding and Major Martindale would continue to rule the roost, and some of them, such as Baines, would make a good thing out of it as well. Perhaps they were meant to. Perhaps a town of this sort had to have half a dozen small-time bosses to keep it going. That mightn't be democracy, as Nat understood it, but it seemed to work. Sandcombe had existed for nearly a thousand years without any newspaper at all, and for the last two generations with a newspaper run on Sam's lines. The town was still there and, if his guess was right, the average person in it was tolerably satisfied with life.

Then what was he doing? Had Mollie been right? Was he throwing away his time and energy and savings in trying to bring out a worthwhile paper? He couldn't be sure if the end was worth the effort. The money didn't matter much. He had never worried unduly about money, and had never been the sort of man to reflect, with calm satisfaction, that he had eight hundred pounds in the bank. If it went it went, and that was that. But the effort, all this struggle and strife, was different. He had himself always tried to avoid strife, and he wanted to go on doing so. All that he really wanted to do was to give the job a fair trial. And it wasn't getting a fair trial, not when he had to face the second week with only a man and a boy behind the scenes.

Well, there was only one thing for it now—to bring out the paper with its Declaration page and see what happened. If it got across, and the town rose to it, Gerald would probably be prepared to compromise. The strike had at least postponed one major worry. There would be no wages to pay on Friday. *That* was Gerald's headache.

Sooner or latter, though, if he persisted in bringing out a newspaper each Friday, the firm would need money. There was paper to be purchased, and power, light and heat to be paid for. His shrunken bank account obviously wouldn't carry the *Clarion* very far, but he could hold out a little longer with the reduced staff. He didn't know it, but he sensed that Burton, or Bumble either for that matter, would not press him for wages. He would have to talk to them about it.

First let him get this week's paper out, and then canvass the town. Perhaps some of the tradesmen would take out shares and he could make Gerald an offer. If a few thousands were subscribed the paper might actually come to be owned by Sandcombe; he had once heard of that happening elsewhere when a local paper was threatened by a big combine. How much would he need? Gerald, of course, would be loath to sell, but if the offer were good enough, and things went on as they were doing, he might be glad to wash his hands of the firm and start afresh elsewhere—in Paxtonbury, perhaps, or in some other town along the coast.

Nat's reflections were checked by an odd silence. He suddenly realized that the Big Machine had stopped running. Burton was bending over the form.

"What's up, Burton? Run out of paper?"

Burton raised his head.

"Our makeup, Nat. Come an' look here; it's dragged out!"

Nat went over to the machine. Page 3 appeared to be crumbling. Part of it had dragged away from the form, and a corner of the page, fortunately comprizing widely spaced advertisements, would need resetting.

"How long will that take?" asked Nat.

"Bumble and I could reset it soon enough," said the printer; "it'll hang us up about an hour."

"Better knock off for lunch, then," Nat told him.

"How about you?"

"I'm going out for a bit. I've got an idea!"

He put on his jacket, took his battered trilby from the rack and went down the wooden steps into the yard. Burton watched him go.

"This would 'ave to happen," he told Bumble, and then, with a grin that revealed the gaps in his teeth, "You'd better fetch a camp bed down 'ere, young 'un. You won't do no more skirt-chasing 'til Friday!"

Nat borrowed Burton's push-cycle and pedaled down to the Harbor. He dismounted at a row of little cottages adjoining the Capstan and went into the yard of the cottage nearest the breakwater. Here he found Peg Leg Baker, painting an upturned dinghy.

Peg Leg was a well-known local character. Outside his back door (Nat had never understood why the board was not transferred to the front) he exhibited a hand-painted sign, which read:

Specialist and Craftsman
Boat-builder, Cabinetmaker
Joiner and Carpenter
Undertaking Done

Underneath this formidable array of talents were the words, painted in much bolder and more businesslike characters: "ANY *Odd Job Tackled.*"

Nat always felt that this was the only part of the notice that really mattered. The rest was Peg Leg's sop to his own vanity. He had never, as far as Nat was aware, built a boat, unless one counted the lopsided toy yachts that he sometimes carved for the children of his wife's seasonal visitors. He had never been seen to make even an orange box, much less a cabinet, and his claim to be an undertaker certainly did not keep Mr. Sleek awake at nights. Peg Leg, indeed, never seemed to do any work of his own account, but spent most of the week stumping round the town engaged in the routine duties of an Honorary General Secretary to the Sandcombe British Legion.

Apart from this he was known as a practical joker who liked to joke on a big scale. Once he had built and painted a huge hoarding and, assisted by some cronies, had slipped out at night to erect it on the open ground immediately facing the large residences on the Ridge.

The hoarding caused great consternation among Ridge dwellers, for the notice read: "Site of Hi Wung Lo's New Chinese Laundry. To be opened here Wednesday next by Hi Wung Lo, Junior." Beneath this startling announcement was a detailed list of prices, the prospective customer being informed that he could get "a shirt washed for 4½d. and a collar laundered for 3d. (plain), 3½d. (glossy)." On the other hand, the notice continued, a pair of socks "could not be washed for less than 1s." For some reason, Hi Wung Lo objected to washing socks.

Nat had enjoyed the joke, and so had other Sandcombians—everybody, in fact, except the residents on the Ridge, who organized a petition to deter the owner of the field from selling the site to Hi Wung Lo and thus contravening an important clause in their leases.

Peg Leg—the name had stuck to him since his return from Jutland with a cork foot—had been the author of other equally fantastic jokes. He had once persuaded young Grimmett, son of the baker in Quay Street, to make a hundred pastries exactly like mushrooms. He and Grimmett had then gone up to the garden of St. Luke's vicarage after dark, planted the mushrooms in a vacant flower bed just inside the front railings, and put up a placard: "The Vicar Invites You To Purchase His Homegrown Mushrooms. His Stipend is Small and his Family is Increasing!"

Notwithstanding the vicar's affection for the writings of Stephen Leacock, the Reverend Galahad Ormsby was slow to see the joke.

In one way or another Peg Leg Baker had done a good deal to brighten life in Sandcombe during years gone by, and Nat had a feeling that he might be useful in the approaching crisis.

The harrassed editor sat down on a vacant trestle near the boat.

"I've heard all about it," volunteered Peg Leg, glad of an excuse to lay down his brush.

"I might need some help," said Nat.

"What sort of help?" asked the Specialist and Craftsman.

"I don't know," said Nat (it was always best to be vague with Peg Leg, for his imagination seldom needed stimulus). "What about the Legion?"

Peg Leg spat, just wide of his paint-pot.

"Dead from the neck up," he said, "leastways, the young 'uns are. Pictures is all that *they* care about. Pictures an' Darts. You won't get much help there."

"It doesn't look like it," agreed Nat gloomily.

"Got a strike down at the *Clarion*, haven't you?" asked Peg Leg.

Nat nodded. "I'm running with two hands—a man and a boy."

"And I hear they're a-gettin' up a meeting," added Mr. Baker cautiously, giving Nat a sidelong glance that made him look not unlike Hi Wung Lo, Jr., declining a dirty pair of socks.

"Hadn't heard that," admitted the journalist. "Who's getting it up?"

"Oh, never mind, if you ain't heard," said Peg Leg, and fixed his eye on a small coaster, beating round Schooner Head, in choppy water. "The pilot's just left her," he said, nodding seaward.

Nat was not interested in the coaster.

"Are you sure that you couldn't stir up the Legion Committee?" he asked, "get them to write me some sort of vote of confidence which I could publish?"

"Vote?" queried Peg Leg, spitting again. "They won't vote for nothing but whist drives an' dugout suppers. But you don't want to worry about *them*. I'll think this job over. I never did like Baines, or that Gelding screecher neither. Besides, I reckon we might get a laugh out of it."

"Thanks, Peg Leg," said Nat, and jumped off the trestle feeling strangely cheered, though he could not have said why. He had not the slightest idea what had been achieved by this casual visit—probably nothing, he thought—but it was good to know that at least one Sandcombian was watching events at the *Clarion* with an unprejudiced eye.

He went out and mounted Burton's cycle again. On re-passing the *Clarion* shop he was surprised to see the door open. So he left the cycle in the yard and went round to investigate.

A girl of about twenty was making a clumsy show of dressing the window. She straightened up when he touched her shoulder. It was Beryl Hopper, the ex-WAAF who had called on him the night when Sam died.

"Hullo!" she said casually. "I heard that there was a flap on; so I told Bumble I'd get weaving."

It occurred vaguely to Nat that Beryl would go on talking like this for the rest of her life. Already the argot seemed dated. Soon words like "flap" would fall as oddly upon the ear as "masher" and "knut." But Beryl would go on using them, in the same way as she used an air of studied boredom to mask enthusiasm. Both words and manner belonged to that part of her life when she had been forced to submerge her personality in a huge collective effort with a definite aim in view. It flashed through his mind also that perhaps this was half the trouble with postwar Sandcombe. All but the greedy and arrogant had surrendered their personalities to the war effort. Then the war had suddenly stopped, leaving them to go on alone. The new goal was not advertised on a poster.

All the same, he could not help feeling cheered. Beryl's nonchalance did not fool him.

"Thanks for coming in," he said. "We can do with some help. I can't promise any wages, though. Did they tell you that?"

Beryl shrugged. "I'm easy. I'm all right for ackers. Still living on my gratuity. I'm signing on again soon. Civvy street's a bind."

"Well... thanks," he said, and left her with a conviction that she had been glad of the chance to come in and occupy her time. Or perhaps this was her way of hitting back at Miss Gelding.

He went out into the works, and found Burton and Bumble still resetting the damaged page. Burton was looking worried.

"I've had a good look at the machine," he told Nat. "The trouble wasn't due to makeup; one o' them cogs is slipping. Skinner coulder fixed it, but I can't."

Nat took a formal look at the machine. He was quite helpless to give advice. "We'll just have to hope for the best; I'll carry on folding."

Burton hesitated a moment, as though making up his mind to say something else. Finally he spoke, "Baines has bin in."

"Baines?" Nat paused in the act of taking off his jacket. "In here?"

Burton nodded.

"What happened?" asked Nat, sensing trouble.

"I kicked him out," said Burton simply.

SEVENTEEN

Burton was speaking the plain truth. He had kicked Baines out of the works—kicked him squarely in the exceptionally large expanse that Baines presented when he turned his back and stooped.

After his quarrel with Nat on the previous Friday, Baines had gone back to his garage to consider his next move. He remained bitterly resentful, but after his first outburst in the *Clarion* office his anger did not show itself, as it usually did, in gruff and irritable handling of his staff at the garage. It was not that sort of anger. It prowled about inside him, like indigestion. It made him vacant and inattentive.

In the succeeding days he began to neglect his business. He had suffered a shock, and it was his pride that took the buffet. Like most men who enter upon public affairs, Baines had an insatiable hunger for popularity. He wanted to be able to walk down the High Street and to imagine that he heard people say to one another, "There goes Old Baines; good sort, Baines, best councillor we've got!" or to walk into the gentlemen's lounge of the Galleon and hear, " 'Evening, Mr. Baines. What'll it be? I owe you one for fixing that chimney o' mine; the surveyor would never have got round to it on his own!"

Baines had no guilty conscience about the Hilltop Housing Scheme. He had long since discussed the matter with the surveyor and with other councillors, like Martindale and Morgan, who also preferred this site to any other. They had helped to convince each other that by choosing this particular area they were acting in the public's best interest. They had ceased to consider alternative sites.

The possibility of a considerably increased revenue from his bus service had, of course, occurred to Baines, just as the likelihood of an increased turnover in the shop had been pondered by Councillor Morgan; but even if he had not owned a bus service, Baines would have been enraged by Nat's opposition. It indicated that, before long, someone else might emerge as town leader, and Baines was happy in limelight himself.

He thought much on the matter throughout the weekend. It interfered with his sleep and spoiled his Saturday evening at the club. Because of it he took little or no interest in the Sunday newspapers, which he usually plowed through column by column, as he sat in his glass box at the garage. By Sunday evening he had decided to do something about it, and called in at the Galleon lounge, where he knew he would meet Angel, the town clerk, and Major Martindale. They were always there from seven till nine on Sunday evenings.

The three men took their drinks over to their special table in the corner farthest from the door. Each knew that the other was thinking about Friday's *Clarion,* for, in addition to the publication of Nat's letter about the housing scheme, the story of the partners' quarrel had gone the local rounds. Skinner and Miss Morgan were inveterate gossips.

After a few sips Angel said, "You're going to have trouble with young Hearn."

Baines did not like the way that Angel said "you" instead of "we." It was as if the shrewd clerk intended to make it perfectly clear from the start that he was a mere employee, and had never given his councillors advice on choice of site.

Martindale frowned into the fire. Like most soldiers, he hated newspapers and newspaper men. Even now it made him wince to see his name in print. He had never quite got rid of the feeling that the colonel would present his compliments and ask him to come in and explain what he thought he was playing at. Like Baines, however, he was not going to stand by and see a newspaper man make a fool of him. The resurrection of the Flats Development Scheme, which he had astutely scotched all those years ago, had disturbed him. If they started shifting the hoi polloi to his perimeter he would soon show them. He would sell his house in the best market and move to another town. He knew that Grimstone-Beech and one or two others of the Ridge dwellers would do the same. The trouble was, where could they find houses half as good at even double the price now?

Baines rang the bell for the waiter, and young Ernie Potter appeared—the Ernie who had outraged Princess Mathilde behind scenes during the opera by informing her, in the heat of the moment, that she was "the outside bloody limit." On this occasion, however, Ernie was deferential. Both Martindale and Baines left a small tip on the tray after every round.

"Three more," said Baines, leaning forward confidentially.

Ernie gathered the glasses and left.

"There'll be a spread in the *Clarion* this week," said Baines solemnly. "There'll be a big spread, mark my words!"

Angel marked them and smiled, a shade scornfully.

"I wouldn't worry about the *spread,* Mr. Baines. The government inquiry is the thing that counts, and, unless I'm mistaken, somebody will put in an appearance there."

Angel was not displeased with the unexpected developments. He liked to see councillors under fire. It gave them something to think about, and prevented them from interfering with his work of running the town. He decided to encourage them a little by giving bad advice.

" 'Ave you got any ideers?" asked Baines bluntly, while Martindale wished heartily that Baines possessed the merest shade of finesse.

"Well, I don't know," said Angel, delicately twirling the stem of the refilled glass that Ernie had placed on the glass-topped table. "The public won't like the housing scheme being delayed. You might get up an informal meeting and sound them."

Baines began to feel better already. Here was something that he understood. He could dominate any meeting that they were likely to stage in Sandcombe. He had done it before, and could do it again, especially if Martindale would undertake to bring in his set and give the assembly tone.

"Would you back me up?" he asked.

"Me?" said Angel, incredulously.

"No, not you, Angel; you, Major!"

Martindale considered.

"I might," he said, "if Grimstone-Beech will come in."

"Okeydoke!" said Baines, consulting his diary. "We've a cahnsel meeting Toosdy. 'Ow about nex' Monday—tomorrer week?"

"Monday will do," said Martindale. "You'd better book the hall."

"Leave it to me," muttered Baines, and immediately relaxed.

They began to talk of other matters. Angel told one or two of his amusing stories—smutty, of course, but so respectably told that they might have been Gospel parables.

The public meeting, however, was not destined to be held on Monday week; it had to be brought forward to the preceding Thursday. The reason for this change of plan (which entailed considerable hustling on the part of Baines, the principal organizer) was a casual visit to the *Clarion* works on Wednesday afternoon, while Nat was sitting on the trestle of the "Specialist and Craftsman" down by the harbor.

Baines had already roped in Miss Gelding and Norton, having heard, by the channels through which all news traveled in Sandcombe, that both these worthies had been considerably put out by the previous week's *Clarion*. He then heard about Gerald's strike. Thornton informed him over the phone when he rang Baines' garage to inquire whether his radio battery had been charged.

On Wednesday afternoon the garage proprietor happened to be passing down St. Luke's Road when he saw Nat cycle off into the Clarion yard. Baines acted on impulse. He went into the yard and up the wooden steps to the works. The door was open and the machinery still. He sauntered across to the Big Machine, where Burton was tinkering with one of the rollers.

Baines, who knew Burton well enough, tapped him on the elbow. The printer straightened up and stared at him, rather uncivilly as Baines thought.

" 'Ullo, Burton," began Baines, pleasantly. This was the fellow Thornton had told him about. He would need careful handling.

"What's the idea, comin' in 'ere?" asked Burton, wiping his hands on cotton waste.

"Oh, I dunno," said Baines. "Thought I might find Nat."

"He's out," replied Burton, preparing to move away.

Baines hesitated for a moment, his eye roving round the empty workshop in the hope of finding something of interest. Then he tilted his bowler hat an inch and thrust his red hands deep into his trouser pockets.

"Where's the men?" he asked, bluntly.

The printer eyed him slowly. Baines' big face retained its good-natured expression.

" 'Olidays!" said Burton, shortly.

"All of 'em?"

"Yes, all of 'em!"

"Funny," said Baines, withdrawing one hand to pick his teeth.

There was a short pause. Burton moved over to the printer's stone, where the Declaration page was being made up, ready to be lifted onto the machine in place of the inside page now being printed. He picked up a type mallet and began tapping. Presently Baines followed him over.

"You've got your name dahn for a cahnsel 'ouse, aven't you?" he asked.

"I 'ave," replied Burton quietly; then he added, unexpectedly, "but I don't see why I should pay you eightpence a day to go to an' from it, do you?"

Baines changed his tactics. It was no good monkeying with this man. He was the sullen type, like one or two of the hands at the garage.

"I'll give you twice the money you're gettin' here an' see that your name goes to the top o' the cahnsel tenants' waiting list, if you'll pack in like the others," he said; but instantly he regretted it, for Burton looked very ugly. His prominent knuckles gleamed over the handle of the type mallet that he was holding.

There was another short pause. Then Burton flung down the mallet and smacked his palm on the page of type in front of him.

"See that?" he said. "It's the lowdown on you. See them blocks? That's the old plan o' the Flats Scheme—the one you 'elped gloss over. See that 'eadin'? I'll read it to yer. It says, 'If You're Satisfied With This, So Are We!' Think they will be? I don't reckon so, Baines. I reckon that you're gonner look pretty soft when this comes out Friday."

Baines lost his temper again.

"You print that an' I'll sue the pair o' yer fer libel!" he shouted.

Burton laughed outright.

"There ain't a word o' libel in it," he told him. "D'you think Nat's barmy?"

"I'll fix you, one way or another; you see if I don't!"

It was here that Burton succumbed to an irresistible desire to lay hands on a councillor. It was something that he had always wanted to do, ever since he had been told to mind his own business when he had climbed the office stairs to inform Sam that some of the councillors were supplying themselves with free tar from the council stores depot. Here was an excellent opportunity. Baines was a virtual trespasser and could legally be ejected.

"You goin'?" he asked, wanting to be quite safe on legal grounds before he acted. He had read somewhere that you always had to ask a trespasser to leave before you threw him out.

Baines played into his hands.

"When I think fit," he said.

"No mate, when *I* think fit," said Burton, and, suddenly seizing the heavier man by his collar and sleeve, ran him across the short space of flooring between the slab and the works door.

Burton never forget the next moment. He relived it every time he passed the *Clarion* office in subsequent years.

Baines was a big man and no coward. It was only the speed of his assault that enabled the wiry old printer to triumph.

Once they were at the head of the short flight of steps

there was no doubt that Baines would descend them in the manner prescribed by Burton. Baines' bowler hat fell off in the struggle and rolled under the platen. Popping his head out of the caster room, Bumble was just in time to see the pair rush by and to hear Baines' shout of rage as his feet were pushed from the edge of the rickety little platform outside.

He fell heavily, rolling on his side and coming to rest on hands and knees in a shallow puddle in the asphalt patch at the foot of the steps.

Burton had just time to retrieve the bowler, stamp on it and throw it after its owner before slamming and locking the works door. He made haste to do this, for Baines scrambled to his feet and rushed up the steps again, bellowing like a wounded buffalo and looking somewhat like one.

Bumble, now a startled onlooker through the caster-room window, did not need Burton to tell him to hurry up the stairs and along the passage to the shop and make sure that the shop bolts were drawn. It was as well he did, for Baines lost no time in hurrying round to the High Street entrance. He was too late. Bumble hurriedly pulled down the blind, and returned to congratulate Burton.

The printer concealed any jubilation he might have felt and went straight back to work. Bumble was having another squint through the window when Beryl Hopper arrived to offer her services. He lost no time in letting her in and enrolling her on the spot. She hadn't quite Marlene's class, but he liked the look of her legs, and Johnny Marlow, at ATC headquarters, had told him that she was hot stuff.

Meanwhile Baines retired to nurse his bruises in the garage, where it occurred to him that whatever he might have to say at Monday's public meeting would be stale and profitless, if it followed the publication of the *Clarion*'s Declaration page. If the meeting was to be held at all, it would have to be held prior to the next issue of the *Clarion*. It was then Wednesday. It would have to be organized for Thursday. In that way Nat Hearn, not Baines, would be left with stale news.

Baines' bulk never curtailed his energy, especially when business advantage was to be gained by prompt action. He did not move from his little glass box. He used the telephone half a dozen times and sent out two or three of his employees with typed notes. By teatime Baines had an impressive following lined up, the contemplation of which took some of the ache out of his right buttock, when it had struck the sharp angle of the safety rail on the *Clarion* works step.

Toward the end of the afternoon Nat went up to his office. He had not been there long when Beryl Hopper looked in at the landing door.

"Sky pilot down in the shop," she told him; "he wants a natter."

Nat told her to send the clergyman up, and was not surprised when the Rev. Galahad Ormsby walked into the room. The vicar looked a good deal more cheerful than he felt.

The Rev. Galahad did not wear black. He belonged to that school of clergymen who believe that it is their business to look as much like other men as possible. He conceded the dog collar, but nothing else. He was generally hatless, and favored a light gray double-breasted flannel suit.

He now greeted Nat warmly. "I know you're busy, old man, but can you spare me a minute?"

Nat invited the vicar to sit down. Ormsby took off his cycle clips and foraged for his pipe.

"It's about this wretched organ-fund business," he began.

"You read the leader, I suppose," said Nat, rather apologetically, for he had no reason to dislike Ormsby. Before the war they had always got on together rather well.

"Let bygones be bygones," said the vicar. "I thought that you were a bit hard on us, but ... you're an ex-serviceman, and you had a perfect right to say what you felt."

"Thanks," said Nat, feeling even more apologetic.

"As a matter of fact I've come round to suggest a compromise. Supposing we call this meeting of young people, as you suggest, will you see that my fund gets an allocation of, say, a hundred or so?"

"How can I do that?" asked Nat. "It'll depend on the popular vote, won't it?"

"All right, let's leave it like this. I'll waive any claim on behalf of the parish, and you, as sponsor of the meeting, will propose a donation of a hundred pounds to the organ fund, leaving the rest of the money for whatever mode of commemoration or distribution the meeting thinks fit? If you move that, the rest of them will vote for it, and we shall all be happy."

Nat hesitated. It seemed an easy way out. A hundred pounds was not much out of a thousand tax free. Nine hundred pounds was a comfortable figure for a club-room endowment or whatever similar project suggested itself since the publication of last week's editorial.

"What does Mr. Norton think of this?" asked Nat, and realized, as soon as he had spoken, that he had said the wrong thing.

Mr. Ormsby did not like anyone to suggest that he was under Norton's thumb. Parishioners might think it if they liked, but no one must actually say it; in parochial circles this proviso was understood and respected.

The Rev. Galahad flushed a little and lifted his pipe from its cosy resting place at the corner of his mouth.

"You would oblige me, Hearn, by leaving Norton out of this."

This time it was Ormsby who said the wrong thing.

Nat had an intense dislike of being addressed as "Hearn" by people whom he had known for years. It seemed to him the very pinnacle of patronage on their part. People might call him "Nat" with impunity, and begin doing so from the first moment of acquaintanceship; they could, if they preferred, call him plain "Mister" and omit the surname altogether, but they could not address him as "Hearn" and expect him to like it. This mode of address always made him feel like a jobbing gardener putting in half a day's work at one of the big houses on the Ridge. The vicar, too, had always called him Nat in the past, and had only used this form of address because he had been stung by the journalist's clumsy reference to Norton. Nat failed to realize this. Instead he concluded that Ormsby's present overtures were insincere, and that the whole matter had been thrashed out at a second meeting of the church council, after which the vicar had been delegated to call on him and patch up a peace. In this supposition he was entirely wrong. The vicar was acting, for once, on his own initiative. The chance of a reconciliation foundered on this snag.

"I'm afraid that I can't promise anything like that, Mr. Ormsby," he said, laying particular stress on the "Mr." and overcoming a spiteful impulse to drop the word altogether. "I came out against this proposal because I felt it to be wrong. I'd look ridiculous now if I stood up at a meeting and proposed splitting the money."

"Don't you think that you are being a little greedy?" said Mr. Ormsby softly.

Nat considered. He didn't; no, he damned well didn't. It was far greedier of the church council to want a share in the money so obviously intended for another and specific purpose. He said as much, and the vicar was silent for a moment, impatiently swinging a crossed leg.

Presently he said. "D'you mind if I speak frankly, old man?"

"Not a bit, Mr. Ormsby," replied Nat, but mentally raised a guard against the "old man"—a term which the vicar always employed when he was about to say something that might be hostilely received.

"Well, then," pursued the vicar, "I'm going to say that I'm not very happy about the provocative note in the new *Clarion.*"

"That's a pity," said Nat, now on firmer ground, "because I was thinking that I ought to get a good deal of support from the church."

"The church," said Mr. Ormsby kindly, "is not a belligerent advocate of sectional strife! Ah . . . ah . . ." as Nat opened his mouth to interrupt, "I know what you're going to say—that certain evils exist in our communal life and that it is the duty of a conscientious journalist to root them out. Naturally that is so. The British press has, I might say, a very good name in this respect. You recall *The Times'* exposure of the conditions of the sick and wounded in the Crimea, of course. Russell's fearless dispatches, I believe, led to the magnificent efforts of Miss Florence Nightingale."

"That was close on a century ago," growled Nat, who was beginning to dislike his visitor.

"Precisely," said the vicar, "but the press can still turn the spotlight of publicity on what it believes to be wrong and unjust without doing as you are doing."

"What *am* I doing?" asked Nat, genuinely anxious to know.

"Hurting people," said the vicar, with the air of a distinguished prosecuting KC, nailing the final lie of the principal witness for the defense. "You are hurting those people who are endeavoring, clumsily, perhaps, to do their best for the town."

Nat now felt more and more certain that Ormsby had been primed by the Baines-Martindale-Gelding bloc. He sounded altogether too glib. The conviction made the editor unreasonably angry. He was still feeling lonely and somewhat depressed, despite his visit to George Baker, Specialist and Craftsman, and despite Burton's account of Baines' unceremonious departure from the works.

If the vicar *had* allowed himself to be sent in as a peacemaker, it was obvious that his sympathies were not with the *Clarion*. Now that he came to think of it, the Rev. Ormsby had always been a wishy-washy creature, willing to compromise with bullies like Norton in order to maintain an uneasy peace within the parish.

"You preach Christ," he argued. "Wasn't Christ a rebel against the existing state of affairs?"

The vicar smiled, reflecting how foolish it was on the part of this self-righteous young man to choose the weapons of a professional opponent.

"Aren't you forgetting your Gospels, old man? Christ suffered Himself to be crucified between two thieves on Calvary."

Worsted, and not liking it, Nat lost his temper for a moment.

"That won't ever happen to you, Mr. Ormsby; you're too well in with the Scribes and Pharisees."

As repartee it was not bad, but Nat was not the sort of man who could get away with this kind of rejoinder. He was too tolerant and too kind-hearted, and it recoiled on him immediately. The vicar rose with the patient shrug of an early Christian martyr.

"I'm sorry, Nat," he said, with a humility that made the other man feel small enough to crawl into one of Sam's abandoned glue bottles lying on the window seat. "I'm quite prepared to discuss this matter quietly and reasonably. I'll do so again, at any time you wish. On the other hand, that sort of talk disarms me. If I preached humility, I must practice it."

So saying he walked out of the room and down the stairs, fully conscious of the editor's acute discomfiture, and so certain of having gained a crushing moral victory that he beamed at Beryl Hopper on his way out of the shop.

Nat lounged over to the window alcove and gloomily surveyed the High Street. He was beginning to wonder what was going wrong. Why had he been so boorish with that ass of a clergyman? Ormsby had probably meant well enough, and his offer to renounce his claim to half of the legacy and to make do with a tenth would, if accepted, have been a spendid advertisement for the *Clarion*'s new policy. It would have passed for a victory among local ex-servicemen, if any of them were sufficiently interested.

That was the point. Was anybody interested? If not, was it because his approach had been wrong and was still wrong? Did he really believe, himself, in what he was doing? Or was he merely paying a twenty-year-old debt of rancor to the *Clarion* readers, and hitting back in an attempt to level scores for a wasted youth? If so, he had better come to terms with Gerald right away, and go off for a tramping holiday somewhere to think things out. The question was, could he ever think things out? He had had enough time, in all conscience, between the arrival of Sam's letter offering him his old job back and his final acceptance last spring. Yet during all that time he never had thought things out. He had mooned and meandered and pottered until he found himself back in the office again.

Outside it was growing dusk. A few lights were beginning to show in the High Street. Opposite he could see Mr. Frobisher crawling in and out of his shop window to dress and undress the row of headless trunks that displayed his corsets. Nat's mind went off at a tangent again. He reflected, not for the first time, how oddly out of key was this occupation with Frobisher's local reputation as a Methodist lay preacher. Did the old man get a mild kick out of sliding brassieres over the generous busts of his decapitated ladies? Was it perhaps some sort of consolation for a life of chastity? He wondered what Frobisher's reactions were to the jokes that must have been made from time to time about those ripe curves that caught the eye of every man who walked past the shop. He must have heard some coarse comments during all the years that he had dressed the window.

Light footsteps sounded on the works stairs. Nat turned as the door opened and the light was switched on. He blinked for a moment in the sudden glare of the naked bulb.

Mollie Thorpe stood just inside the threshold, one gloved hand on the latch, the other holding a small leather attaché case.

EIGHTEEN

They regarded one another for a full half minute. Nat was too stunned to speak, and Mollie remained by the door, enjoying his astonishment. Then she closed the door, laid the attaché case on the editor's desk, went across and kissed him.

He did not ask for an explanation. That could wait. For the moment he was too overwhelmed, too warmed and too happy to have her again, to say anything at all. He remained for a moment, his arms round her waist, and then, abruptly, stood up and kissed her mouth over and over again.

After a while she gently disengaged herself and went back to the attaché case. Nat heard it jingle and wondered. She unclipped the fasteners and emptied the contents onto the desk. A cascade of small change poured out, coppers mostly, but a few folded and dirty notes and some small silver also.

"What the hell . . . ?" he began.

Mollie laughed. It was good to hear her laugh again.

"It's *Clarion* money," she said. "I knew that you'd never have the sense to collect it. I made a round of the agents on my way down from home. You're pretty short, aren't you, and I knew that you wouldn't borrow."

"I'll say I'm short!"

Imagine her thinking of that! Who said that women weren't practical when it came to pounds, shillings and pence?

"There's about eight-ten there," she told him. "It's your money, and you aren't obliged to bank it." She swept it into a soiled cotton bag which she had taken from the drawer of her old desk. "Now then, what's the latest?"

Nat told her everything over a pot of tea. She listened patiently, but most of it was known to her already. There were even one or two items of news that she could tell him. Gerald was trying to get into touch with the Imperial Press, a newspaper combine, at Paxtonbury. The Imperial Press, in addition to owning a daily and several periodicals, published the *Paxtonbury County Herald*, the *Clarion*'s nearest newspaper rival, covering the Sandcombe district. These people had made one or two tentative approaches to Sam in the past, and Sam had indignantly turned them down. Their price was not sufficiently high, for Sam had always held an inflated view of his firm's market value.

Nat was not greatly disturbed. Gerald couldn't sell out to the Imperial Press while he continued to hold shares.

Mollie had also heard about Baines' meeting. She had learned of it from Curzon, one of the garage proprietor's conductors, on the way up in the station bus. The conductor was not sure when it was to be, but had told her it would be soon. The Old Man had been in a proper stew for the last few days.

When they were both up to date with the news, Nat asked her the question which he had been afraid to ask since they began to talk.

"Mollie ... does this mean ... have you changed your mind? Have you come back for good?"

"I don't know, Nat; I honestly don't know," she said.

"But I thought ..."

She put down the kettle she was holding and came over to him again.

"Look, Nat. Don't let's go into that now; let's wait and see how it works out. I'm here now; that's all that matters, isn't it?"

"Yes," he said quietly, "that's all that matters, Mollie. Only, if you go again, I'm coming with you."

She kissed him, maternally, on the top of his head.

"Poor old Nat!" she said, and this time he did not mind the implied diminutive. It even seemed appropriate.

Mollie had not been unaware of what was happening at the *Clarion* office since her flight to London. Her father, who knew her rather better than she imagined, had posted on Nat's first *Clarion* and kept her informed by letter of developments inside the firm. This he found it easy to do, for his daily charwoman was the wife of Bert Hole, one of the compositors, and Mrs. Hole liked nothing better than to hover at the door of his study and gossip. She was ignorant of his link with the editor, and so talked without restraint. She herself had come down heavily on the side of the strikers, of whom her husband was one. Mr. Thorpe had let her run on, and supplemented his information from this source by a cosy chat with the manager of the Vane family's bank. On learning of Gerald's last move he had phoned his daughter, and casually let slip the information. He was not surprised, therefore, to see her absurd little hat bob round the laurels soon after the afternoon train arrived in town. He would have liked to talk it over with her, and half hoped that she would ask his advice, but she did not. After a quick wash and change she was out of the house again. He knew that she would make straight for the *Clarion*.

Even Mollie woud have found it difficult to explain to herself the reasons that prompted her sudden return. She had not enjoyed her stay in town—her first since prewar days. In the middle of a show she found herself thinking about the *Clarion* and the sort of stuff Nat would write during his first week as editor. When the paper arrived on Saturday morning she tore off the wrapping and let her breakfast go cold while she read through every word of the issue. In spite of herself, she began to giggle over the opera write-up, and only just prevented herself from shouting "Hear, hear!" when she had finished reading the attack on the church council. These were the sort of articles she had often longed to write, and she had to admit that Nat, when he had something to say, could write very well.

She tucked the paper into her bag—the huge bag that Nat had always teased her about—and hurried off to Kew Gardens. The beds looked disappointing and dismal in the late autumn sunshine, and she caught a bus to Hampton Court.

Here, in the Peter Lely gallery, she saw a seventeenth-century alderman looking exactly like Baines immediately after one of his motions had been defeated. Two portraits away there was a matron who might have been Miss Gelding's great-great-grandmother.

So it continued all the time. When she went shopping in Knightsbridge she found herself comparing the prices with those marked on handwritten tickets in Mr. Frobisher's window. She could not get Sandcombe and Nat out of her mind. Twenty or thirty times a day she wondered how Baines and Gerald and Gelding would react to Nat's first broadside. She hung about in her room hoping that her father would ring up again. When he did, she bombarded him with questions.

By Wednesday morning, about ten days after her flight, Mollie had had enough. She still put off making a final decision, but admitted to herself that staying on there, hearing everything at second or third hand, was merely stupid. She bought a pile of magazines to read on the train journey home, but she did not open them. Instead she sat and mused, wondering what she would do when she arrived back in Sandcombe. She felt that it would not do to rush breathlessly back to the works and give Nat the chance of gloating. But this was precisely what she did after hearing the bus conductor's remarks about Baines' protest meeting.

It was sweet of Nat not to gloat. As soon as she saw him she felt unutterably glad that she had returned. It was so good to feel that she was back in Sandcombe, on the one occasion when something mildly exciting was about to happen—was, indeed, already happening. And it was equally good to discover how badly he had missed her. She put off thinking about the future, about settling down in this odd little town. It was enough, for the present, to see the new *Clarion* on its feet, and then take stock.

She worked all the evening, folding with Beryl. Nat lent her one of Miss Morgan's abandoned overalls, and it hung about her like a small, brown tent.

Most of Thursday was spent making up the page adjacent to Nat's Declaration. The presence of Mollie and Beryl to do the folding enabled Nat to expand a little and cover some of the shorter items of general news. But before the front and back pages were on the machine the latter broke down again, and Burton, muttering blasphemies, had to spend nearly an hour fiddling with that complicated assortment of cog wheels, rollers and levers that was the womb of the *Sandcombe and District Clarion.*

"Bloody lucky job Bill Caxton never 'ad the 'andling o' this," grinned Bumble. "We'd've never 'eard no more about printin'!"

Burton got the machine running again by about five-thirty. For a worrying half hour he had been endeavoring to swallow his pride and go up to beg information from Skinner, who knew the machine better than a conscientious monk knows his beads. Under Skinner's dispensation the flatbed had often stopped, but it had always started again. Burton had not this amount of confidence in his own repairs.

Before they commenced the final run they held a brief conference in the editorial office.

Nat felt that Baines' meeting, which had been billed throughout the town and promised to be well attended, should be officially covered. Burton felt that the works ought not to be left unguarded, and, anyhow, there was too much folding and interleaving to be done.

The supplements were already folded, and had been stacked on trestle tables near the cropper. But, whereas one person could easily fold a double sheet, it needed two pairs of hands to insert the supplement into the freshly printed outside pages, and fold again to hold the inside sheet in position.

The men and girls on the *Clarion* staff had always worked in pairs at this stage of the weekly routine. Hole, Bennett and Miss Morgan—the quickest folders on the staff—had faced Bumble, and two of Miss Morgan's binding-room girls. The latter trio had "fed" the former and, in the course of years, their teamwork had acquired a speed much admired by Nat in happier days.

The same job had now to be done that evening, and there were more papers to fold, for Nat had budgeted for an extra five hundred. Burton, who would be feeding the machine, was not available for folding. Of the remaining members of the staff only Bumble had any experience in the work. It was agreed finally that Bumble should fold and Beryl feed him, and Nat would do his clumsy best on another folding board, feeding in his own supplements at the rate of about five per minute. Meanwhile Mollie could attend the meeting.

Nat had been anxious to cover the meeting himself, even if it meant slipping in through the stage door and keeping out of sight in one of the dressing rooms.

After discussion, however, they all agreed that if he was caught and thrown out by the stewards he would do their cause far more harm than good, whereas Mollie's entrance, via the front door, would hardly be questioned, especially if she chose her moment carefully. She was known to have left the staff a fortnight back.

So they got down to their respective tasks, and Mollie, tucking a fat notebook into her handbag, went down the yard steps and out into St. Luke's Road. It was already dotted with people, moving in ones and twos up the hill toward the lighted hall. As she closed the yard gates Mollie heard the preliminary, high-pitched whine of the Big Machine, when Burton threw the starter up to begin the final run.

The sound gave her an odd, queerly pleasant sensation in the solar plexus.

NINETEEN

St. Luke's hall held just over four hundred and fifty people, and it was very nearly full.

It had been drizzling outside, so that the entrance was stacked with damp umbrellas and mackintoshes. Two of Baines' garage staff, uncomfortable in stiff collars and self-conscious above buttonholes, had been pressed into service as ushers. They were both heavily built men, and Mollie felt that their employer had had in mind their possible use as chuckers-out. They were genial enough at the moment, however, and did their best to persuade townspeople to occupy the front seats. She noticed that their endeavors in this direction met with little success. Sandcombians always preferred back seats at public meetings and, while the first two rows of stalls were still empty, people were already standing at the rear of the hall.

The meeting had been advertised to begin at 7:15 P.M. By ten minutes past seven the platform was occupied, and Mollie was somewhat dismayed by its display of council solidarity.

Part of the operatic society's scenery remained in position. There was a highly colored backcloth depicting the ramparts of the castle in which Mr. Ivor Morgan, the ambitious hussar, had been incarcerated. Both wings, featuring stone staircases, had been moved back to make room for a semicircle of chairs, centering on the speaker's table. Pinned on the backcloth was a single handwritten bill. It read, "Speak Your Mind About Your Houses."

Mollie surveyed the platform from right to left.

On the extreme right, looking as though he was there on sufferance, was Major Martindale. He sat bolt upright and looked straight before him. Mollie guessed that Baines had been obliged to use all his powers of persuasion to get Martindale onto the platform. He was known to hate display of any sort, and seldom spoke in council. He was carefully dressed, however, down to the dazzling polish on his brown shoes. Mollie wondered if Baines had managed to persuade him to speak. It did not look like it, for the major's disapproving stare remained fixed on the audience, much as the eye of a doomed aristocrat must have rested upon the outer circle of the rabble in *Place de la Guillotine.*

On the major's right sat Colonel Grimstone-Beech. He had not yet had an opportunity to doze, and was constantly turning to Miss Gelding, on his right, cupping his ear and shouting, "Hey what?"

Miss Gelding was the one member of the platform group who looked as if she meant business. She had been offered, and had accepted, the only padded chair on the platform. It was one of the gilded properties not yet returned by the operatic society's stage manager, and, sitting erectly against its ornate back, it made her look not unlike Queen Victoria shortly after the lady-in-waiting had told the rude story. Her hands clasped the gold lions that reared at the extremity of the padded arms of the chair, and whenever she spoke to the colonel on her left, or to Mr. Norton on her right, she jerked herself out of alignment and then jerked upright again. Once the colonel must have made a little joke, for the stern cast of her features relaxed slightly and then, within a matter of seconds, reassumed their regal impassivity.

Norton's eyebrows were in evidence again, thick, bushy and forbidding. Mollie wondered how Norton could be maneuvered into the program without making it obvious to the audience that he was present that evening to promote church organs, not dwelling houses. The bill on the backcloth implied that the business of the meeting would be concerned, not with the general policy of the *Clarion,* but with the *Clarion's* forthcoming attack upon the current housing scheme of the council. Presumably Baines, the brain of the opposition, had worked upon the wounded vanity of all those whom the *Clarion* had attacked. He seemed to have been successful. The vicar, although not on the platform, was present in the hall, and Miss Gelding looked as though she had every intention of adding her voice to the general protest against the newspaper's recent policy.

Baines himself, as principal speaker of the evening, was helping Councillor Morgan with the duties of chairman, to which the little Welshman was not accustomed. Mollie guessed, and guessed correctly, that Baines had failed to persuade Major Martindale to occupy the chair, and had fallen back on Morgan as a substitute. Morgan was obviously flustered. He darted across the platform, almost knocking over the water carafe, which was gravely retrieved by the watchful Norton.

Angel, the town clerk, was also in attendance, but not on the platform, having been careful to point out that he attended "as a ratepayer, not as a town official." He was determined to sit on the fence as long as possible.

Having completed her inspection of the platform and front stalls, Mollie surveyed the body of the hall.

Almost all Sandcombe's prominent citizens were present.

Before the house lights were dimmed she noticed Mr. and Mrs. Frobisher, from the High Street, the latter still looking as if she could do with one of her husband's corsets. Close by was Mr. Frost, the milkman, chatting with Coates, the ironmonger. Mrs. Gage, of the Galleon, had responded to an invitation from one of her best customers, and left both bars in the charge of Ernie Potter, the erstwhile stage manager, reposing in him a trust that was subsequently betrayed, and might have cost him his job had he been less popular in the public bar.

Mr. and Mrs. Sleek were sitting near the center aisle, halfway down the hall. Even inside a hall Sleek continued to wear his tall hat—a source of some annoyance to Mrs. Scratton, the beach donkey-woman, who sat immediately behind him, and was not at all sure whether or not she was missing something on that account.

Twigger, the Free Church Union Secretary, was there. He attended every public meeting in Sandcombe, always on the lookout for somebody in need of redemption.

Twigger felt that any meeting, no matter how it began, might end in religious revival, and so offer unique opportunities to sharp-eyed shepherds. He was already pressing pamphlets into the unresisting hand of Giocomo, the Italian proprietor of the seafront café. The Italian, whose good nature was a byword as far away as Cragmouth, saw no harm in accepting them or in promising to study the literature before retiring to bed that night. He was a good Catholic, and loved everybody, even pamphlet evangelists. He stuffed so many of the folders into his pockets that Mr. Twigger was already regretting that he had brought along only a limited supply.

Vince, the young surveyor, was there too, but, like Angel, had wisely refrained from taking a seat on the platform. Eyeing him from the back of the hall sat Mr. Wainer, his predecessor, whom Baines' stewards had been doubtful of admitting, until they had received a whispered "Yerse, yerse, let 'em all come!" from their employer.

Eddie Nunn, the cycle agent's son, turned up, tactfully avoiding the stony glances of Beryl's father, Mr. Hopper, who had done a little detective work on his own since his daughter's appearance in court, and was now quite certain of the fact that Beryl had been led astray by a young waster whose father, he recalled, had once appeared in court himself on the far more serious charge of stealing a tire from a military vehicle.

The Thursday Whist Club was there to a tongue. The meeting clashed with their weekly drive in the institute hall adjoining, but such an occasion was not to be missed for the sake of a few hands of cards, particularly as Mrs. Stenner, the president, had been laid up with bronchitis during the weekend and had forgotten to send down her usual basket of fruit for the first prize.

The St. John's Ambulance duty squad attended, just in case of accidents. So did PC Tremlett, of the War Reserve, having turned out in response to the local inspector's request, the police being notoriously short of manpower at the time.

Nobody questioned Mollie's entry. She found a seat two rows from the back, next to a thickset little man with very prominent teeth, who had something to do with the opening and shutting of the harbor lock gates. Mollie did not know his name, but became more interested in him as the evening progressed, for he punctuated the speakers' remarks with all manner of weird interjections, none of which sounded like real words but more like a Congo dialect, such as "Uggereah!" "Zwotysay!" and "Caneer, caneer, s'pkup!" Shortly before the climax of the meeting Mollie translated the last bellow into "Can't hear, can't hear, speak up!" but she never found the hidden meaning of the menacing "Uggereah!" or "Zwotysay!"

The hum of greeting and casual conversation faded as the lights went down and Chairman Morgan stood up. There was an expectant hush in obedience to the Welshman's raps on the speaker's table; but somebody not very expert at the job was handling the lights offstage. The ambers were suddenly switched off and replaced by blues, a change that made the semicircle on the platform look like pantomime demons. Hearing a shout of alarm, the fumbling electrician hurriedly transformed the platform into a storm at sea by nervously tugging red, blue and amber switches in quick succession.

" 'Ere, 'arf a tick, 'arf a tick!" shouted Baines, above the laughter. "We ain't made no charge to the audience, Charlie."

Another, less satirical, burst of laughter greeted this sally, and Mollie rather admired the garage proprietor for thus saving the situation.

The amber glow returned to the platform to reveal Miss Gelding looking like Queen Victoria being shot at in The Mall.

The audience settled down. Chairman Morgan, with a nervous glance at Charlie in the wings, advanced to the footlights.

He was greeted by a faint clapping, which was just what the chairman needed.

His introduction, notwithstanding, proved rather flat, for Morgan was anything but a good public speaker, and had not had much opportunity to get his briefing from Baines.

He drifted on aimlessly for a few moments—wouldn't detain them long, plenty of other speakers better qualified to talk—the usual preamble of the formal chairman who is put up to break the ice but somehow only succeeds in lowering the temperature for the next speaker.

Mr. Morgan, however, had a minor duty to perform, in addition to that of introducing Baines and his fellow speakers. He had been charged with presenting the resolution.

The resolution had been composed by Major Martindale. It had the simplicity and directness of an ultimatum issued to recalcitrant tribesmen.

Having arrived at the point in his speech where he had used up every well-worn phrase in his vocabulary, Mr. Morgan groped for the resolution, which he felt certain had been in his hand when he began to speak. He glanced down, and was disconcerted to find both hands empty. He tried his left-hand jacket pocket, then his right, then his left-hand trouser pocket, then his right trouser pocket, but nothing emerged. He was about to stake everything on a plunge into his hip pocket when Baines leaned forward and thrust a sheet of paper into his hand. The chairman said, "Ahhhh, here it is!" and added, to anticipate the general titter, "I was beginning to be afraid that I'd lost it."

The resolution read:

> That this meeting expresses complete confidence in the council's endeavors to select a suitable site for Sandecombe's housing estate; that the townspeople present this evening prefer *an immediate solution* of the pressing housing problem to any alternative scheme involving indefinite delay.

It was certainly cunning, thought Mollie. There was nothing about hills, nothing about distance from the town, nothing that any ratepayer could criticize. The sole emphasis was on speedy solution to a problem that was bound to concern, in one way or another, every man, woman and child in the hall. Just houses! Houses now or at some far distant date?

Quite properly, the reading of the resolution was greeted with a burst of clapping and a few scattered shouts of "Hear, hear!"

The man with the prominent teeth sitting next to Mollie cried "Uggereah!" but immediately qualified it with "Caneer, caneer, s'pkup!"

Morgan now thought it time to retire, and backed toward the speaker's table, where Baines had already half risen in his chair. Martindale so far relaxed as to give a fierce, emphatic nod, while Grimstone-Beech stirred in the dream that was taking him across the Modder River in a bullock cart.

Miss Gelding began to look more like Queen Victoria receiving an illuminated address from the loyal citizens of Stoke-on-Trent.

Baines advanced to the footlights. He enjoyed public speaking, having the invaluable asset of immense self-assurance, notwithstanding his strong Middlesex accent, which took complete control when he began to address an assembly of more than three people.

He had a naïve trick of taking an audience into his confidence, almost as though he were persuading them to accept rationed goods without coupons. His humor was a little ponderous, but it usually went over quite well, for he ensured the success of all his little jokes by starting the laugh himself and encouraging his listeners to join in when it was well established.

"Now les looker this 'ousin' problem fair an' square," he began, raising both arms as though the entire estate was held firmly between his huge, red palms. "I called this meetin' because o' certain hundercurrents in the town. I'm not goin' ter say wot these hundercurrents har. But I don't mind sayin' what they'll end up in, an' that's delay, hindeffernit delay, ladies an' gentlemen."

He waited for encouragement from the hall, but none came, either because the audience was too interested in what he was saying, or else because it imperfectly understood his veiled reference to last week's letter in the *Clarion*, which hardly anybody in the hall had read.

So he brought his extended palms together with a resounding smack and continued.

"You want 'ouses. We all want 'ouses. Ah, my friends . . ." and here Mollie knew that Baines was about to adopt his familiar role of public benefactor, who wept to see the miseries of the inadequately housed, clothed and fed, "you don't see these things like I see 'em. You don't 'ave the 'eart-renderin' letters pushed under yer door, letters from some of our lads 'oo was quick enough ter leave their 'omes when Ole Narstie was knockin' at the door."

The popular reference to the late Adolf Hitler brought its reward in the form of a polite giggle. Baines decided that the vein was worth exploiting.

They (our lads) downed tools quick enough *then,* and secured Sandcombe from the attentions of Mr. Himmler. What of today? They had come home to share front-parlor floors with their brothers and sisters, in the dilapidated homes of their aged parents. His heart, having already been rendered, now bled. It was indeed a poor reward for Alamein, for Arnhem and for D Day.

At this point Councillor Baines suddenly ceased rolling his head from side to side, and struck the attitude of Lord North defending Gibraltar.

All this was true. Nobody could deny it. Yet there were some—yes, he'd go as far as to name them—there were some, including the local editor, himself an ex-serviceman, who dared to question the council's wisdom in tackling the housing problem without delay, and were actually pestering the committee to adopt some hare-brained scheme of laying out the Flats as a pleasure ground!

Put like this, Nat's case seemed dangerously thin, and Mollie got the impression that Baines was on the way to securing a notable victory. She glanced round the hall. Everyone seemed to be listening attentively. There was no sign of heckling or of opposition.

Baines must have sensed this, for his rocklike features relaxed into a warm and generous smile.

"You won't stand for that, ladies an' gentlemen, you won't be done aht of yer 'ouses at this stage? If you do stand for it, all I can say is that you deserve to live in coal cellars for good. I alwus say, ladies an' gentlemen, that a town gets the guvvernment it deserves. Some of us up here 'ave tried to do our best fer the tahn. If you give us yer backin' we'll stick inter the job, good an' proper. That's why I'm astin' you, 'ere an' now, to raise yer 'ands an' vote on this proposition that the chairman's read to yer."

There was a stir in the hall, but Baines was not quite ready to hand over to the next speaker, presumably Miss Gelding, or Colonel Grimstone-Beech. He fluttered his hand for silence.

"Now, 'arf a tick, 'arf a tick," he shouted. "I'm not standin' up 'ere and 'avin' all the say. Is there anyone 'ere who'd like to ast a question or two on the 'ousin' scheme? They're welcome. We don't mind standin' to our guns, none of us."

Mollie looked anxiously round the hall. There was absolute silence. Sandcombe audiences were not afraid to ask questions at public meetings, but they were always afraid to ask the first question. Mollie felt that if only somebody would get up and ask something—anything—questions would soon follow and the trend of the meeting would become less one-sided. It seemed to her that the silence lasted for fully five minutes. Finally it was broken by Baines himself, who said, "Well, ladies an' gents, it looks to me as if everybody was . . ."

TWENTY

Mollie found herself on her feet. She hated this sort of thing. It always made her feel slightly sick. But if nobody was going to get up and question Baines, the resolution would certainly be passed, and, if it was passed, all those who had voted for it would feel obliged to stand by it when the Declaration page of the *Clarion* revealed the true facts the following morning.

She held fast to the back of the chair immediately in front of her. The man with the prominent teeth hissed "Caneer, caneer, s'pkup!" and, for some reason, Mollie found his gibberish encouraging.

She called out in a clear voice, "Mr. Chairman!"

Four hundred and fifty faces turned on her like so many searchlights. She felt rather like a bomber caught in enemy beams.

These faces were not hostile, however, but merely curious.

Baines saw Mollie standing away at the back of the hall, and grinned. He liked an intelligent question or two, for lack of questions always implied lack of interest.

"Lady down there . . . she's not afraid . . . trust the ladies to ast the questions I always say . . ."

There was a titter, and Mollie felt her cheeks burning. It was obvious that Baines had failed to recognize her over the distance separating her row from the brightly lit platform.

"I'd like to know," began Mollie, and the pitch of her voice seemed to her unnaturally high, "I'd like to know, assuming that the houses are built at Hilltop, how the council propose that their tenants should get to and fro from work, especially at lunchtime?"

Baines pulled one end of his nicotine-stained mustache. Odd question that! Genuine or inspired? Hard to say. Possibly genuine, the originator being a prospective tenant—shop girl, perhaps. He made a quick decision. Better give her a civil answer, particularly as her question must have been heard by everyone present.

But he was hardly the person to answer a question dealing with transport facilities. Might look bad—bound to, in fact. He turned hastily to Morgan, the chairman, and the Welshman, accurately interpreting his look, jumped to his feet.

"Sensible question that," he said. "The council has been into it already. I think we can be sure of extended bus services. The traffic commissioners have been approached by Councillor Baines."

It was, in one way, a stupid reply. Until the word was out the majority of the audience had not linked Baines with bus routes. Everyone in the hall, of course, knew that he controlled local transport, but he had been speaking that evening as a councillor, not as a garage proprietor, and as a councillor he and his comments had been accepted. It was not that Morgan's indiscretion let the cat out of the bag, but it revealed the tip of the cat's ear, and a restrained murmur from the hall signified as much.

Mollie took maximum advantage of the slip. Her voice, steadier now, rang clearly across the hall.

"Is it not a fact, Mr. Chairman, that Councillor Baines controls all the local bus services?"

The effect of the remark was immediate. A roar, half humorous, half protesting, rose from the hall, and above the general din odd and scattered shouts of "Shame!" were heard. The main effect on the audience, however, was one of amusement. Baines might be a popular councillor, but even popular councillors are fair game, and it was exhilarating to see civic legs pulled in public.

If Baines himself had not been brooding about the matter for nearly a week, he would have kept his head and bellowed with laughter. In that way he would have beaten Mollie on her own ground. If he could have rapped out a humorous reply, "Me? Why, I'm going to make me blinkin' forchune, didn't y'know?" the danger would have passed. As it was, he neither laughed nor joked. Leaping to his feet, he shouted something to Morgan, of which the only word that the audience could catch was "personal."

Morgan, looking very flustered, turned back to the hall again and shouted, just as the roar was subsiding, "That question is out of order. We think it's very personal."

The roar broke out again—shouts of "Hear hear!" and "Shame!" mingling with "No, no!" and renewed laughter. For a few moments the chairman lost control of the meeting.

Mollie, who was standing up again, quite failed to make herself heard, but across the hall she saw one or two other members of the audience on their feet. At her elbow the lock-gate attendant was still shouting "Uggereah!" occasionally varied by a sinister "Zwotsay!"

It was Major Martindale who restored order for a brief period. Realizing that Morgan was going to pieces, he stood up, adjusted his broad cravat, and marched downstage, dismissing the unhappy chairman with a peremptory tap on the shoulder. Morgan retired, still talking, and Baines, who had now realized his error and was attempting to repair the breach in his defenses, moved up beside the major, the two of them standing side by side in front of the speaker's table.

With the advance of Major Martindale, for whom most Sandcombians felt a grudging respect, the audience became quiet for a moment. It was quite obvious, however, that they had begun to enjoy themselves, and a number of appreciative chuckles were heard.

"The chairman is fully justified in ruling that question out of order," began Major Martindale. "In my opinion it is both unfair and irrevelant. We are not here to question our good friend's personal honor as a councillor."

A man in a raincoat stood up at the back of the hall.

"Nobody has questioned it," he began, and the major, satisfied that the interrupter was pro-Baines, did not shout "Silence!" as he was inclined to do. It was a pity that he did not, for the man in the raincoat added, after a brief pause, *"But if the cap fits, wear it!"*

Uproar began again. There were more cries of "Shame!" "Shut up!" "Sit down!" "Mr. Chairman!" and, of course, "Caneer, caneer s'pkup!" from Mollie's neighbor, who was not alone in being unable to hear.

Mollie glanced to her right, and noticed that the man in the raincoat had advanced into the center aisle. When he moved within the orbit of the platform lights she recognized him. It was Otto, and he appeared to be slightly tipsy. He waved his arms as he moved forward.

"If it is all above board, why are you holding this meeting . . . ?" shouted Otto, moving nearer the platform.

"Stewards! Where are the stewards!" called Martindale, standing firm in front of the agitated occupants of the platform.

Baines' two garage hands moved up in Otto's wake, and one of them laid a firm hand on the belt of his coat. A scuffle began in the aisle, so that Baines, now very red in the face, again shouted "Order, order!"

Mollie got a good deal of subsequent entertainment from speculating what might have happened if the climax of the evening had not occurred at that precise moment. Otto might have been ejected with the acquiescence of most of those present. Baines might have preached another little sermon, concerning the folly of allowing town rowdies to interrupt public meetings. With Martindale's expert help he might well have restored order and brought the meeting to a satisfactory conclusion.

But at that moment Otto, and the two stewards in tow, drew level with a gangway seat occupied by Dan Brewer, who delivered coals for the Sandcombe Fuel Company and was one of Otto's regular drinking companions. Brewer, a big, good-natured fellow, fond of his beer in the Galleon public bar, was greatly attached to Otto, who had paid for several vats of it over the last ten years.

Observing one of Baines' henchmen lay a hand on his benefactor's shoulder, as a preliminary to getting a good grip and running him down the gangway to the foyer, Brewer lumbered to his feet and hitched his trousers. Ignoring his wife's shrill advice to "Let-be-an'-mind out!"

the coalman hit the nearest steward very firmly on the ear, demanding of him, somewhat too late for it to matter, "Who he thought he was a-pushing of?"

The steward, reeling from the blow, fell against Mr. Sleek, and his impact did more damage to the famous stovepipe hat than twenty-five years' wear and tear of winter funerals had achieved. Mr. Sleek's protests were lost in the uproar, Brewer's shrewd blow being vociferously cheered from the back of the hall.

Several things then began to happen at once. Mollie had a fleeting glance of Otto, shouting up at Major Martindale from the edge of the shallow orchestra pit. Close by, the second steward seemed to be measuring an operation scar with Brewer (for, although not actually hitting one another, they were pressing their chests together and exchanging shouts at a range of about an inch and a half). At this moment Special Constable Tremlett came into action, moving with the finality of the Imperial Guard at Waterloo, and not even turning aside to examine Sleek's battered hat, indignantly thrust forward for his inspection.

The platform group had all edged toward the footlights, and Mollie's neighbor, the winch minder, was on his feet, spraying the collar of the man in front with a fine rain of saliva.

Miss Gelding, now standing, looked like Queen Victoria receiving the news that Albert would not recover.

Then it happened.

Something stirred in the fringes above the stage, and there was a noticeable dwindling of interruptions. Inch by inch, as though operated by an uncertain hand, a large canvas backcloth came down in front of the serried battlements of the Hapsburg fortress. By the time that the cloth was halfway down an awed silence had supplanted the bedlam preceding it, a silence enduring for some ten seconds while the audience took in the change of scenery. Then the silence gave way to a gale of laughter, a din that was heard as far away as the bar of the Maltster's Arms, across the road.

The backcloth carried a rough but easily recognizable cartoon. It depicted a huge Baines, in the somewhat gaudy uniform of one of his own busmen, taking fares from an endless stream of passengers labeled "Ratepayers," who were being shepherded into a bus parked at the foot of a winding mountain road. At the summit of the mountain, in the top left-hand corner of the picture, was a huddle of red-roofed houses marked "Homes for Heroes."

The cartoon was extraordinarily well done. It was, in fact, the work of a Specialist and Craftsman, who at that moment was descending the ladder from the stage catwalk to the stage door. Another figure slipped out into St. Luke's Road behind him—Ernie Potter, barman of the Galleon, and sometime stage manager of the Sandcombe Amateur Operatic Society. Ernie also was fond of a joke, and had not yet forgiven Miss Gelding.

With their backs to the source of the audience's laughter, it was a moment or two before the platform group turned to inspect the backcloth. Even then they were too close to the caricature to appreciate all its implications. Baines, however, quickly recognized himself, and dashed for the catwalk ladder, followed by Norton and Martindale. He was just in time to hear the stage door slam. Grimstone-Beech dozed on. Miss Gelding sought the cover of the familiar dressing room. She looked like Queen Victoria when they said that Albert was dead.

TWENTY-ONE

Gerald had not put in an appearance at the public meeting. He thought it best to keep out of sight.

Having contacted the Imperial Press and made an appointment with one of their directors for the following week, he felt that there was nothing more he could do but wait developments. But Gerald was not a man able to clear his mind of immediate problems and relax. He felt that he ought to be doing something—anything was better than to sit at home reading the papers or to drift cautiously around the town avoiding people who might wish to discuss his troubles with him.

Gerald hated discussing his private affairs with townspeople whose sympathy was in doubt. It seemed to him, on the few occasions when he had discussed recent events with acquaintances, that they did not care two straws who was in command of the Clarion Press, but were merely interested in the personal relationships of the directors. Gerald did not feel inclined to satisfy that sort of curiosity.

Quite apart from all this, he was homesick—homesick for his office, his customers and his efficiency charts. He seemed to have walked out of his beloved surroundings twenty years ago.

There had been times during the last few days when Gerald would have patched it up with Nat at almost any price. He worshiped law and order, and the strike distressed him. He had no real faith in its effectiveness, and it hurt him to see old employees like Skinner and Bennett, who should have been bending over *his* typecases, lounging at street corners and taking the air on the seafront. The previous week most of his resentment had been reserved for Nat, as author of all the idiotic strife and wastage. The meeting poster changed that. He began to feel more resentful against interfering customers.

Gerald saw the poster exhibited on a rotting hoarding

on the half-cleared site of Sandcombe's sole bomb crater, near the dock. Its handwritten crudity offended him. He read the announcement of Thursday night's meeting, and moved thoughtfully away, nursing a grievance that seemed to grow bigger and more irksome every day.

What right had that coarse fellow Baines to hold a public meeting about the Clarion Press? What business had he, a man who crawled about under secondhand cars, to express views on how a printing works and newspaper should be conducted? Gerald found himself almost sympathizing with Nat, and certainly sharing some of the editor's indignation. People like that wanted showing up. Gerald quite hoped Nat would lay it on good and hard in Friday's *Clarion*.

He drifted home to Cliff Terrace and reread the previous week's letter in the *Clarion* correspondence columns. It did not seem strong enough to express all that he now felt about Baines. So he reread the operatic notice and was surprised to discover that it no longer frightened him. If Nat had been there at that moment they might have shaken hands right away.

By 7 o'clock on Thursday evening Gerald, unable to settle to a book, had put on his neat black greatcoat, pulled his black trilby hat rather lower than usual over his brow, and strolled down to St. Luke's hall, where he stood at a distance and watched the people enter. Ten minutes later he skirted the building and passed round behind the church institute to approach the stage door.

He hung about for a while feeling rather like a burglar's lookout man. Then he tried the door, and found it open. After another cautious pause he entered and made his way along the narrow corridor behind the scenery to the gents' dressing room. He could have heard the speeches a good deal better from the ladies' lavatory, but Gerald felt that his dignity would suffer if he was caught eavesdropping inside a powder room.

He sat down just inside the door, and did not switch the light on. By leaving the door ajar he could hear fairly well, although he felt rather miserable sitting there alone in the dark.

He heard Councillor Morgan's faulty opening, and was glad when Baines began to speak, for the garage proprietor's voice penetrated the dressing room, and Gerald could easily hear all that was said. Soon after Baines started, Gerald's attentive ear caught the sound of stealthy footsteps in the passage outside. Two men passed the open door. They were whispering, and all he caught of their remarks was ". . . I'd like to be in front and see his dial"— a comment which gave him the impression that at any rate the two newcomers did not belong to the platform party. The impression was strengthened by their stealthy conduct.

Reassured after they had passed the dressing-room door he peeped into the passage. There was just sufficient light issuing from the wings for him to see Mr. Baker, Specialist and Craftsman, climbing the ladder that led to the catwalk.

Gerald had as much curiosity as the next man. He crept along to the foot of the ladder and stared into the darkness above him. He heard the other man say, "When did you fix it?"

And Baker's laconic reply, "Dinnertime!"

That was all, but there followed quite a lot of rustling and creeping about twenty feet above the stage. It seemed to Gerald that Baker was monkeying with the scenery on the far side of the catwalk and that his companion, the younger man, was doing the same thing immediately above Gerald's head.

So interested did Gerald become that he forgot Baines' speech for a brief interval, and his attention was only reclaimed by the councillor's loud demand for questions.

After that Gerald went back to the dressing room, where he heard, with growing satisfaction, the increasing tempo of the disturbances in the hall. He recognized Mollie's voice, and found himself thinking, a little sourly, "She wouldn't have stood up there and spoken like that for me!" The thought made him harden his heart against Nat. His memory went back to the first day when Nat had returned and had asked him about the girl who had filled his place during the war. He might have known that something would come of it. Nat Hearn was infernally sure of himself, despite his reputation for excessive amiability. He wondered if Mollie Thorpe was in love with the idiot, or whether she regarded all this ridiculous business as an enjoyable piece of tomfoolery of which full advantage should be taken in such a dull town as Sandcombe.

As the uproar in the hall increased, Gerald was tempted from his retreat, and crept down almost as far as the electricians' switchboard. He heard a few bad-tempered exchanges between platform personalities as the meeting got out of hand. Baines shouted across to Morgan ". . . Well, do something, cancher? You're the blarsted chairman!"

Gerald had his eye glued to a chink in the backcloth when he heard a prolonged rustle over his head. He flinched, instinctively, suddenly remembering the two men on the catwalk, but before he could move something hissed down from above and completely shut off his view of the stage. He heard the roar of laughter that greeted the appearance of the cartoon, and only then, as he scampered down the stairs a few yards in front of Baker and his partner, did he remember the former's reputation for undignified practical jokes.

The recollection doubled the speed of his retreat. Gerald scuttled round behind the church institute and into the dripping shrubbery beyond. Pausing here for a moment to catch his breath, he could still hear the noise of the audience inside the hall. There could be no doubt about it; Baines' meeting had been a complete flop, and that meant that, when the next *Clarion* appeared, Nat ought to be in a position to enlist considerable support.

During the past few days Gerald had felt outraged. His whole conception of business methods, of how to conduct oneself among one's neighbors, of life itself as lived in Sandcombe, had been turned upside down. He had been successively alarmed, disappointed, flouted, maddened, humiliated and mocked. He had known that some of the people whom he passed in the street were laughing at him, and this hurt more than anything else. He had seen the thing that counted most in his life—his business—in what he considered grave danger of closing down. And most of the time, during this nightmare period, he had been lonely and miserable. But all this had not caused him to lose his head. He could still think clearly, and without allowing vindictiveness to warp his judgment.

As the tempest of sound reached him through the open vents of St. Luke's hall he knew, with absolute certainty, that somehow, at some time, he must make his peace with his partner.

He groped his way out of the shrubbery and hurried off down St. Luke's Road to the yard entrance of the Clarion works.

Climbing the steps, he tried the works door. Before he passed inside he noticed something odd. The Big Machine was silent. It was Thursday evening, about 8:30, and for the first time within his memory he failed to hear the steady clumpety-clump of the flatbed at that hour. He knew then that something was wrong.

Gerald found Bumble just inside the door. He was sitting disconsolately on a bale of newsprint, eating from a bag of chips.

Across the works he saw Burton, picking glumly through a pile of type on the machine bed. Nat was nowhere to be seen. Gerald walked across to Burton, who looked up, still glumly, and then went on working.

"What's up, Burton?" asked Gerald, trying to conceal the excitement in his voice.

For answer Burton waved a grimy hand over the type.

"Lug snapped," he grunted, and turned away again.

Gerald made a closer inspection of the flatbed. One of the lugs—a little tongue of steel that held the worn rollers in place beside the bed—was missing. Its short base was a jagged spur of new-looking metal. A clean break.

Gerald knew then what must have occurred. When the lug snapped, the roller which it held had skidded across the typeface, breaking off and deeply scarring the type. The Declaration page had suffered severly and it was obvious that no *Sandcombe and District Clarion* would emerge from that machine for some time to come. Glancing at the jagged lug again, Gerald doubted whether even

Skinner would be able to put the machine back into commission.

He stood there for a moment longer, wondering why this had never happened before. They had had trouble—minor, adjustable trouble—with that machine for years, but never anything like this. Nobody could possibly have forseen such a freak occurrence.

"Where's Nat?" he asked, and his voice was almost gentle. Gerald had been a printer all his life. He could imagine, none better, how Nat was feeling now that this had happened.

Burton jerked his head toward the wooden steps that led to the office, and Gerald left him.

When he reached the landing he could see a light in the editorial. The door was ajar. He walked quietly across the uncarpeted floor and looked in. Nat was sitting in the window seat with his back to the door. He called.

"Hullo, Nat!"

The journalist started and looked round. Gerald thought that he had never seen a man look more tired or dispirited. Nat looked as if he had not eaten or slept for days. His face gave Gerald a physical shock. He came into the room and closed the door.

"I suppose you've seen it," said Nat, feeling in his pockets for a cigarette and bringing out an empty packet, which he flung down.

Gerald nodded and fumbled for his cigarette case—the case he kept for customers. It was full. Gerald had had no customers lately. He pushed it across to his partner, who took one, absently.

"We've got to make it up, Nat!" he said, quietly.

Nat did not answer immediately. The initiative had passed to Gerald. In their other two encounters since the quarrel it had been Nat who attacked and Gerald who remained on the defensive. Tonight it was different, not only because of the broken machine downstairs, but because Gerald possessed the latest information regarding the town meeting. These two factors gave Gerald more confidence.

"Come on, Nat. Call it a day. There's no sense in keeping this up; it'll ruin the pair of us. Tone down the paper and I'm with you, even against Baines, if you don't lose your head."

It was a generous offer, and Nat, hearing Gerald's voice as though he were hailing him from a passing ship across a hundred yards of water, knew that it was generous. He felt glad that he had never disliked Gerald. The crash, which had wrecked the Declaration page of the *Clarion* half an hour before, had revealed to the journalist the utter futility of fighting this battle alone, without money, without influence, with plant that would always break down at crucial moments and leave him with less than a quarter of his quota printed. He felt, after a mere glance at the machine bed, that Mollie had been right all along. The struggle was not worth the effort. If he had had a few thousand in the bank or, even without capital, if a section of the town had shown some indication of supporting him, of wanting a good weekly paper, then the struggle might have been worth while. As it was, the whole thing had become tiresome and absurd. One couldn't run a business without money. Every crusade needed a fighting fund. He and Mollie between them would be hard put to it to raise two hundred pounds.

He had forgotten Baines' meeting. It had ceased to count, in any case. He only wished that Mollie would come back so that he could tell her that he was ready to accept her advice and pack in, now, at this moment. The next day's *Clarion* might go hang. Sandcombe could do without it for once.

It was a moment or two before Nat replied. When he spoke, it seemed to Gerald that he weighed every word. The tone that he employed matched his haggard appearance.

"I've been a bit of an ass, Gerald. I know that now and, as far as you're concerned, I'm genuinely sorry. I hope you'll believe that, because I know what this place means to you, what it has always meant to you. As far as I can see, it doesn't matter what a person's sold on so long as he's sold on something. The trouble is that most of the people round here aren't sold on anything, not even on their own futures. It's because of that, that I'm going to pack in."

"Pack in?"

Gerald was more than surprised; he was a little alarmed. Pack in and hand the business, paper and all, back to him! What the devil would he do with it on his own? It dawned on Gerald, as never before, that the responsibility of a newspaper, even of a local rag, was a frightening thing. He did not want it unshared. He did not want to begin sharing it with anyone else—a new, perhaps modern, young man, with even more dangerous ideas. Nat's ideas about editorial policy might be heretical, they might even lose the firm a certain amount of business, but they at least emanated from somebody with whom he was familiar. He could, of course, sell out, but in contacting the Imperial Press earlier in the week he had never intended going so far.

He had only toyed with the idea of holding an Imperial Press offer over Nat's head as a bargaining weapon. At this moment he was sure of two things: first, that he did not want to sell, and second, that he did not want to start all over again with a new partner.

He was about to protest, with an eagerness that would have puzzled Nat, but at that moment a hubbub broke out from below. It sounded as though several people had entered the works, and their voices were raised in argument. Gerald experienced a new surge of indignation. What did people take the premises for? The local forum?

He would have hurried down into the works himself, but almost immediately hurrying footsteps were heard on the staircase, and Mollie, her cheeks bright with excitement, flung open the works door.

She ignored Gerald, directly addressing Nat.

"You've got to do something about that machine, Nat. Baines' meeting was a huge flop, and half the town'll be with you."

Gerald bit his lip. He was half inclined to order the girl out of the office, but he saw Nat's expression change. It told him that the man's professional appetite for news, for sensation, had been whetted.

"A flop? Go on. Tell me!"

Mollie hurried across and seized both his hands. Gerald felt that she behaved as though they were alone, and that he had ceased to count.

She began to pour out the story of the meeting, the questions, the scuffle, the cartoon. She had later news than Gerald, who had left during the first big laugh. The meeting had broken up in disorder. Baines had tried to speak again, and had been shouted down. The cartoon, primarily intended as a joke, had had a deadly effect on the main purpose of the assembly. Sandcombe had seen through Baines' camouflage, and jeered, though more out of high spirits, it is true, than indignation.

All at once the office seemed full. Odd people, some of whom had no business to be there at all, kept crowding up from the works. Burton was there, arguing with Nat and doing most of the talking, the girl Beryl Hopper was there, with her father, still wearing his trilby hat, confound him, and in earnest consultation with old Mr. Wainer, as though the pair of them had been directors of the firm discussing a new line of stock. Skinner appeared from below, and Gerald noted, uneasily, that he was already in his shirt-sleeves. Bumble was shouting something to Mollie, who was still describing the meeting, and with far too much gesticulation, as Gerald thought.

There was nothing but talk, talk, talk, and Gerald felt that none of it had much to do with him or his business. It was all about the *Clarion,* the housing scheme, Baines, the council and the meeting. Suddenly he felt defeated, sick to death of all this silly chatter and petty strife. He turned to leave the place, but Nat, noticing the movements, called across to him.

"Just a minute, Gerald. . . . You're in on this!"

Gerald paused on the threshold of the landing.

"What have all these people got to do with us?" he asked sulkily, and looked round the room with evident disapproval.

Nat came across to him and caught him by his arm.

"They're going to help, if it's OK with you."

"I don't see . . ." began Gerald, but Nat cut him short. He seemed repossessed of all his old confidence. What an

oddly mercurial sort of fellow he was, to be sure! thought
Gerald; but he edged into the room, and the chatter died
away.

"It's Skinner's idea," said Nat, nodding at the little foreman, who stood sucking his cherrywood pipe just inside
the works door. "He's suggested that we dig out Aunt
Maria and finish the run on her. If we can get away with
it tonight, we can make other arrangements next week."

It was odd how they had all forgotten Aunt Maria—the
old, old flatbed (born 1881) that had printed Sam's first
Clarion all those years ago. Sam never bought new machinery. Maria was thirdhand when he assembled her in
the nineties. She had been partially dismantled and used
as a dumping ground for spare parts, type and cleaning
materials by two generations of untidy printers, too lazy to
find accommodation in the overcrowded premises. Subsequently she had been replaced by a slightly more modern
machine, the one that had broken down now. Sam, accustomed to keeping his eye on bargain columns of county
weeklies, had picked that one up for a few pounds in a
Paxtonbury auction room.

Skinner had remained faithful to Maria. Nat recalled
his comments of years past, when he had been tinkering
with the present machine during temporary breakdowns
on Thursday nights. "We'd've done better ter stick by
Maria," he used to say. "She took 'er time, but she never
went back on us."

And here was Skinner, ringleader of the strike, suggest-
ing that they set to and rehabilitate Maria at this time of
night.

Skinner's change of heart had not been engendered by
the meeting. He had not been present in St. Luke's hall,
although he had heard all about it by now. He had heard
also that the flatbed had collapsed a quarter of the way
through the final run, and that news, notwithstanding the
strike, drew him into the works as though he had been a
blob of quicksilver and the broken flatbed a magnet.

For nearly forty-two years Skinner had stood on his little
box beside one or other of the *Clarion*'s big machines and
fed the newsprint into the guides. His life had become

a rhythm which reached its weekly climax every Thursday evening. Not once had he missed a Thursday night through illness; even his annual holiday began on a Friday morning and ended on Thursday midday, just before the paper went to press. It was the strength of this habit that had caused him to strike, for fear of being forced to seek work elsewhere, but all that day, Thursday, he had been ill at ease.

He had drifted about the town in a state of nervous misery. Bennett and Hole tried, and failed, to comfort him. He could not help reminding himself that down at the works someone—a clumsy amateur, no doubt—would be feeding *Clarions* into the Big Machine. By 10:30 P.M. a new paper would be born, and he would not be there. He felt like Napoleon's chief of staff watching, from a neutral window, the Prussian troops marching on Waterloo; but Skinner was not the type to fling himself from the window in a fit of remorse, as Bertheir had done. Instead he dawdled down toward the Clarion yard and listened to the unsteady clumpety-clump of the Big Machine, trundling out the first copies of the paper. He remained there for the best part of an hour, and then mooched up to the Maltster's Arms opposite St. Luke's hall. His beer tasted flat.

There he heard the news of the crash from Bert Hole, who had it from Bennett, who got it from Bumble via Beryl Hopper in the chip shop. Skinner hesitated no longer. He stayed only long enough to collect Bennett and Hole from the public bar of the Galleon. Then he went off round to the yard as fast as his short legs could carry him, arriving soon after Gerald.

Gerald did not hear about this until much later. Standing on the threshold of the office, he heard Nat outline his plan. Skinner and the two journeymen were to assemble Maria and connect her to the power. Burton was to reset the damaged columns. Bumble was to watch the casting. Meanwhile Nat himself, Mollie and Beryl would push on with folding. Mr. Hopper volunteered to clear away the stitching machine, which occupied such a position as to preclude the reemployment of Aunt Maria. He was an expert handyman, and the job was perfectly straight-forward. Even old Wainer, the surveyor, offered to stay on and count out the *Clarions*, stacking them in dozens and parceling them up for the newsagents. He had caught a glimpse of his plans on the front page, and was fired by a thrill of professional pride.

For Gerald the choice had to be made there and then. All these people—some of them mere amateurs—would be monkeying about in his works. He caught, in spite of himself, the excitement of the moment, the race against the clock amid all the hazards of impatient fingers wres-tling with ancient plant. He could not hesitate for long.

Nat simply said, "What about it, Gerald? Are you with us or not?"

Gerald pursed his girl's mouth, his finger and thumb began the rapid lapel massage.

"I ... I ... er ... should like to stay, Nat. We'll talk it over later. It won't do to miss an edition; it might be dis-astrous."

Then, trying to look as if he saw nothing undignified in Nat's painful slap on the shoulder, he carefully peeled off his black jacket and uncoupled his gleaming cuff links, as an earnest of his intention to haul with the mariners.

TWENTY-TWO

Aunt Maria was in working order by 3:25 A.M. They shifted four typeracks as well as the insignificant stitcher, and even then Skinner had to clamber on top of the machine in order to adjust the belt to the driving shaft above.

By that time the broken columns of the Declaration page had been reset, proofread and the forms locked up.

There was an anxious moment when the motor was switched on and the machine started, for the belt snapped. They stood round in glum silence while the sweating foreman rejoined the belt. It held for three revolutions, and then snapped again.

Skinner, however, was inspired. He broke through the gloomy circle and made for the belt attached to the broken machine. Within ten minutes Skinner, Hole and Burton had torn it down and coupled it up to Aunt Maria. They started up for the third time, and the ancient machine, after an understandable shudder or two, grumbled into action. Skinner hopped about within inches of the squeaking cogs, using an oilcan like a duelist's rapier.

When Maria was, as Skinner put it, "warmed up an' second winded," the foreman dropped the oilcan and mounted his box. He swept the first blank sheet into the guides with an air of modest triumph. It disappeared for a second, and then reappeared above his head, hovering for a bit before coming to rest in the correct place.

Bumble, devouring his third bag of chips (reheated in a saucepan over the stove), said, "Stick it, Skinny. She'll have the whole ruddy lot printed by Friday week!"

But although Aunt Maria seemed painfully slow—so slow that they had to give her half an hour's start before they began folding her output—she trundled along gamely enough, and did not reject more than one in ten of the sheets that Skinner fed into the guides. The blotched, half-printed discards littered the machine-room floor, wrapping themselves round the folders' legs, as men and girls plodded to and fro for fresh supplies.

By 6:15 A.M. the run was finished. Almost five thousand *Clarion*s were stacked and parceled on the folding boards, ready to be dumped at the head of the yard steps, where they would be collected by agents soon after dawn.

Nat went round and said a word of thanks to everyone. To Gerald he only winked, for he noticed that his partner had a neatly folded *Clarion* in his inside jacket pocket. Gerald said "Good night" and went out behind the men.

Nat had promised to lock up. He felt quite light-headed as he washed the ink from his palms with paraffin. He wondered, vaguely, what would happen next. Gerald and he had agreed to reopen the works at 11 A.M., and doubtless they would talk things over. There would be further argument, of course—perhaps many arguments in the years ahead—but that did not seem to matter anymore. They had gone through this night together. Both of them had held their breath when Maria's belt snapped, and both had counted heartbeats when the fourth, fifth and sixth *Clarion*s slipped uneventfully through the guides. Perhaps they would call in Thornton and redraft the agreement. Perhaps they would wait for Baines and present him with a united front. They would still be short of regular advertisements. The machinery would have to be renewed within a matter of days. But the main problem—that of the relationship between the partners—looked like being solved, and, with that cleared up, anything might happen. He was too tired now to speculate.

Nat went slowly up the stairs to the landing, and found Mollie, looking almost unbelievably fresh, dozing in the leather chair, waiting for the dented kettle to boil.

He went over to kiss the top of her head, and she squeezed his hand. He noticed the ink under her fingernails. She saw that he noticed, and pouted, humorously.

"Will you pay for a manicure in Paxtonbury every Saturday, if I stay on in this filthy business?" she asked.

"Battle scars," he replied. "Look at mine." He spread his hands, and she noticed how white and unworkmanlike they were, despite all the inky folds they had made.

The kettle began to sing, and she spooned the dipper

into the caddy—a battered caddy with red and gold pictures of Shanghai on its six sides. He remembered that caddy from his earliest days on the *Clarion*. A missionary had given it to Sam after one of the evangelical rallies.

He went over to the window and tugged back the brown, fraying curtains. It was just growing light. The High Street was completely empty and the sky was clear. He pushed open the window—the window that Sam would never open—and a fresh sea breeze dispersed the fug of the office. Across the street the first pale gleam of wintry sunshine was sparkling on the chromium of Frobisher's shop window, just below the central trunk in the pink corsets. The breeze swung the Galleon's signboard. Its faint creak was the only sound that broke the silence.

Nat lingered there for a moment, just long enough to hear the first of the agents' newsboys arriving with his three-wheeled trolley at the yard gates round the corner—Dalley's lad, no doubt. He was always the first. The boy took four and a half dozen, never more, never less. The boy was whistling "The Isle of Capri." Nat thought it a curious tune to choose at 7 o'clock on a November morning in a British seaside town. He heard the first few *Clarions* rattle onto Dalley's trolley and the sound of the wheels and the boy's whistle die away up St. Luke's Road.

"Tea's ready," said Mollie.

Nat yawned and turned back into the room, taking the steaming cup from her hand. It was strong and good.

He caught her smiling up at him, as he stifled a yawn.

"You can sleep all day tomorrow, Nat."

He shook his head.

"Not tomorrow, Mollie. Tomorrow I'd like to get married."

She gave a little ripple of laughter, in which he joined from the sheer joy of hearing her laugh.

They finished their tea in silence. The Galleon sign went on creaking. Down by the seafront milk cans rattled on the pavement. At the top end of the town the first train chuffed out of the station toward Paxtonbury. Up the High Street the self-starter of one of Baines' buses was heard and nearer the office Mr. Richards' milk float rattled by.

Sandcombe came alive again.